FORGIVENESS

Cover photo manipulation by JLB Works
www.jlbworks.com
Editing assistance from AutoCrit www.autocrit.com
Printed by Ingram Spark www1.ingramspark.com

Visit secondchancebook.org for more information on this and other titles from Second Chance Publishing.

ISBN- 978-0-9911052-4-3

10 9 8 7 6 5 4 3 2 1

Thank you, Mom, for always believing in me when I lost faith in myself – so many times.

Prologue

Myrtle Beach, South Carolina
Sunday, May 14, 2017

Since the day he moved to the beach to begin his second career, he has found the natural, relaxing rhythm of the waves crashing against the shore quite conducive to enticing creative thoughts and energies. He pondered whether to write about the experience, triggered by the news.

The sea, in its perceived infiniteness, conveyed the notion of the vastness of life's possibilities. One simply picked a course, or followed a certain star, as their guide. Though the seas, like life, inevitably can get rough, if one held straight and true to their plan, the journey would end in a safe haven. Then the trip will have fulfilled its purpose.

The coastline, where ocean met land in a roar betraying the differences between the two, spoke its own unique language, one he tried to understand. Unbounded possibilities met with a singular force where one discovered the true destination of the voyage, however long. Sometimes he mused the shore was the great storyteller, and he relegated to mere interpreter. Nevertheless, the water and the man had functioned quite well together in the written world, before.

The chill in the late spring air sent a mild shiver up his spine, and he poured himself another brandy, only partially for warmth. He glanced down through his glasses once again at the newspaper discarded at his feet in disgust ten minutes earlier. Most had abandoned the printed word altogether for video or the Internet, but to him nothing compared with leisurely dissecting a Sunday paper, starting at a late breakfast and usually ending in the early afternoon when he, on a good day, finished both the crossword and Sudoku puzzles.

He possessed no enthusiasm for attacking those challenges today, thanks to the news of the bastard's death at the hands of another inmate in a brutal manner. He was somewhat glad, though, he lived to see this day, and not the other way around, a feat he did not take for granted. Jake Stockman was not a vindictive man, except in this case. Surely, some measure of justice had finally been served.

Although many years removed from that moment, he still held regret deep within, unmatched by anything else in his life. It was not just guilt, as that beast had died when he almost did.

He had chosen the course that led to the disastrous effects of his decisions. He would have to share the lessons, if he ever learned them, just to fulfill his promise to her. But he had never been able to grow past the hurt and the resulting agonizing, caustic pain; he only stifled it one drop at a time.

"That bastard."

He once cherished the words first heard by the lake, convinced all regret and guilt had passed, yet forgiveness of ones mistakes was difficult. The message of forgiveness as the key to inner peace still rang in his head, but while he had forgiven himself for most of his mistakes before, and after, regrets remained within.

He could have, should have prevented it.

He never forgave the bastard, nor would he ever. The bastard had robbed them of their one shot at a second chance in just one second. Never mind Albert's words. The bastard, he was different, he was pure evil. Jake held some comfort, ever so slight and fleeting, in visualizing the bastard rotting in agony on the other side of the River Styx.

The fantasy still did not bring her back.

There may be peace in forgiveness, but when compassion is impossible, the soul is constantly at war with itself. He mourned the life he could have lived, robbed from him. Loneliness defined his last twenty-five years.

Ages, a lifetime in fact, passed since the terrible moment at The Oasis, yet every consideration of what happened brought pain as sharp as if events of yesterday. Only the infrequency of those thoughts provided him with some escape, however temporary, that he had craved and perfected for decades.

He looked up with a yearning to run away from the feelings now. The news of the bastard's killing brought the memories of that night back, stronger, an unstoppable progression of an army of pain, individual bayonets stabbing at his heart.

He teetered on the edge of the cliff of depression, and feared opening old wounds would push him over it, again.

He stared at the bottle of brandy, glassy eyes devoid of any emotion beyond hate. Without his permission, past events returned to rip open those emotional scars. They stung, as the memories burned like salt in the wounded soul.

"I need this escape," he convinced himself as he poured another brandy. As he took a healthy gulp, he barely acknowledged the clock above his desk. He did not want to acknowledge drinking in the morning, again, and likely would be drunk before noon.

He cradled the brandy in his hand and thought about writing again. Perhaps this event, the bastard's death, was exactly the catalyst he needed. For in all the years that had passed, he always felt something was missing. He shook his head. He knew what that something was.

Perhaps now he should finally stop running, again, and face the pain head on, he thought. Maybe this is the time to tell the story. "Time," he said aloud to nobody, with a muted chuckle.

He sat in quiet reflection for many minutes, and then rubbed his temple, the discomfort a bit more prevalent than usual, although expected. He understood he would succumb to the issue someday. Indications over the last few weeks suggested that day was not as far off as he would like. But tests could be wrong, and he has beaten them before.

He gave a slight smile. "Besides, I outlived that bastard," he reminded himself.

His solitary existence for so many years allowed for deep reflection on his self and his past.

He had never envisioned a life of living alone, and in an external sense, he was not by himself at all. There were many casual friends at the flying club, church, and the American Legion, where war stories, some true, were told over and over.

Those who lived on the same small stretch of the beach seemed to harbor a sort of dysfunction, most if not all quasi loners by choice. The mix included couple of retired fisherman, another writer also drawn to the shore for inspiration, and an ex-football star turned real estate agent after a career ending injury his first year in the NFL back in '06.

No families lived near him, certainly no children.

The bastard's death should have closed a significant chapter from his past, and his story would follow the same path soon enough. He had looked forward to this day as much as the one his own physical discomfort will end. Yet he was saddened, because the emotional pain remained.

"What am I looking for? What should I have expected?"

Albert had given him an answer back at the lake, but his words had lost all meaning that horrible night which had started out with so much happiness and celebration. The years he spent searching for the reason why, visiting various churches and listening to the preaching of forgiveness, did not produce the desire to forgive the bastard, their messages as empty as Albert's became to him.

He found forgetting much easier, to run away in his mind, again, and when difficult to do so on his own a few beers or some brandy would usually help. At least the drinks put him out until the morning greeted him with a bright sunrise enhanced by the shimmering waters, providing additional cranial stabs to his already painful hangover.

Albert spoke of forgiveness. "Forgive and find peace," he repeated to himself. He closed his eyes and imagined forgiving the one who caused the most pain, but more aching resulted. He looked at the bottle again and poured another drink. He was not planning to fly today, or tomorrow for that matter.

Semi-retired at age fifty, he gave flying lessons as often, or not, as he desired. A few successful novels he authored provided him with a small, somewhat steady income through continued sales. Some smart investments he made before he lost his engineering career and a very low-key lifestyle contributed to his financial freedom. He rarely acknowledged the other factor.

He had no family to support.

He lived in a converted vacation beach bungalow a century old, the remaining one left standing from an original row of several dozen or so. This year marked his tenth living in the single story structure with two bedrooms and just shy of a thousand square feet; ample in size for this simple man with simple needs.

It was a good place to spend the last years.

He still held his medical so his life during the day, when he desired, consisted of giving flight instruction at the north Myrtle Beach airport. His

Cessna 172M airplane was solid and his piloting skills acceptable, despite what the FAA might say. On non-flying days, activities often involved beach cookouts with plenty of beer with his dysfunctional neighbors. One could peg him a sort of beach bum, and he was comfortable in an odd, warm way with such a label.

Three novels in various stages of completion, none past eighty pages or modified in over eighteen months, resided on his iPad. The desire to write any more words had left him a long time ago.

When the mood hit he would pick a random destination to fly to and enjoy a mini vacation, often lasting several weeks. Not many things provided him moments of pleasure, but flying vacations still did, cognizant of the importance of making the most of his limited days.

Once or twice a year he would fly to Chicago to visit his brother Steve, his only family remaining. The Stockman lineage would end with them, at least their branch. He could handle flying over land without issues.

In previous years, he flew to The Keys to hang with Tom and reminisce about days in Buffalo. But his days flying over open water ended more than eighteen months ago, when the dizziness started.

He only flew to Buffalo to visit her, and only once a year.

The thought of flying to Buffalo to visit her again to serve as a catalyst for telling the story entered his mind, but he quickly dismissed it in favor of a third brandy. "Maybe I need to first decide why

I want to do this now. Besides, I'll see her in about six weeks anyway."

He consumed three more brandies before passing out on the couch in the living room watching CNN, no closer to any answers.

*   *   *

The rising sun poured through the large bedroom window facing the ocean and shone on his face. With a slight moan, he got up out of bed, limped to the bathroom, and pissed a river. His regular morning routine included instinctively reaching for the bottle of Extra Strength Tylenol situated at its permanent location on the left side of the small sink.

While he had quit smoking ages ago, except for an occasional cigar, beer and brandy continued as constant companions. In some ways, alcohol had provided a path to a new career and fueled his creative mind to write, providing success when he found little during his days in the corporate nine to five rat race. Sometimes though he wondered if he still perhaps self-medicated too much, particularly now as the physical pain grew worse, on average, day by day.

He looked at the yellow ruled pad on the desk with mild disdain. This time, writing would mean plunging back into bad emotions and feelings. He shook at the prospect.

Too early for brandy, but bacon, eggs, hash browns, and coffee sounded good, so he made himself a hearty breakfast for fuel and consumed the meal on the deck. The ocean again roared, encouraging him, and he found clarity in his mind as he sipped his coffee.

He must write the story, now, as time was short. Dreams from the previous night again provided the answer to where to begin, and more importantly, when.

He leaned back in the beach chair and closed his eyes for a moment to acquire a mental picture of 1992. Despite the number of years passed, with minimal effort he could produce the images and feel the emotions of time, almost all at once, a patchwork quilt of primary colors woven together to form a bright, white light, dimming to reveal the lake.

Opening his eyes, he bent down and picked up the pad and pen, and the sea against the shore seemed to roar a bit louder. Through the waves, both told him they needed him to do this.

He soaked in their presence as he clicked his pen. Using his iPad as a laptop desk to support the pad of paper, Jake Stockman began to write.

PART I
Pride

One
Control

Buffalo, New York
Thursday, May 7, 1992

In discipline, there is control, and when in control, you own your destiny.

Those words Lucas Robinson lived, dreamed, ate, slept, and breathed. He strived to be in absolute control, always. If the situation was not his, then he made it his. If those around him did not agree with his point of view, then he made them agree, or ridiculed them harshly until he came out on top.

He believed owning any situation as the highest, most important aspiration in life, because control led to respect. His father taught him so, instilling it in Lucas' brain before first grade.

His father should know. Thousands of men grew to respect him at Parris Island. The military factory took in innocent, scared, apprehensive, weak young men, most looking at a future of challenge and service, some trying to escape the so-called real world. He fashioned the raw material into hardened warriors.

Fourteen weeks later, and the same boys who pleaded for their mothers and their teddy bears methodically cleaned rifles, marched in perfect unison to a bellowing cadence, and turned fear into a fighting tool. Individuals no more, they functioned as a collective team, strong, disciplined, always in control. Those weeks built up character in addition to muscle. Not all who entered survived to the end of boot camp; those that did represented the best of the best - the few, the proud, the Marines. Charles Robinson created thousands of young soldiers to serve. He not only worked for the Marines, he was the Marines.

Such indulgence of the military way of discipline and obedience translated to Charles' family life as well. Married to the perfect woman for him, a cheerleader with a flawless body and an attitude of servitude, she learned to agree with her husband, just as he desired, and without hesitation. Although early in their marriage Mary Baker Robinson had occasionally disagreed with Charles, she had not crossed the defined line for years, to avoid the physical and emotional pains from the beatings. She instilled the same respect of obedience in her two sons, for she did not wish them punished any harsher than necessary for proper discipline.

With Charles' stern guidance, they created a happy home and family life, so long as no one noticed the bruises, the busted lips, and the black eyes. Charles was not a bad man, she always told others, including those meddling social workers with the nerve to recommend she and her sons leave Charles. "Leave Charles! What an absurd thing to say!" she thought. "Leave Charles for what, their safety? What did they mean by that? We're safe with him; we're a family, why didn't everyone see that?"

Lucas loved his mother, and respected his father. He never told his father he loved him, since doing so would show weakness. The strong respected all, the strong followed, and the strong obeyed; thus the strong led.

Lucas remembered those words well, and they served as fuel for his determination to be strong like his father when he became an adult. His father's words, filled with purpose and power, had strengthened him enough to make the varsity football team in high school. He heard the same words in his helmet when he was in the trenches on the O-line, and they pushed him a bit further when the game was on the line. His coach always encouraged healthy competition but considered Lucas' passion counterproductive and dangerous, hence the dismissal from the team after Westlake's quarterback suffered a near life ending helmet-to-helmet hit from Lucas.

Lucas never agreed with the dismissal, as in his mind he did what he had to do. His father had certainly supported his style of play. "How can they say there was excessive roughness in football?" both had wondered. "Football is a physical game, a strong man's game, not one for the weak, and not one for crybabies." His father always made sure Lucas understood the importance of strength, preparation, hitting hard and following through. Lucas yearned to please his father. But his father never said "I'm proud of you, son."

The whistle blew, indicating the end of his shift, and Lucas jogged to the locker room for a quick shower. He held a good job with a solid future as a union employee transporting materials to and from the store yard at Grappone Lumber. "She knows I can provide," he thought as he toweled down, anxious to change for his date with her at Manchester's while he rushed through his normal post shift routine. He remembered to bring a clean set of clothes to work so he would not be too late to meet her, this time.

He looked at the analog wall clock above the sink and realized he was about fifteen minutes behind schedule, but she would understand his arriving late. She always tolerated his tardiness, and that bothered him in an odd way. He gave much of himself to her, and although sometimes she got out of line because of her husband, she eventually came back around, occasionally with some encouragement.

She was divorcing that weak idiot anyway.

Whether her divorce was final yet or not did not concern him, though. She had told him much about her marriage, and he had no respect for her puny husband. In Lucas' mind, her brainiac partner went happily about his engineering work, neglecting Nina's needs. Not surprisingly to him, Nina turned to Lucas because she needed a real man, which he loved, as he despised stuck up, arrogant, and full of themselves "nerds." They all thought they were better than he was. "Better than me? That's a laugh."

Well, Nina certainly found more in Lucas, and he recognized why she had naturally grown sick of the pathetic Jake and turned to a man to satisfy her. He gladly obliged, in ways she only may have dreamed about before. Sure, he also talked with her, and he understood her, the depth of her loneliness, and the incredibleness of her beauty. The more she confided in him, the more he owned her. Lucas did not regret screwing a married woman, particularly one as worldly and hot as her. She deserved the best, and if her husband did not fulfill her needs, then she did right to find someone else.

On the edge of something great, they would get married soon, he thought. He loved her and almost owned her, convincing her to move in with him next month. At twenty-six, he was sick of his father getting on his case about not having found a proper wife yet. Now at least his old man would shut up, because Nina wanted to marry him.

He looked at himself in the mirror, a man disciplined, strong, and in control. He smiled.

He left the locker room, exited the lumberyard employee building, and jumped in his truck parked near the door. He sat behind the wheel of the '88 black Dodge Ram and played with the radio to find a good song on a good station, confident the sole reason he held his destiny in his hands was since he was strong, and in control.

He knew, because his father had said so.

*   *   *

Nina Thater Stockman did not understand happiness anymore, at least not joy within a romantic, committed relationship. She had experienced as close as possible love at first sight the early days with Jake. Handsome, smart, and funny, he had brought out the best in her. Their oneness had been obvious to anyone who observed them together, and she had a glowing aura around her. "The perfect couple," people used to remark about them.

Of course, the fairy tale was years ago, and she never did figure out just when they lost the spark. Their magic burned out sometime over the span of the short marriage. Nothing they tried rekindled the energy. No fire, no smoke, and no shared future remained for them.

Her current concern, though, focused on her lack of a similar spark of love for Lucas. All of her divorced friends who found love again, without exception, told her the next time was always different. "You'll never have that spark again, but it's ok, that's natural," they said.

"How do you know if it's the real thing or if you're just settling?" was her question, with always the same answer. She would know, somehow.

She sipped the Café Mocha as she studied for her Issues in Child Psychology exam, dedicated to completing the requirements for her master's degree in Social Work with a concentration on abnormal child behavior. She was not a mother but, by helping children in bad situations, she found healing, and her calling.

She enjoyed studying at Peter's, a small coffee shop on Delaware Avenue, midway between Buffalo State College and her apartment. A full renovation of the turn of the century three-story building several years ago left the original first floor interior brick walls intact, with portions of ragged drywall added in random places to create a crumbling but classical look. The sanded and refinished oak hardwood floors showed off their marvelous grain while preserving the imperfections from decades of service as a community grocery store.

Shelves lined one side of the shop and held books patrons were free to read when enjoying a Café Mocha, a Cappuccino, an Espresso, or whatever the beverage of choice. The light classical music strengthened the relaxed atmosphere. Although a portion of the clientele was Bohemian, more mainstream professionals in their late twenties or early thirties made up the majority.

Nina did not fool herself. She enjoyed studying and relaxing at Peter's without interruption from Lucas. He hated coffeehouses, and considered them dull, boring, and a waste of time. Lucas preferred Brookhaven's, a small bar up the street from her apartment, or Matt's, a sports tavern in Tonawanda. In those places, he could have beer and whiskey, his drinks of choice. Eventually Nina tired of his alcoholic, late night partying ways.

He dried out for a while after Nina threatened to leave him, and she had hoped the changes would be permanent. Nonetheless, he slipped, and Nina would not accept the slaps, the bruises, or the humiliations any more. She had earned respect back for herself, and although she did have Lucas to thank, at least partially, for her growth in an odd sort of way, she blamed him for her bitterness about her period of lost esteem.

She sat back, recalling the night a year and a half earlier when she, sad and vulnerable, first ran into him at Brookhaven's. Their lives had crossed before, twice in fact. She knew he had been attracted to her, and perhaps she felt some for him as well. After many short conversations of small talk and lengthy exchanges of cash and booze with the bartender, they settled into a booth together for a more private environment. The ground war had started, and she needed to escape the drama of tangled love and frustration that defined her relationship with Jake. Her emotional gates opened and her loneliness spilled out from her insecurities.

Lucas talked and listened to her for hours while they both drank. When the time was right, he leaned over to kiss her. They started caressing passionately in the semi-private booth, until Nina put an abrupt stop to the touching, disgusted through the drunken haze at herself.

She talked with Jake stationed in the desert in the Middle East two days later. The phone call, a twice a week ritual, kept both of them as close as possible while separated. She stayed mostly silent during their conversation. As much as she wanted to, she could not bring herself to tell him about Lucas, not with him on the other side of the world fighting in a war.

Already depressed with Jake gone, she slipped deeper into emotional darkness, the guilt of the drunken make out session with Lucas always present. To escape the emptiness and sadness she went out more often for a few drinks after class with friends. During those times, she would on occasion notice Lucas at Brookhaven's. Initially she had avoided him, but somewhere along the line, her loneliness won.

Slowly she drew closer to Lucas, and he relished it. The night she and Lucas slept together for the first time, she hid her tears from him in the darkness. Even while engaged in the act, she recognized she had lost control of herself.

She sighed. She never wanted to hurt, let alone lose Jake. Their break had not been definitive, as both had difficulty letting go. Yet all attempts at reconciliation resulted in failure. Inside, she desired everything with Jake as it was before, but she did not expect forgiveness from him when she struggled with forgiving herself. By the time she realized such, the boat had sailed.

The constant confusion of the direction of her heart also strained her relationship with Lucas. Lucas had a jealous streak, and he correctly sensed something was wrong between him and Nina. This led to arguments that sometimes did not stop at just words.

The first time Lucas hit Nina, accusing her of having been with Jake, she did not talk to him for three days. She eventually returned to Lucas, though, figuring she tolerated the abuses from her father. Besides, she had nothing else, and was painfully lonely.

Yet, she grew. After returning to school, her work at Buffalo State became more important to her than any other aspects of her life. She had a primary purpose again, helping children. Lucas did not understand, nor like, her seemingly newfound tenacity.

"You have a good job with the real estate agency, why do you need more?" Lucas asked in frustration the night before. But she did need more. She needed to resume her destined path.

She concluded her goals and aspirations did not include Lucas.

She sighed as she put the empty cup down and glanced at the clock on the wall at Peter's. She guessed he was probably heading to Manchester's on the waterfront at that moment. They had agreed to meet at the bar instead of him picking her up, at his insistence, his setup for the same tired ritual of her driving Lucas home after he drank too much. She would then drive him back to pick up his truck early the next morning, before he reported to work and her first class.

Tonight was going to be different, as she made up her mind, and she was very sure about herself.

*   *   *

The music from the stereo reverberated throughout the house after he pressed "play" on the cassette deck, a common ritual every afternoon after Jake Stockman returned home from the plant. He pulled off his tie and tossed it over the chair in front of the old, wooden desk. In rapid succession, he stripped off the blue long sleeved dress shirt, undershirt, gray pleated pants and black wingtip shoes, the uniform of his profession, and donned a more comfortable shorts and tank top ensemble.

The mail of the day held no surprises and included the electric bill, a postcard from his brother Steve from a visit to the new Oriole Park at Camden Yards, and an ad from a record company requesting him back as a member. The enticement of thirteen free cassette tape albums for the price of one was designed as too hard to resist, yet he had no problem doing so. He tore the offer up and tossed it in the trashcan.

He pondered the song playing on the stereo, a melody he remembered well from his senior year in high school in the mid-eighties. The tune instantly brought back memories of Courtney, and the happiness and sadness of their time together. Sorrow prevailed in the end, as the letters she promised never came.

So much had changed since those times of innocence, dreams of his future, dreams featuring a house in the country with some land and a couple of horses, raising a family. "Dreams are the seeds of the future, and you must plant them properly and cultivate them with care," his high school principal once told him. He had not heeded those words, at least early on, as his years of disciplinary problems in high school reflected.

However, he had made a niche for himself in life, and a rather comfortable one at that. Twenty-five and a college graduate, he was pursuing his Master's degree in Mechanical Engineering at the University at Buffalo while employed as a Materials

Engineer at Buffalo Steel. He had been a part of a war and a marriage, the former a success by conventional measures and the latter an utter failure, ending in a nearly finalized divorce.

He lived in a moderate ranch house with a reasonable mortgage in a nice suburban neighborhood, but with no horses, no family, and no children to populate the scene. He projected success and enjoyed controlling the illusion, so long as his inner truth remained hidden. With thirty not far ahead, he recognized deviating from his apparent destiny, one he did not like, became more difficult. He was resentful about that safe stability that defined his lonely existence.

With a sigh, Jake grabbed his weight belt and sauntered to his mini home gym in the basement. His setup included a free weights bench, some dumbbells, and a treadmill. Several sets of lifts and triceps extensions would provide him with the release he needed from the stresses accumulated from a long workday. He also admitted to himself that the rough week at Buffalo Steel was not the main cause of his tension.

The doorbell rang as he started his final set on the bench. There was no reason to stop his routine to answer the ring. Tom walked through the unlocked door and down the stairs to the basement, as he did every Thursday after work. Jake was not sure why Tom even rang the bell anymore. Today was Tom's turn to drive to the Amherst Fitness Club to play their weekly racquetball match. In addition to weight training, Jake found racquetball an effective stress relief.

Tom appeared at the base of the stairs as Jake emerged from the basement gym, stretching his shoulder. The lifting loosened him up enough for the upcoming hour or so of intense competition on the court.

"We still on? Tom asked, knowing the answer.

"Of course. Let me get my stuff."

*　　*　　*

The usual after work crowd filled the Amherst Fitness Club. Jake joined the gym for the free weights, the indoor pool, the racquetball courts, and the women. Tom frequently said the club was one of the best places for hooking up, and Jake needed no other reason to become a member after he and Nina separated.

His college years had installed within him a dislike for what some referred to as the "bar scene" for meeting women. He found it impossible to meet a potential mate in a local tavern. A gym, however, possessed much potential for socializing, filled with prospects working to improve themselves.

But this was not the time for socializing, as racquetball held the higher priority. After a quick warm up volley, Tom aced three serves in a row with low drives to Jake's backhand.

"Man, Jake, you usually don't have such a problem with those."

Jake rolled his neck to initiate a successful vertebrae crack. "Bad day at work slowing me down, I guess," he said as he bolted to return another corner serve, this time with success.

"He's not biting," Tom thought as he raced across the court but could not reach Jake's low hit. "Brutal. Chuck giving you a hard time about the Eiberman Contract?"

Jake nodded as he picked up the ball. "Uh huh. He expects the overhaul of '17 Roll' to be completed in three weeks, and the plans were just approved by the home office. Hell, it'll take that amount of time just to redesign the hydraulics. The modifications are just too much. God knows when the electricians will have the time to install the circuits to run that damn thing. The existing wiring doesn't come close to the specs."

"17 Roll," the largest metal roller in the northeast, pressed huge slabs of brass into thin sheets. Management indecisiveness delayed Jake's project to modify the roll to reduce the need for maintenance downtime, thereby increasing production yields. Jake hated bureaucracy, as to him it seemed to always get in the way of engineering progress, or any advancement, for that matter.

Jake loved engineering with all of his heart but he despised the associated political dancing. He learned after descending into the so-called "real world" after college that the greatest obstacles to progress were often not the limits of physics or economics but rather man made ones consisting of posturing and establishments of fiefdoms. The

Challenger accident had solidified the belief for him during his first year of college. Back in 1986 engineers vehemently protested the launch of the space shuttle because of the cold temperatures, but management overruled the subject matter experts, with tragic results.

Tom returned Jake's serve with vigor, but the ball skipped before hitting the front wall. "He knows of the backlog."

"Nah, it's not him, though. Marv's putting the pressure on him, because the second quarter projections are shitty at best. Without that contract we'd be in shit-ass shape."

Tom whacked Jake's next serve, handcuffing Jake with a well-placed Z shot. Jake flipped the ball to Tom as they traded positions. "If they aren't fully functional, Jake, it won't kill them. And it's not worth killing yourself trying to accomplish the impossible."

Jake stopped. "You think I'm killing myself?"

Tom nodded. "Yup. You're letting the politics eat you up again, and you know you shouldn't."

But Tom wondered if something else was amiss with Jake, again.

*　　　*　　　*

She arrived at Manchester's shortly before seven and immediately spotted Lucas at the bar, watching a Bisons game on the television. He held a half-consumed beer in his hand like so many times before. As she approached him, she noticed with mild relief that he was not drunk, yet. She cringed at the thought of the explosive reaction to her announcement if he was plastered.

He smiled when his eyes met hers, and motioned to get the bartender's attention. She accepted the beer he bought for her, knowing it would probably be her only one for the night, at least with him.

"Want to go outside?" she asked, no hesitation in her voice.

The sun, partially obscured by high clouds, hung low in the sky over the Niagara River and produced a stunning array of colors and shadows. Nina Thater Stockman sighed as she considered the chromatic display near the horizon. She shivered, although not cold, and her silent thoughts turned to past dreams. Not long ago she had envisioned a career in psychology, a loving husband, and a family, yet like Jake she found herself having not realized those aspirations.

Nina accepted she had made mistakes. Unlike Jake, however, she did not dwell on her faults anymore, nor did she identify a need to assign blame or guilt. She also now recognized just how more fulfilled her life may have been, if she had learned not to obsess about the past earlier.

The ability to forgive herself for her mistakes was still rather new to her, and something Jake did not seem to understand. She now concentrated on improving her future. Doing so meant no more conversations with Lucas, or Jake.

Lucas slowly put his arm around her, and she half smiled. "Beautiful sky," he said.

Nina nodded, and felt his hand grab hers, not a comfortable sensation to her anymore. She firmly pulled away. The one thing she was sure of was her uncertainty of what she wanted. The only way to find any answers was to travel her path, alone.

"Lucas," she started.

"Yes?" Lucas looked in her eyes, and Nina paused. She had thought he gave her back a measure of confidence, when in reality she gained her independence herself. The more self-reliant she became, the greater he tried to rip that from her.

She resented him, bitterly, for trying to control her. Now she had to tell him goodbye.

*   *   *

The previous year, Jake's failing marriage and readjustment to civilian life had taken an extreme toll on his personality and appearance. Those who knew him found it difficult to recognize Jake at times. He had dropped about twenty pounds, a change he laughed off, stating he needed to lose some weight anyway. He became gaunt in the face, skin pale. The dark bags under the eyes and his moodiness betrayed his physical and emotional exhaustion.

Tom had taken the responsibility upon himself as Jake's friend to help him through the separation with Nina, starting with the day Jake moved out. He gave Jake much leeway, understanding he held significant pain. Direct inquiries or conversations about Nina had been for the most part out of the question. The few times Tom asked, the response from Jake was more often than not a terse "I'm fine," or "I don't want to talk about it."

Tom instead helped to keep Jake busy, and racquetball was one activity that successfully distracted Jake. Tom, though, grew to somewhat regret introducing the sport to Jake. Tom now found himself on the losing side of their matches often.

Nights at The Oasis also provided suitable distractions, although in a not as healthy setting. Jake enjoyed the pool and darts more than the drinking, but imbibing was a part of the ritual as well. Tom noticed as Jake had gingerly progressed through the recovery he consumed less alcohol, but following every failed reconciliation attempt, Jake imbibed more.

On average, though, Tom noticed significant progress in Jake. Jake had regained most of his weight lost following the separation, and had started dating again. However, except for Christina, his relationships did not last past the second date. Tom figured not committing early was for the best. "Give it time," he told Jake. "No need to rush into things."

Something changed recently, though, based on Jake's sullen demeanor. The pressure at Buffalo Steel was not behind the change, or at least Tom suspected as much. He observed Jake acting exactly as he had following his unsuccessful attempts to reconcile with Nina. The last time was over six months ago, but Tom was certain Jake must have talked with Nina again, or was planning to, despite having signed the divorce papers.

Only the judge's decree, the pardon needed to win release from his self-imposed prison, stood between Jake's freedom from Nina. Still, Jake was reluctant to walk out of the cell.

Tom made the conscious choice again to not confront Jake directly about his suspicions. The best strategy was still to heap distractions on Jake to prevent his retreat into an emotional cave. Jake would take the bait to open up on his own, when ready.

The possibility how one woman could have such an effect on an otherwise normal, intelligent man had always puzzled Tom. He had never been in love, or at least he did not think so, except for perhaps Becky Matheson in the tenth grade. Tom thoroughly enjoyed dating women but remained wary of commitment. He had seen too many couples, beginning with his parents and continuing with Jake and Nina, who appeared deeply in love but ended up focusing on the other as the prime enemy in life.

Tom prided himself on his rationality, and if being in love could strip his logic then he did not want to have any part of a deep romantic relationship. He became quite bitter over the past few years, sure any "perfect" marriage had just not yet entered the cosmic soul-churning blender that spits out remnants of once happy people. Ironically,

Jake had almost convinced Tom otherwise until Jake's own marriage dissolved.

For Tom, a committed relationship was in fact more dangerous than its possible benefits, so he steadfastly avoided entering one. Dodging the inevitable pain associated with long-term relationships was less risky, and Tom liked the safe harbor.

*   *   *

Jake sat in front of his computer, nursing a mental block with a Sam Adams. At about seventeen years old, he discovered writing fiction countered the boredom of his classes and provided escape from the pressures of adolescence. He had penned several short stories and a novel, though he never completed the latter or been satisfied with what he had written.

Jake eventually shelved the book effort but never forgot the joy filling an empty canvas on a typewriter or later a word processor evoked. Creating stories provided a break from the troubles and tribulations of the real world, if only for a short while, and he craved the escape again. Earlier in the week, he returned to working on the novel. Despite his efforts, however, he realized shoehorning a situation into a mismatched storyline produced unfavorable results. The words did not flow.

He stared at the screen again, and acknowledged crap instead of an intriguing story. He sighed, leaned back in his chair, lit a cigarette, and finished his beer.

While writing fiction years earlier had been an effective vacation from the pressures of dealing with teenage angst, he experienced no such relief this night, or this week for that matter. He could not blame the low quality of the product displayed on his monitor. Writing did not push away the strong pains of the reality of their last meeting.

"There will be no more meetings," he sighed, knowing he had vowed the same many times before.

He put out the final cigarette of the day, thinking maybe tomorrow would be a good time to start the next effort at quitting. With nothing more to write, he shut down the computer and flopped on the spacious and lonely bed.

The eleven o'clock news began, the television muted from when Jake turned to writing earlier. He had no interest in hearing the newscast, and lazily watched the images on the screen in silence. The lead story showed images of former President Bush and Saddam Hussein, and Jake theorized the report related to the President's visit last month to Kuwait.

Memories of his days in the war returned, particularly the letters from Nina. Her notes always contained elements of hope and desire to resuming their happy times after the war ended.

However, poignant bitterness from the subsequent betrayal and hurt remained. Jake held on to the past love and yearning for the happy times but also lived in reality. There would be no more second chances. Each time they tried, their individual situations ended up worse.

Sports soon followed on the television, and Jake groggily registered the Yankees lost to the Angels. Footage of Don Mattingly's base hit reminded him of the days working at the hospital, when he and Courtney would dissect USA Today's baseball statistics during the dinner break while following Mattingly's pursuit of the batting title.

As he dosed off to sleep, he thought more about his times in high school, at the hospital, and with Courtney. Those days of dreams, of innocence, of exploring held hope, now absent from his bitter, hardened heart.

Those days were gone forever, drowned in the lake of the lost souls.

*   *   *

Lucas did not take her words particularly well, in line with her expectations. She had correctly predicted his reaction of angrily accusing her of being with Jake. She steadfastly denied any attraction or desire for Jake, perhaps hiding some element of wishful thinking, even from herself.

She needed to start fresh, to find herself. Lucas never understood her need for independence. For the first time in months, she stared at her image in the mirror in the bedroom where she and Jake, and later Lucas, had shared many moments. She focused on the lines around her eyes, formed from hours of tears and fear. She wondered if she truly ever had been close to either of them, at all.

"It doesn't matter anymore," she thought to herself. The positive feelings of confidence and independence, both fresh to her and like an old friend returning, provided a new hope. She craved space and time alone to chart her course away from withdrawing inwardly and letting others control her direction.

The abuse she suffered at the hands of her father many years earlier had closed her up, forcing her to adopt a sheltered attitude of withdrawal. By not sharing her inner self with any man, she gave herself a false sense of protection from further hurt. Living through a failed marriage and an abusive relationship with another man brought her to the realization she needed a different existence.

Now she focused on positive change, the key to releasing her self-imposed bondages. Still, an element of living in the past remained, as she sometimes thought if Jake could recognize, and truly understand, her evolution, perhaps things might be different between them.

"No, stop thinking that," she chastised herself.

Only recently she fully accepted the effect of her father's dominating presence and controlling demands on her. She figured she had been attracted to Lucas because he reminded her of her father, not necessarily in a good way but a comfortable, familiar one. But being under control again stifled her growth, her individuality, and her soul.

She wondered how differently things would have turned out if these revelations had manifested themselves before her marriage disintegrated.

Nina sighed as she turned away from the mirror. To learn from the past was one thing, to dwell on mistakes was another, she reminded herself. With a determined spirit she would continue her life and stop wishing for things she had no control over.

*   *   *

He sat, shaking his head side to side in the dark silence. He had consumed nearly half of the liter bottle in less than an hour, yet took another long swig. He would not just let her go, at least not this easily, and not this way.

True, their relationship had been rocky at best, what with her never able to get over Jake, no matter how persistently he encouraged her. He did not understand why she wanted Jake. He was stronger, much more powerful than Jake. He was more of a man. He was "The Man."

"How could she not see that?" he wondered as he tilted the bottle back and gulped another mouthful of whiskey. Weakness crept into his being, and he hated anything that reduced his strength. No methods to control her worked.

Ever since he met her, starting with the kiss, he wanted to own her forever.

But that ass, Jake, stood in the way.

The song request would not work, a pathetic attempt to win her, spawned from his earlier softness. But he regained his posture, fueled by the whiskey, and formulated the beginnings of a solid plan to get her back where she belonged.

Lucas Robinson smirked as he put the bottle down and pulled on his boots, confident what his next destination would be.

Two
Chance

Buffalo, New York
Friday, May 8, 1992

Jake relished Fridays for two reasons. First, although he found his career to be both satisfying and enjoyable, he welcomed the prospect of the weekend away from Buffalo Steel. Second, the weekly "17 Roll" update inspection took up most of the day. The checkup of the giant machinery got him out of the office and provided an excuse to wear leisure clothes as opposed to a stiff shirt and tie.

The best engineers were hands-on workers, not behind-the-desk bureaucrats, and should dress as such, he maintained. From personal experience, confining attire often stifled creativity, the engineer's most important and versatile tool. Getting dirty is a fact when performing field work, and all engineering starts and ends in the field. He had pressed the issue with management early in his career at the plant, with moderate success, in part due to the nineties relaxed attitude on dress. Previously, corporate rules mandated engineers working the floor wear a button down collar shirt, tie, and dress pants. Now, permitted apparel included polo shirts and khakis.

He began his tour of "17 Roll" as he had done every Friday for the past six weeks, starting at the massive rollers situated at dead center of the nearly one hundred foot long machinery. The rolls take the brunt of working huge metal slabs into sheets. The enormous brass fashioning machine performed as it had for the last three years, with the older, stressed rollers, while awaiting the replacement of the four largest ones.

He stared at the massive twenty-five ton rectangular slab of searing, glowing brass passing back and forth between the huge roller assemblies, each the size of a gas station tank. The heat emanating from the slab stung Jake's face, but he enjoyed being close to the machine. The soft shifting air currents above the slab distorted the view, an effect similar to a wavering television screen, its signal momentarily interfered by a jet.

Jake pondered if what his vision registered is a mirage, a huge three-dimensional projection, and nothing his eyes detected in fact real. Perhaps the thermals rising from the brass block constituted some sort of localized "reality interference." Could it be possible to generate sufficient energy, such as with a nuclear explosion, to radically expand the interference, and even rip the fabric of space and time? Jake wondered if such blasts, and indeed the interior of stars themselves, might be cosmic portholes revealing the hellish nature of "true reality."

He shook his head at the absurdity of the notion and cleared his mind, once again concentrating on the operation of the rolls. He made a mental note to ratchet back his watching of "Twilight Zone" reruns.

As the inspection capped the end of the work week, a timely completion meant an early beginning to the weekend. By working through lunch, Jake guaranteed a prompt finish, and was out of the plant and "wheels up" before three thirty.

He lit his cigarette, and fumbled for the tuner on the car stereo after getting on the I-190. Buffalo's radio options included two classic rock stations, one concentrated on disco and pop music, one devoted to country, and two offering a lighter mix. Jake stopped on one of the latter, and took a drag.

He contemplated the meaning of the song playing, while not devoting much attention to the analysis. The tune spoke of one pouring all of their caring effort into a relationship, only to face the frustration and heartbreak of rejection. He frowned. "Been there, done that," he thought.

Jake's eyes widened when he heard the dedication after the music ended. "That was from Lucas to Nina. Hope it works out for you, buddy!"

The strong rush of jealousy, anger, love, and sadness made his extremities tingle, emotions he struggled often to suppress. He remembered their disastrous talk two weeks earlier. He had violated his "no contact" promise to himself.

"Obsession," Tom has said on many occasions. "He's right," Jake thought. Every time he saw her, a part of him still wanted her back.

The jealousy and anger subsided in a few minutes, the normal course, replaced by lucid thinking, curiosity, and an element of hope. The context of the lyrics did not infer a couple enjoying a stable, loving relationship.

"Maybe the song really was for her. Maybe she did reject him, finally. If she is over him, then maybe there's a chance," he rationalized.

He exited I-190 on the north side of Buffalo, not at his usual turnoff. Rather, he followed the route from his past, the familiar path to her apartment, the same abode they once shared.

He was not sure though how far he would go, this time.

A right turn and three blocks later he pulled into a street parking spot across from the front of Nina's apartment building. From his vantage he could see her car parked in the residential lot and her living room window. Interior lights betrayed her presence. He shut off the ignition, and leaned his head against the steering wheel, then looked up and pounded the wheel with his fists.

"Damn it, damn it, damn it, what am I doing here, what am I doing here, what am I doing here?" he said aloud, to nobody in particular.

He glanced at the building and his stomach churned. "This isn't right. C'mon Stock, grow a pair." Suddenly he started the engine and pulled away, hoping she had not seen his car.

But he was drawn to her, like a moth to a porch light. Despite the disappointments in the past, he convinced himself of his adequate strength to talk to her with civility. His mind persuaded him he could do so without expectations and jealousy ruling his words. "If the 'Lucas distraction' is gone, maybe there is a chance," he again rationalized.

He had to find out.

Three right turns later and he approached the same spot he vacated minutes earlier. He parked, shut off the car, put his head in his hands, and sighed, before gathering up a measure of courage.

He exited the Camaro and zippered up his jacket. Although not cold, he shivered. He walked up the familiar stone walkway and rang the bell. He waited for what seemed like an eternity to him until the door opened, but only a few inches. He found himself staring at Nina, dressed up and with fresh makeup, as if ready to go out.

"Jake," she said, her face devoid of emotion and expression.

"Uh, hi Nina. How are you?"

"I'm good, good."

"Nina, do you mind if I, uh, can we talk? I promise I'll be civil this time." So many times, he had made the same assurance before, but as with other pledges, he often betrayed those words, a victim of his own insecurity and stupidity.

Her expression changed, and she did not attempt to hide her distress at his visit. "Well, Jake, I don't know, I'm getting ready to go out."

"Nina, Nina, please. I only want to talk. It won't be long, I promise. It'll be cool," Jake pleaded. He hated himself for the obvious begging.

Nina sighed and, without saying a word, stepped aside while flinging the door along the rest of its arc. With her arm, she motioned for Jake to step inside as she rolled her eyes.

Every time Jake entered into the apartment they shared in happier times, uneasiness at the familiarity no longer familiar gripped him. He noticed the furniture arranged as it had been when he lived with her, with minor exceptions; a new television and changed end tables.

"And a different bed in the bedroom," he said to himself as he glanced through the open master bedroom door.

"Do you want something to drink?" Nina asked, projecting cardboard hospitality.

"Sure. What do you have?"

"Well, I've got pop, beer, milk."

"I'll take a beer."

Nina returned with two beers, and handed one to Jake. He opened the can and sat down on the couch, not sure where to start, so he began as he usually did.

"Nina, I'm so sorry. I wish I could take things back. I'm not talking about getting back together, reconciliation or anything like that. I'm just talking about things that I had said in anger that I wished I hadn't said."

"We were both angry, Jake. Besides, you can't go back."

"I know. But if I had a second chance to do things differently, I would. But I was thinking that, well, you know we did share a lot of things together, Nina. Good things."

She thought about last night. "I know," she said, her voice just above a whisper.

"And that was something that was borne from a friendship."

"Still, you know, Jake, you always said that you wished you'd gotten to know me better in the beginning."

"Well I know, I know, I know. I understand. But we did know each other. I mean we were friends. We did have good times together that didn't involve anything romantic, before."

Nina focused on her can. Jake scanned the living room, and contemplated the song on the radio, the trigger of this visit. The words came out of his mouth before he thought about them. "So, getting ready to go out with Lucas?"

Any chance of her opening up vanished. "No," she said, with a hard, firm voice.

"Why not?" He hated to ask, but he had to know.

Nina did not look at Jake. "Well, if you must know, we broke up."

A surge of hope passed through Jake, again. He looked at Nina, noticing she seemed dressed for a date. "Was it for someone else?" he wondered to himself.

"You broke up? Why?"

"It wasn't right, it wasn't what I wanted. Not that it's any of your business," she added with more than a hint of irritation in her voice.

"Good, it serves that asshole right," he thought to himself.

"I'm sorry to hear that" he replied with little honesty.

"Yeah, right." Nina's sarcasm returned the serve and began the volley in a game they played so well, as perfect practice makes perfect. Their matches always ended with a score of zero - zero.

Jake did not offer an immediate verbal response, rather he sighed in proactive defeat, deciding to let this lob go unreturned. "Well, I just wanted you to know I still care for you very much. If you need anything, I, uh well . . ."

She looked up and interrupted him. "That's sweet," she said in a low tone, serving up another round of coldness borne from hurt. In her eyes, he again started the trip down "guilt trip lane."

The walls were going up. The "Cold War" was returning.

"No, I mean it. I know things were rough, but maybe, maybe we could talk." Jake was saying what he promised himself he would not say; doing what he swore he would not do.

Nina stood up, a surge of energy and disgust in her speech. "No, Jake, I know what you're talking about. Not again!"

"Why not?" He wanted to hit himself for continuing.

"It's always the same. For you it becomes a 'conditional relationship,' and quite frankly I'm tired of your rules."

"No, not this time."

She walked across the room, turned, and returned to Jake. "Sure it will, and you end up trying to make me feel guiltier than shit. You always do it. I'm not saying what I did was right but damn it, I did try to talk to you. You were always so damned busy studying or something."

"I was working for us," he protested.

"Bullshit, it was more for yourself. And I'm not gonna live the rest of my life being second, or being made to feel like shit! I deserve better! It's been too long, and I'm not gonna spend the rest of my life regretting it. I'm not going to destroy the rest of my life paining because of a mistake I made. Fuck it, Jake, I'm sorry, I'm the one who fucked up, but it's over. Get over it!"

"Nina," Jake said as he stood up and reached for her.

She turned away from his outstretched arm and stared at him with wide eyes. "No, no, don't you touch me. Just don't. Move on, will you! It's over."

"It doesn't have to be," Jake muttered.

She faced him in anger. "Yes it does, Jake. It's over, it's been over, and we will never share what we did before. We've tried, it didn't work, and it's been too long. Jake, do us both a favor and forget about it. Why can't you get over it?"

"Doesn't a fool know just when to let go?" Jake thought as the phone in the kitchen rang, prompting Nina to get up to answer it. Jake was thankful for the unscripted respite from their bout and took a sip of his beer. He positioned himself on the edge of the couch, not for comfort out of habit, to better eavesdrop on her call.

"No, I said that's it," he heard Nina say into the receiver. "No. Listen, I can't talk. No, no, no! Look, yes I heard it. No, I don't care. Lucas, look. Look. All right, fine! Well you can go to hell! Fuck off!" The sound of plastic hitting plastic echoed throughout the apartment when Nina slammed down the receiver.

Jake stood up, having let jealousy overcome his thinking, as Nina returned to the living room. "That was Lucas, wasn't it." It was not a question.

"Yeah, so?"

"So you guys didn't really break up, you're still seeing each other, still getting it on, aren't you?"

"No!" Nina shot back defensively.

Jake continued. "No, that's ok, I can tell," he said with the sarcasm he had failed to leave behind.

"Jake, get the hell out of here. Just leave my home! MY home!"

"Fine! Fine, I'll fucking leave! I can't believe I actually thought we could at least be friends." Jake rose and slammed the door as he left the apartment.

*   *   *

She sat down on the floor, the anger having dissipated in the twenty minutes after his exit, replaced with all too familiar frustration mixed with sadness. Every time she argued with Jake, she always ended up completely exhausted.

She was sorry for the affair with Lucas, but the experience in some way did help her grow and come to terms with many issues. Deep down, her relationship with Lucas was not the real cause of their breakup, although her infidelity certainly provided a convenient excuse. Jake would not let go of his bitterness and guilt from the mistake they shared, well before Lucas.

They had tried marriage counseling to work through the pain and the guilt from their fateful decision, but Jake refused to open up and share his wounds. With solo therapy and the support from her divorce care group at church, she regained her emotional and spiritual strength.

She remembered the early times, prior to all of the hurt, how she and Jake had been "better than perfect." Their relationship had started as a fairy tale, but had ended in an emotional nightmare. Each had used the other to release their feelings of guilt, and "better than perfect" had not been strong enough to withstand such an assault.

"Why couldn't he just forgive and move on?" she pined.

She raised herself off the floor and walked into the bathroom. Her mascara had run from the tears of regret, and she would have to fix her makeup before she went out. She looked at the clock above the vanity and accepted that she still had more than enough time before she needed to be at choir practice.

Jake likely assumed she had a date or was going out partying. She sighed. The idea of her preparing for a church function on a Friday night would have been foreign to Jake. He always assumed the worst of her, and that alone hurt Nina more than anything else did.

*　　*　　*

Lucas ignored the ringing phone once again as he came back inside, having completed the next step. The message from the lumberyard added to the other two they had left on the answering machine. With too many tasks to accomplish, he would not waste time working the night shift. He had to concentrate, and for him it was harder with the throbbing in his head still resident from last night's whiskey. He had to be sure he addressed the smallest details.

Nina hanging up on him earlier solidified his resolve.

He was strong, and smart, smarter than the feeble ass Jake. He was "The Man with a Plan," a plan his father would approve of. More importantly, Nina would be his, but only if this night he executed the mission successfully.

The plan was beautiful in its simplicity, because of his preparation. "That's how you win, as victory is not in the trying but in the training," he said to himself, echoing his father.

He put the box wrench away, having removed the evidence just in case. He would have to take side roads to reduce his chance of a cop pulling him over for lack of plates.

He had driven the route before on many occasions, in planning. Tonight he would follow the now familiar path one last time, and tomorrow Nina would be his.

*   *   *

Tom was already at The Oasis when Jake arrived, waiting with a pitcher of Killian's and two glasses, one half-consumed. Tom always liked to arrive at the bar early on Friday nights to get in a couple of warm up games of darts or pool to be ready in case he found himself in a money game later on.

Tom passed Jake a beer as he sat down. It was not long before Jake confirmed his suspicions.

"So anyway, I don't know. It just fucking pisses me off, Tom," Jake said as he finished his monologue about his talk with Nina earlier.

"Jake, let me ask, why do you do this? Why do you put yourself though this every time?" he said as he refilled both of their glasses from the pitcher. Before Jake answered Tom added, "You talked to her a couple weeks ago, too, didn't you?"

Jake nodded his head. "Yup."

"I knew it. I could tell. So why do you do it?" he asked again.

"I don't know," Jake sighed and paused. "Well, I do know. I still love her. There's still something inside that keeps me there. I can't get away from it. There's no ifs, ands, or buts about it."

"So you love her but you both always end up arguing."

"Yeah, go figure. I wish she'd just be able to see my point of view sometimes. I mean, I know it sounds stupid, but it's like I still think of her as a soul mate of sorts."

"Well, soul mate or not, it doesn't seem like you guys have much left anymore," Tom retorted as he took a healthy swig of Killian's.

"I know, but sometimes, sometimes, well, Tom, sometimes I think it's just because we don't know how to handle what's happened." Jake hung his head. "You know what I mean."

Tom nodded. "Yes, I know. But you both made the choice. You know what I think? I think you both haven't come to grips with it yourselves, first. So you dump your guilt on her, and vice versa."

Jake stared ahead. "Maybe we just need more time," he said, softly.

"More time? How much more time? Tom asked, his words tinged with a hint of disgust. "How long has it already been? The divorce, you know, that thing you've worked so hard for, is almost done. Are you going to again put that on hold? Are you gonna waste the rest of your life going after something that may never show itself? You've been banging your head against a wall for too long."

"No I haven't."

"Yes, you have. I'll be blunt, Jake. I don't know if you're obsessed, depressed, or whatever. But I do know that you not letting her go, it go, is not healthy. It's not healthy for you or her. You're letting your past rule your present and destroy your future."

"Funny, Nina kinda said the same thing, almost," Jake said, staring blankly ahead.

"Well, hallelujah, I actually agree with her for once," Tom spouted. "Remember Christina? You guys were an awesome couple, always together and always smiling, and what did you do? Almost three months into it you drop her, just because one night Nina walked into here — this is your haven, remember — and said she may still have feelings for you. A couple weeks later, you were without both Nina and Christina."

Jake stayed silent as Tom continued. "Well, it sounds like Nina finally got her senses straight, so maybe you should do the same."

Jake rolled his eyes. "I don't know. You're right. I don't care. I'm really upset about it. Not so much with her, I suppose, more so with me." He chugged what remained of his beer and lit a cigarette, hoping his actions signified to Tom he did not want to talk about Nina anymore.

He exhaled the smoke from the long drag and looked at the bottles above the bar. The desire to escape overwhelmed him. "Man, I just want to get drunk tonight. I wanna forget about Nina and the whole cluster fuck at work and this shit. I wanna get toasted. Like the old times."

"Well, I'm up in pool in a few games," Tom offered, knowing another distraction opportunity was presenting itself.

"Yeah?"

"In for vodka gimlets?" he asked.

Jake knew what he meant. "Oh, geez! Tom, we haven't done 'shot for shot' in ages!"

"Yeah, so?" Tom asked with a glimmer in his eye. "What, you feeling old or something?"

"Tom, the last time I did 'shot for shot' they nearly had to pump my stomach. Man, I had a three day hangover!"

"Well, you played four games that night. You should've limited yourself, considering how piss poor you play," Tom replied, egging him on.

"Well, nah."

Tom assumed a more pragmatic approach. "Jake, you wanted to get drunk, right? One shot, one shot. You make a shot. I drink a shot. Last one left standing wins!

Jake thought for a second. "Well, ok. I'll do a game, but just one game."

"Cool." Tom motioned to the bartender. "Brad, another pitcher. And mix up some vodka gimlets." Brad shook his head as he got out the plastic shot glasses from behind the bar, and wondered when the first wave of puke would hit the floor.

"Jake, my good friend," Tom said after lighting a cigarette, "prepare for a journey into the twilight zone!"

PART II
Past

Three
Reverse

Binghamton, New York
Thursday, April 25, 1985

Jake let out a low groan. Each movement of his head brought a barrage of mini sledgehammers upon his brain. His mouth was bone dry as if he had consumed a cotton dinner. He stayed still for a few moments, eyes closed, to avoid the pain the slightest movement and light produced. When he realized he was lying on grass, he decided he needed to move.

"This can't be good," he thought as he opened his eyes and sat up. He expected the accompanying nausea and pain but did not welcome the discomfort. He was sitting in an unfamiliar field or an enormous back yard of a large house in the distance.

He was alone.

He tried to remember where he had parked his car, and instinctively reached for his keys in his right front jeans pocket. The search produced only some loose change.

"Shit," he thought as memories of events from the night before began dripping into his conscience. "The Oasis. I am never touching vodka gimlets again!" The mere thought of alcohol overpowered him, and he leaned to his left to throw up. Once finished, he brushed his hair back and drew in a deep breath. The spring air refreshed him.

Regurgitating provided some relief from the hangover, even if it amounted to little more than dry heaves.

He studied his surroundings. "Where the hell am I? Looks like Williamsville, off of Eggert somewhere," he thought, based on the style of the house in the distance and the lay of the land. He struggled, but did not remember anything past the "shot for shot" game a few hours earlier.

He glanced at his watch. "Damn, I was supposed to talk to Joe about the introductory flight lesson this morning." He mustered the strength to stand up, and as he did so, dizziness enveloped him. "Wouldn't be a good day to begin flying lessons anyway," he thought. He tucked in his shirt and walked towards the driveway at edge of the large lawn that led to whatever street existed ahead.

He wanted to buy a pop to quench his extreme thirst. His hand reached for his back pocket, relieved as he retrieved the billfold and examined the contents. "Seven dollars. Now all I have to do is find something to drink."

He reached the unfamiliar road and turned right. If he correctly identified his location as Amherst, he would eventually reach Main Street, where likely he would come upon convenience store to satisfy his thirst and need to piss. A busier street did loom ahead, but its identification escaped him. Nothing he saw spoke of Amherst.

Still, he had been at this place before.

He reached the busy street and read the sign, confused. "Riverside Drive? There's no Riverside

Drive in Amherst or Williamsville," he thought. "Hell, the only major river anywhere close was the Niagara. Maybe Tonawanda Creek or Ellicott Creek."

A sense of déjà vu enveloped him. "This is wrong," he considered, as he began the walk along Riverside Drive.

He had traveled about a quarter of a mile when he noticed a large rounded, wooded hill in the distance. Jake stopped to rest and to collect his thoughts as a pertinent fact struck him.

The hill was out of place. Amherst was for the most part flat.

A twinge of horror hit Jake as he identified the river and the surrounding scenery. He had indeed spent many years here in the past. He recognized the hills overlooking the Susquehanna River.

He sighed in mild disbelief. "Binghamton. Damn it, how'd I get to Binghamton?"

He tried, but still did not recall past the middle of the "shot for shot" game. He remembered he drank the first four shots because Tom sank the first four balls, but nothing after that. His alcohol-induced amnesia had locked away any clues on how he ended up two hundred miles from The Oasis.

He had grown up in Binghamton so he knew the area quite well, and determined his next step. The nearest pay phone resided a few blocks away in the high school where he had spent four years of his life. Tom would be royally pissed but calling him for a ride was his best option. "Kinda his fault, anyway," he reasoned. "But I'll never live this down."

*   *   *

He produced his AT&T calling card from his wallet as he reached the bank of pay phones beyond the student lounge off the high school's main lobby. He thought it strange the main doors were unlocked on a Saturday, but he heard activity in some of the rooms in the distance, likely from a club meeting or other school function. He dialed zero and his calling card number on the first phone's numeric keypad, only to hear an error message from the telecommunications company informing him the code was invalid.

"Damn these 'clone' phone companies," he complained to himself as he clicked the receiver. He pressed "10ATT" to access the AT&T telephone network directly.

"AT and T, this is Julie, how can I help you?"

"Hi, I'd like to place a call to Amherst New York with my calling card."

"The number you're trying to reach and card number please." Jake provided Tom's phone number and the information on the calling card, again.

Jake sighed and checked his watch during the short delay. The operator returned after a few moments. "Could you give me that card number again?" Jake repeated the calling card number, slower than before, enunciating every digit.

"How did I get myself into this?" he thought as he waited for the operator to return.

"Sir, I'm sorry, but that number is invalid."

"Are you sure?"

"Yes, sir."

"But I've been a customer for years."

"Sir, we show no record of that number ever being issued. Are you sure you have the right number?"

Jake thought of another option. "Forget the card. Could you make this a collect call?"

"Sure, one moment please." After a slight pause, "Sir, we show that number as not being in service."

"Man I do not need this," he said to himself as he leaned his head against his left hand. "What do you mean, not in service?" he asked. "It's the number for Tom Schultz, Amherst, New York. Please try again. This is somewhat of an emergency."

He endured another wait, much longer than before. When the operator returned, Jake sensed a slight edge of disgust in her voice. "Sir, I show no listing for a Tom Schultz in Amherst, New York."

Jake sighed and considered his options. Seven dollars and change would not pay for cab fare back to Buffalo. "Okay, let's try one more." He retrieved a scrap of paper from his wallet with mother's phone number in his scribbled handwriting. He recited it, beginning with the area code for San Diego.

"One moment please," the operator said, again.

"I hope she'll wire me some money to get home," he reasoned. With a sense of irony, he noted he could have simply walked to their old apartment if this had happened just six months earlier, before Julie Stockman had moved from Binghamton to California.

"The 'got drunk, passed out, and woke up a couple hundred miles away' story won't win me any sympathy, or funds," he guessed. He hated to lie, realizing with a sense of irony he was about to do so in his old high school, again. Back in the eighties, to avoid trouble from skipping classes and instigating fights, he had become a pro at the con in the same building.

Jake heard a phone ringing, and he sighed in relief. "Car problems, yeah that'll work," he concluded as the other end rang a third time. It was not a lie, as his problem was he did not have a car, although he hated rationalizing the situation.

"Hello?"

"This is AT and T. I have a collect call from Jake Stockman. Would you like to accept the charges?"

"Who?" Jake found it odd his mother's voice sounded so different. Calls to the West Coast always sounded more distant, though.

"Jake Stockman."

"I don't know any Jake Stockman," the woman said before she hung up.

Mystified, nauseous, and quite hung over, Jake needed to throw up again. Calling for assistance was going nowhere. "Thanks anyway, operator," he said as he placed the receiver back in the cradle.

The sickness overwhelmed him, and he found the nearest bathroom to engage in a series of dry heaves. After finishing his business, he cleaned himself up, walked to the hall, and bent over at a fountain for a much-needed drink of water.

"Do you have a hall pass?" said an older female voice behind him after he took his fifth gulp.

Jake turned while realizing he likely still reeked of alcohol from the vodka gimlets and beer the night before. "No, ma'am, I don't. I'm not a student here. I had car problems and needed to use a phone."

"You should have cleared it with the main office," she replied with authority.

Jake tried to muster up as much charm as permitted through the anvil squeezing his temples. "Ma'am, I'm sorry, but . . ."

She sniffed and interrupted him. "Have you been drinking?" She turned and yelled in the opposite direction. "Louis, call the police. We have a transient here!" She focused back on Jake. "Now, just stay here."

Jake froze for a moment, looking at her wide-eyed, before sprinting for an exit. He raced down the hall with the "hall monitor lady" chasing but falling behind. He rounded a corner and diverted to a stairwell. After bounding down a flight of stairs and stumbling through a door, he found himself outside. He spun around, and looked up at the back of the school.

As "hall monitor lady" emerged from the same stairwell egress, he spotted two men who had paused their painting of a window frame to his left. "Hall monitor lady" walked to the two men, briefly said something, then all three started moving towards him.

"Oh, jeez, this is not what I needed!" he thought. He whirled around to the opposite direction and resumed running.

His path ended abruptly after he rounded the school's corner. An eight-foot wall directly in front of him blocked his escape.

Jake studied the obstacle. "Only way out is up, Stockman."

Looking up from the base of the old wall, he positioned one foot in a crevice about two feet up, grabbed a rock above him with his left hand, and began the climb. He flipped over the top as his posse arrived.

The sense of immediate danger subsided as he realized his getaway was successful, yet the adrenaline still lingered, as he knew the chase might not be over. Quite sure jail would not be a good ending to this situation, he continued to traverse a winding path through two yards and the back of a business before emerging on Court Street. He continued to run, although slower, as he crossed the bridge spanning the Chenango River. He stopped after reaching the other side and turned. His pursuers were gone.

Grateful he had escaped, and consumed with thirst, he walked a block and purchased a Coke from a CVS drugstore on the corner. He eagerly took two large gulps of the carbonated goodness as he exited the store. A bus stop bench to the right near the corner of Main and Washington Street beckoned to him, and he sat down, welcoming the rest.

"Place hasn't changed much. Kinda busy for a Saturday though," he thought as he sipped his soda, surveying the scene.

He briefly studied the busy lunchtime crowd then leaned back to admire the serene, near cloudless sky. He had many fond memories of downtown Binghamton. The library where he had spent extra time studying to make up for the months he had not taken his schooling as seriously as he should have during his senior year sat off to his right a couple of blocks away.

He turned his attention to Christiano's, an Italian restaurant converted from an old abandoned bank. Jake smiled at the thought of the establishment where he had taken Courtney on their second date. Except the "Christiano's" sign was gone, and the building appeared gutted.

He sighed. "Everything changes."

He finished his soda and lazily stared at the entrance to the mall besides the now defunct Italian restaurant, trying to decide whom to call next. As he thought, he noticed the Washington Street Mall next to Christiano's was also under renovation.

He stood up and tossed out the empty Coke can in a trash bin. "Two points," he thought with a smile. As he walked across the street towards the mall's main entrance, a growing sense of uncertainty settled upon him.

Something was wrong. The entrance to the mall appeared to be under construction, not renovation. "Odd, that they have knocked down the original, not more than ten years old, and are replacing it with what looks to be the same," he thought.

He shrugged his shoulders and walked towards another pay phone near a department store, close to the river. He knew he needed to get in contact with someone for help, anyone, even Nina. Walking back to Buffalo is not an option. He resigned himself to the lecture Nina would give him, but he hoped at least a bit of caring remained in her to help him.

Given the events of yesterday, he did not hold out much hope Nina would come to his aid.

As he approached the phone, Christiano's and the mall stayed foremost in his mind. To him, the reconstruction seemed out of place and odd. Both appeared today as they did when he was a senior in high school, before they opened.

He halted in his tracks, startled by one of the most irrational thoughts one could have.

He slowly turned to look back at the mall, and started back across the street to Christiano's. His stomach sank when he poked his head through an uncovered window of the restaurant.

The old bank vault stood in the same spot it had been for decades.

"No, it's not possible. It makes no sense," he said aloud.

He knew of one way to test his theory. He crossed the street again and headed back to CVS, remembering the wire frame rack near the cash registers held copies of the day's newspapers.

He picked up the top paper from the rack, with exaggerated slowness, not immediately processing the words on the front page. His eyes widened and his hand shook as acceptance and rejection were struggling for control of his being.

The headlines confirmed Jake's suspicions.

"Reagan Pushes Budget"

"'Star Wars' Developers Named"

"Challenger Readied for Flight"

His gaze moved to the printed date. "Thursday, April 25, 1985."

"Sir, are you going to buy that?"

"Huh?" he said, startled, as he looked up.

"Are you going to buy the paper?" the cashier asked, pointing at Jake's hand.

"Uh, no," Jake said as he set the paper back on top of the stack, beads of shock sweat forming on his forehead.

He collected his breath and walked outside in a daze. "Seven years! How in the hell could I be back seven years? This has to be a bad dream, or one hell of a hangover," he thought.

Another possibility entered his mind. Perhaps this experience was a manifestation in his comatose mind while he laid in the intensive care unit at

Buffalo's Erie County Medical Center from too many gimlets.

"No, this seems too real," he ascertained, studying the detail of the Corinthian columns, a prominent feature of the facade of the corner building.

"What to do now, Stockman?" he deliberated as he weakly sat down on the bench in front of the store. "This has to be real. I couldn't have remembered everything in such detail," he thought as he considered the bus schedule sign in front of him.

A quick inventory check of the change in his pockets confirmed he had enough coins to cover the seventy-cent bus fare. "I could take the bus back to the old home," he thought, as he pondered the ramifications of such an action.

Not ready to make a decision, with the throbbing in his head increasing in intensity, he took a deep breath, stood up, and walked towards the river. He sat on the concrete wall overlooking the water. He marveled at the beautiful day in Binghamton, the bright blue skies and gentle breeze providing a comforting backdrop, but he was far from comfortable. He needed a moment to analyze the situation with logic and rationality.

He let his legs dangle over the river as he pondered his dilemma. "Say I really did somehow, as incredible as it may seem, go back in time through some sort of colossal mistake. What if I went home, and saw Mom? Could I alter my future, uh, present by interacting strongly with this present, my past?"

"What if I saw the 1985 Jake or if he saw me?"

"What if I replaced me?"

"I don't remember meeting myself. But is that because I never tried to see myself? Maybe that was the way out of this, a sort of cosmic shock."

"Maybe I stared for too long at the thermals at Buffalo Steel rising from that slab of molten brass yesterday, and I crossed over to some place from my reality in the plant into 'thermal land', and maybe Rod Serling is about to appear. He's from here, after all," he thought, recalling what Tom had said to him the night before at The Oasis.

He jumped off the wall and kicked a can in disgust. "Stop it, Jake! That's crazy. There has to be a logical answer." Tired, hung over, hungry, and low on funds, he had to do something.

"Play along with the dream, that's what I'll do," he decided, his options limited.

He checked his watch. "Seven thirty-two. That can't be right," he thought, then realized that was the "before" time. The digital sign outside of the department store read twelve fifty-nine. He convinced himself he had time to go home before "he" or his mother arrived, grab a quick bite to eat, shower, and regroup. "Maybe take some of my younger self's cash also."

The diesel fumes from a passing bus reminded him all buses at the central route terminus departed on the hour. He sprinted across the street and two blocks up to the proper bus as it began to pull out from the stop.

"Didn't think you'd make it," the driver said as Jake jumped through the door.

"Neither did I," Jake replied between breaths as he dropped the correct change in the collector.

*   *   *

He retrieved the key to the front door of the duplex apartment from the hiding place. "Guess it is true," he admitted, recalling he had retrieved the key from this spot when he had helped his mother pack the van for her move to San Diego late last year.

What happened next shocked him. When he opened the door, the companion he grew up with, his best friend from his youth, ran eagerly to greet him.

"My God, Stoley, is it really you?" The canine responded with an affectionate nuzzle against Jake's arm and several tongue laps on his nose. Gladness and sadness flooded Jake as he rubbed Stoley's head, recalling the dog's last moments at the veterinarian four years ago.

"Ok, ok, let's go outside," he said, laughing, remembering their routine.

Once done and back in the apartment Jake sat down on the kitchen floor and affectionately played with Stoley. He gently rocked back and forth on the floor as he petted the German Shepherd's fur, overcome with love and nostalgia.

He studied his surroundings as Stoley playfully licked his chin. The kitchen table was the same as he had remembered. The ugly yellow wall phone, a staple of the early eighties, hung above the counter, and his old red ten-speed bike leaned against the wall. The hand written notes held by a variety of magnets on the refrigerator reflected a familiar lived in state.

One of the clippings caught his eye. He stopped petting Stoley, rose, and walked to the refrigerator door. He removed the scrap of paper and stared at the name and phone number.

"Courtney," he whispered.

The sensual stimuli of Courtney Wilson returned to him in a flash, her stunning, shimmering blond shoulder length hair, her petite yet quite womanly figure, her soft touch, her favorite perfume, and her lips.

He also remembered the twisted mass his stomach became whenever he thought of her, especially when those memories turned to their relationship's end.

"Courtney," he repeated, louder. He thought back to Bob's birthday party at the park. First, he had played in an impromptu game of Frisbee football, and later he had walked with her by the lake. A boy never forgets the woman that made him feel like a man for the first time, and Jake had never forgotten Courtney.

He toured the apartment, stopping at almost every step to examine closely another article from his past. He picked up a picture off the top of the television of him, his brother, and his mother. He remembered when they had posed for the picture as if had been taken yesterday. "Pretty close," he smirked.

Julie Stockman and his father divorced not long after Jake's birth. Jake had no memories of his father, as Raul Stockman never visited or contacted his children. Abandoned, Julie cared for and raised her two children on her own.

"Mom, you'd be proud. We became a lawyer and an engineer," he said as he placed the framed picture back on the television.

He thought of how tired, hungry, and dirty he was. He noted the analogue clock hanging on the living room wall above the couch and realized the "1985 Jake" would return from school in a few hours, if he had in fact attended this day. Although academically gifted, Jake had little interest in school back then.

He returned to the kitchen, opened the refrigerator, and studied its contents. "Mom always did make good meatloaf," he thought as he removed a container, grabbed a fork from the utensil drawer, and began to eat from the Tupperware bowl.

Recognizing his time constraints, he returned the remaining meatloaf to the refrigerator, cleaned and put away the fork, and vaulted up the stairs two by two to the bathroom. He stripped off the jeans and t-shirt, glad none of his puking episodes had resulted in residue on his clothes. He turned the shower valve and, as he waited for the water temperature to rise, he opened the medicine cabinet, produced three aspirin from a bottle, and swallowed them. He cupped his hands and filled them with water from the sink's faucet to chase the pills. When he finished drinking, he splashed cool water on his face and stared at his reflection in the mirror.

"Old. I feel so damn old."

Following the long, hot shower, he dried off, and replaced the towel on the rack in the bathroom. He dressed and walked back to the living room, Stoley following close behind. He looked at the clock again. "I still have some time, it's only two thirty-five," he thought. The warmth of the shower had relaxed him and the aspirin had defeated the headache. He stretched out on the couch and closed his eyes, intent on resting for a few minutes before heading back out to confront his problem again.

Though not the best idea, he needed a short time to rejuvenate. He did not resist the attractive draw a fifteen-minute power nap promised. "Maybe I'll wake up on The Oasis floor, surrounded by empty plastic shot glasses," he hoped as he closed his eyes.

Four
Dream

Camel Air Base, United Arab Emirates
Tuesday, January 29, 1991

The loud turboprop engines from a C-130 cargo airplane taking off abruptly plucked Staff Sergeant Stockman from deep sleep and the dream of his high school days. Disoriented, he hopped down from his bunk in the tent situated about 100 feet from the runway and stretched his arms over his head.

The makeshift desert base established to provide air support for Operation Desert Storm had been his home for four long months. The war had started only a week earlier, and while all indications pointed to the coalition forces exceeding objectives, Jake knew the fighting could last for months, or years. The uncertainty of not knowing when the deployment would end had begun to wear him down.

All he wanted was to return to the familiar life in Buffalo with Nina.

He grabbed a note pad, walked outside of the tent to its plywood-floored porch, and plopped down on the couch made from a bunk and two mattresses. As he began writing his daily letter to Nina, his tent mates Erik and Simon returned and sat next to Jake. He caught part of their conversation as they approached and realized the banter was going to continue. He sighed and quietly closed the pad, knowing the letter writing would need to wait.

"How was breakfast?" he asked as he tossed the pad on the table in front of him.

"Stay away from the eggs, man. Stay away from the eggs!" Erik said.

"So, like I was saying, me and the old lady have already planned to go to Hawaii once this shit is over. We're gonna leave the kids at her ma's house and just lay on the beaches all day!" Simon proclaimed.

"Great. More fucking sand! Like you really need it," Erik replied.

"Man, sand is ok, as long as you've got blue water nearby and a nice cool margarita in your hand," Simon said.

Erik looked over at Jake. "Hey, Stock, what about you? What's the first thing you're gonna do when you get home?"

"Forget him man, he's writing another one of his love notes!"

"Hey, I love her," Jake said, irritated. "We've been through a lot of shit together, and I can't wait to see her."

"Ok, ok, so what's the *second* thing you're going to do when you get home?" Erik said with a chuckle.

"Hope that's the case. Bernie just got a 'Dear John' letter from his wife last week. It turns out she'd been fucking his best friend ever since he left for Jeddah." Simon said.

"Shut up, asshole, that's just what he needs to hear," Erik countered.

"No, man, it's ok," Jake said as he lit a cigarette. "No. Nina wouldn't do something like that. If you saw us together, you'd be amazed. It's like a fucking fairy tale, man."

"Yeah, just don't eat the apple!"

Jake slowly blew the smoke out of his nose. "You know, I have the most amazing dream last night. I was back in my hometown, in 1985. Man, everything was so real, even my dog."

"Aw, he misses his dog!"

"Shut up, man, I loved that dog."

A loud bang less than a hundred feet away shocked them to alert, bringing the three men to their feet. Intelligence briefings about possible terrorist attacks on the base were a daily occurrence, and they understood the threat environment all too well. After a couple of tense seconds, they chuckled when they saw the creator of the disturbance.

"Aw, man, it's just a fucking dog trying to get food out of that garbage can," Simon said.

"Damn, they've got the ugliest dogs here," Erik exclaimed.

"Let's waste him!" Simon grabbed an M-16 rifle. Jake had not noticed the weapon before.

"What?" Jake thought. "It's just a dog!"

In horror, Jake recognized the canine. "No! Don't shoot! It's Stoley!" he screamed as he ran towards Stoley. A bullet from Simon's M-16 struck him in the back before he reached halfway to the trashcan.

Five
Paradox

Binghamton, New York
Thursday, April 25, 1985

The sound of the front door slamming woke Jake up. He heard feet walking down the hall as he glanced at the clock, and he realized his fifteen-minute power nap had lasted nearly five hours. Disoriented from the dream about the war but quite aware, and afraid, of what would happen if he did not move fast, he dashed across the living room towards the sliding glass patio door to escape.

He was too late.

"Jake!" He recognized the stern voice behind him and stopped. Slowly he turned to face its source.

He stared at Julie Stockman, his mother, seven years younger from when he had last seen her. He did not say a word, certain of temporary paralysis to his vocal chords.

"Jake," Julie Stockman repeated, "I got a call from the school again today. You can't keep doing this!"

"Did they report finding me hung over?" he thought as he tried to shake the disorientation from his head. He swallowed and then softly asked, "Doing what?"

"Jake, Principal Blanchard said you cut school again today. After this, if you miss one more day of school, that's it, you will be expelled." She sighed in frustration. "And don't think I'm going to let you stay here. You mess up one more time you might as well consider getting your own place to live. You are old enough to take responsibility for your actions."

With the edict delivered, Julie Stockman turned, marched up the stairs, and slammed the bathroom door behind her.

Jake sat on the couch and cupped his head in his hands as he remembered the incident his mother referenced. Bored with high school, and somewhat of a nonconformist, Jake had attempted to bend every institution rule to satisfy his whims. His senior year he had cut classes, picked fights, and argued with his teachers, and his actions and attitude had often landed him in trouble. By the middle of April 1985, he recalled, he had been suspended from school twice before. Principal Blanchard had advised him he would get no more chances.

But he had heeded the warnings, and had graduated with his classmates.

He found it strange, and lucky, that "he" – the 1985 Jake – had not yet arrived home. "Maybe I replaced him, uh me." He thought. "I have to figure out the rules of this dream as quickly as possible."

Jake looked at the clock. "Seven thirty-eight. He – I – should have been home by now," he thought. He wondered for a moment about 1985 Jake's reaction when his – their mother referenced seeing him, then shook his head. "Not my problem." He had his own pressing dilemma.

The brief interaction with his mother probably would have no bearing on future events, but if he met his 1985 self, the effects may be disastrous, he surmised, again conjuring up images of space and time imploding. He gave Stoley a final pet on the head, grabbed the 1985 Jake's Members Only jacket, and snuck out the patio door.

With no other reasonable choices, he planned to spend the night in the woods. The apartment backed up to the side of an undeveloped hill, tree covered with the exception of an access road to a large water tank at the top. He shivered in the chilly Binghamton air, yet he predicted with the jacket he would endure a night of fifty-something degree weather without major issues.

As he walked up the path behind the split-level duplex through the woods to the ancient concrete tank, he wondered about the location of the 1985 Jake. A few moments later voices up ahead where the woods ended in a small clearing surrounding the water tank triggered the answer. "Of course! I'm at the tank partying with Bob and Dave. We did that almost every Thursday night during the spring of my senior year."

He stopped at the tree line, knelt down behind a bush, and strained to look through the darkness, remaining as silent as possible. Spotting the 1985 Jake would confirm his theory of coexisting with his younger self in this past timeline. Although not sure what he would learn, he had to figure out the rules of this dream.

Through the diminishing twilight, he made out the figures of Bob and Dave. They appeared to each have a can in hand. He did not see the youthful Jake, though. He moved cautiously through the trees to gain a better view. "I'm probably on the other side of the tank," he deduced before a stick snapped under his foot. Bob and Dave turned at the sound and began walking towards him.

Jake had no time to debate running or staying.

"Stock! Where the hell you been?" asked Dave as they approached Jake.

Spotted and unable to escape, he emerged from the edge of the woods. Jake Stockman interacted with people from his past for the second time in less than an hour. "Uh, my ma had a few words to say."

"She found out about you and Courtney goin' off last night. I told you Elsie would tell!" Bob said as he brought the can of Budweiser up to his mouth and took a swig.

"Uh, yeah, something like that," he replied, nervously studying the scene. He expected 1985 Jake to walk up the same path he had traversed only minutes before.

"Well, you got here just in time. Dave got his old man to grab us a case, and Karen and Lynn are on the way. You get ahold of Courtney?"

"Damn it, how'd I get myself into this?" he thought. "Better play it cool, and get outta here as quick as possible."

"Nah. She's got some sort of family thing," Jake replied.

"Too bad. Have a brew, man."

Jake received the offering from Dave's hand, opened the can and took a large drink, then lit a cigarette. The beer tasted good, and he let himself relax a bit.

"Here they come."

Jake looked in the direction Bob indicated. Three female figures climbed up the other path opposite from the one Jake traversed. He did not immediately recognize two of them, but instantly identified the third.

"Courtney," he thought as feelings, good and bad and buried long ago, returned with the sight of her. He had not prepared himself for seeing let alone interacting with her. He chugged the remaining Budweiser, crushed the can in his hand, tossed it aside, and grabbed another from the case.

Jake swallowed as Courtney sauntered up to him and put her arm around his waist. "Hey," she said before pulling him into a tight embrace and engaging in a passionate kiss. Her body felt welcome against his, as adolescent hormonal feelings at the cutting edge raced back to Jake.

He returned the kiss.

"Get a room!" Bob shouted.

"This isn't right," he thought as he eased her away while letting out a long sigh. "Hey."

"Yo, Stock, I thought you said she couldn't make it," Bob said.

Courtney looked at him, and he could not help but stare into her beautiful green eyes. "Why'd you tell them that? I told you last night I'd come." She arched her neck back, opened her mouth, and savored a long drink of the brew. "And where were you today, anyway?"

"What do you mean?" Jake asked while having difficulty thinking straight. His eyes remained focused on her entire being, all he had remembered, and yet more. Her wavy blond hair fell about her shoulders, softy reflecting the moonlight. Her perfume danced in his nostrils, exciting desires from within.

"Whoa. Stop. Wrong," he thought, again.

"You know, Mrs. Thomas is really pissed that you missed that exam today," she said as she ran her fingers along the sides of his face.

Jake gently moved Courtney's hands away from his head and said, "What test? We had a test?"

"You jerk! We've only been studying chemistry for the past several nights," Courtney replied.

"I bet I know the kind of chemistry they were studying!" Kathy said.

"Chemistry. You know, atoms, protons, electrons, attractive forces," Courtney said as she slipped her tongue into Jake's mouth.

This time he did not push her away.

The memory of the day at the lake rushed back to Jake. He and Courtney had been laughing at the shore, alone together after a full afternoon at the party. Their moment had lasted longer, and laughter had turned into kissing, and then more. They had both been uncertain, but willing, as they stripped off their clothes and explored each other's bodies, secluded from the rest attending Bob's birthday bash. She quivered, he laughed nervously, and it was beautiful, that day when they both lost their virginity, together.

"Mmm, Jake, I want you to be the first. I love you," she said as she broke the embrace.

Jake snapped out of the trance. The afternoon at the lake years ago sat months in the future. He eased Courtney away again, knowing the younger version of him who belonged in this timeline sharing these events, would show up soon. While he enjoyed reliving a snippet of his past with Courtney, he did not want to violate the rules of this dream.

"I have to go."

"Go? Go where? We're just starting to party!"

"I have to study for that test tomorrow. I fucked up."

"Fuck it. You can reschedule it for next week. Besides, we don't have chemistry tomorrow. We've got that assembly for that military presentation crap," Bob said.

"Yeah, just what I want to do, join the fucking Marines and die in some damn jungle like my old man did in 'Nam," Dave added.

"Hey, don't knock the military 'til you've tried it" Jake wanted to say but fought the temptation to push further the boundaries he sensed.

"I'm going, see you later," he said with a sternness in his voice as he turned to walk away.

"Later, Stock."

Courtney ran after him. "Jake, is there something wrong?"

Jake stopped after she caught up with him, and shook his head. "No. I just gotta take care of things."

"I'll see you tomorrow?"

He kissed her on the forehead. "Maybe sooner," he said mysteriously and disappeared into the woods, aware 1985 Jake would arrive soon.

Puzzled but relieved he had not encountered himself on the hill, Jake thought about his next action. He inferred a primary rule of "The Dream" meant no interaction with people from his past, even for only a few minutes. Still, to him seeing Courtney again was worth a penalty in this game.

He maneuvered down the wooded path, not sure of where he would make his nest for the night, thinking of this day in the past. He remembered missing the chemistry test because of fear of a failing grade due to inadequate studying. He also recalled snippets of drinking the case at the tower with the group, although unclear of how much he combined or mixed memories of similar nights.

He halted his descent, jarred as another memory fragment of this night entered his consciousness. Lynn had lost her footing navigating down the slippery mud path, but Jake had grabbed her before she slid down a steep embankment to the ravine below. They figured he prevented her from at minimum getting several bruises if not a broken leg or something worse.

He recognized the key point. He was with them.

Memories of this day continued to return in rapid succession. He had spent much of the time at the public library studying, hopeful for a second chance to take the chemistry exam the next day. Yet he avoided returning home early in the evening, aware Blanchard had likely called his mother, to avoid a confrontation with her.

Bypassing the apartment led him to be first at the water tower. "When Dave and Bob drove up the maintenance road, I carried the case from Dave's pickup," he remembered. "I was there when they got there."

It then became obvious to him why he had not run into himself. The Jake of the past never showed because he did not exist.

"It's me. I'm him. I replaced myself," he said aloud.

He learned the first rule of "The Dream."

His revelation determined his next step. With not much time before Lynn would slip, he took a deep breath, extinguishing any lingering doubt of his conclusion. He reversed course and started back up the hill to save Lynn from injury, and to interact with Courtney for a second time.

He smiled as he reached the edge of the woods again and paused, but only for a moment. He realized in some ways living this dream may actually be fun.

Six
School

Binghamton, New York
Friday, April 26, 1985

The alarm on the clock radio buzzed, and Jake's mind centered on "17 Roll" and the associated nightmarish scheduling problems. He hoisted himself up, in the process striking his head against the metal rail holding the upper bed in place, cursing the pain. He eased his legs around to arrive at a seated position on the edge of the mattress.

The thoughts of the problems at Buffalo Steel faded as he recognized his current reality. "Man, it's still real, it still is 1985," he thought as he rubbed his temple. He sensed a slight headache beginning to take hold.

Steve did not come home anymore for semester breaks, Jake recalled, so he had the bedroom to himself. The infrequent times Steve visited Binghamton he preferred to stay at a friends' house. Their mother kept the bunk beds in place should Steve ever reconsider and remain more than an hour at a time.

He scanned the room, finding his objective, his high school chemistry book. "I should have looked this over last night instead of spending several hours at the tank," he reprimanded himself. He did not deny, however, he savored reliving the previous night, especially with Courtney.

A knock at the door interrupted his examination of the chapter on alloys. "Come in."

Jake's mother entered. "Jake, I have to leave. Are you going to go to school today?" she pointedly asked.

Jake got up and faced her. "Yes, Mom, I promise," he said with assertiveness, remembering he had guaranteed the same thing many times before. He did not expect a sympathetic response, nor did he get one.

"If you don't, Jake, consider looking for your own place. You're eighteen and need to start acting like a responsible adult. I can't take this anymore," she said, her voice falling soft.

"I know, Mom. Believe it or not, I appreciate all you've done for me. I love you." He kissed her left cheek.

She recoiled from her offensive posture, not expecting the sincerity of Jake's response. "It's what's best for you, you know."

"I know, Mom," he repeated as he grabbed a towel. "Now, I've got to shower and get ready for that chemistry test!"

*   *   *

"I didn't think you were going to make it."

"Neither did I," Jake said with a sheepish smile to the Binghamton High School parking lot attendant as he climbed out of the 1977 Pacer. He had purchased his first car in early 1984 from a Vestal dealership based on the impressive audio quality of the stereo, without having the vehicle inspected by a mechanic prior. Subsequent repair bills had cut into his part time job earnings and taught him a difficult and costly lesson.

While the auto needed additional mechanical work, it ran well enough. He had learned to perform some simple repairs himself, including adjusting the timing and replacing the head gasket. Yet the Pacer still had the tendency to stall under slow speeds, a fact Jake remembered when the engine quit as he pulled into the student parking lot at Binghamton High School.

He kept his gaze down to avoid talking with anyone as he walked towards the rear entrance to the school. Any eye contact may open the door to unwanted conversation.

Once indoors, he climbed a back staircase to the second floor and entered the library. He had arrived forty-five minutes early to allow time to review for the exam. He sat down at an unoccupied table far from the library's entrance, opened up his chemistry notebook, and examined the contents. Based on his notations, he ascertained the topics to be covered. "Metal and alloy structures, my specialty," he chuckled to himself. "This is going to be easy."

He leaned back as he overheard two girls seated at a table behind him discussing the superstar status of Michael Jackson. "Life was so much simpler in these days," he thought. "We had nothing to worry about beyond teenage interests."

He rubbed his chin again as he had done several times since earlier in the morning. The smoothness reassured him he had shaved as close as possible. He concluded he likely replaced himself but his body appeared no different from 1992. He hoped a good, clean shave and the right clothes would help him pass for as a high school senior. "Of course, when I was eighteen I looked fifteen," he mused.

He flipped open the notebook's cover. As a manner of habit, he had always taped his class schedule to the inside of the binder. Until he figured out what had happened and how to return to his own time, he decided he had no other viable choice but to relive his life. The itinerary provided the necessary information on his classes, and he hoped he could successfully locate the rooms in the large building.

He noted the time the wall clock above the circulation desk reported. "I still have ten minutes before the bell," he calculated. "I definitely can head down to Ernie's for the paper and a cup of coffee."

*　　*　　*

He glanced around his homeroom classroom as the teacher completed the attendance check. He recognized some of the students, and began the mental game of matching names with faces.

"Everyone looks so young," he observed while rubbing his chin yet again.

The bell rang for the second time and he checked his class schedule before leaving his seat. "'Introduction to Calculus' with Mr. Douglas, wonderful," he said sarcastically to himself as he walked down the hall, still avoiding interaction with the other students. Of all his high school teachers, Blake Douglas had been his least favorite. He remembered Douglas as an overweight, unreasonable, and temperamental individual who had always attempted to project an aura of self-grandiose.

The newspaper and coffee provided a needed distraction from the class. Thinking about Douglas attempting to teach pre-calculus, a subject Jake excelled at, made him wince. Douglas did not excel at instructing, from Jake's vantage point. Subsequently, Jake had taught himself most of the subject before, out of boredom and necessity. With a sigh, he sat down in a seat in the back of the room.

Douglas began with the collection of the previous night's homework. Jake fumbled through his notebook, hoping in vain that his younger self had finished the work. As Douglas worked his way towards the rear of the room, Jake buried himself in his newspaper with nothing to offer, hoping he could hide in obscurity.

"Mr. Stockman, it is nice of you to join us today. Do you have your completed assignment?" Douglas asked, a slight smirk betraying his prediction of the answer.

The overpowering odor of Old Spice sickened Jake's nostrils. "Damn, does he bathe in that stuff?" he thought as he put on his 'best behavior' face. "No, sir," he answered.

"Really?" A strange, almost sadistic touch of amusement shone through Douglas' voice. "And why not, Mr. Stockman?"

"I was out of time," he said, as truthful a response as he could give.

A few chuckles from the class enhanced Jake's discomfort. He hated whenever anyone, and particularly someone like Douglas, put him on the spot like this.

"'Out of time' is not a valid excuse. See me after class. Oh, I suppose we also forgot that attention must be paid to me at all times in this class," Douglas said as he grabbed the newspaper out of Jake's hands.

"Hey, I just bought that!" Jake recoiled.

"You may retrieve it after class," Douglas said as he continued to collect homework from the students.

Jake started to protest, but forced himself to remain silent knowing any further confrontation would be counterproductive at best and may complicate matters at worst. He did not need to create issues as he tried to determine what he had to do to get back home in space and time.

As Douglas returned, Jake took a long, deep breath and surveyed his surroundings. A typical mix of teenagers filled the room, from those more studious in the front to the non-conformists near the windows, his location. He recognized several faces but was having difficulty again matching names to them.

He was acutely aware though of how young everyone looked, and how out of place he felt.

As Douglas began the lecture on integrals, Jake let his mind drift. He tried to recall more of the night before last at The Oasis. He remembered talking with Tom about something physics related during the "shot for shot" game. Sometimes a healthy quantity of beer would provoke philosophical discussions of scientific principles between the two.

"Time travel. We were discussing time travel when we were playing," he suddenly remembered.

"Boy, he'd love this."

The possibility of time travel had often been a favorite of their alcohol fueled existential conversations. Each favored his own theories, but the simple paradox of "what if you went back in time and killed your father before your conception" always seemed to be an insurmountable contradiction. Yet the impossibility of an idea often made the topic more appealing for discussion.

"So, what had happened? Suppose this is in fact reality. How did this happen, and why, why Binghamton, and why now?" Jake mused. He did not recall any event of fantastic significance in his or his family's lives at this time to draw him here, assuming a reason related to such for going back to 1985 existed.

"Of course, it could be some sort of freak cosmic accident, or someone's way of pulling a really bad joke, or an illusion," he deliberated. "Damn, I wish Tom were here to help figure this out." His head had started to throb, so he closed his eyelids and began to rub his temples.

"Mr. Stockman. Mr. Stockman!"

"Huh?" Jake said as he opened his eyes, startled.

Blake Douglas stood directly next to him. "Mr. Stockman, did you enjoy your nap?"

"I wasn't sleeping."

"Then answer my question. What is the integral equation for that?" Douglas asked as he pointed to the blackboard at the front of the classroom.

Jake studied the diagram on the board displaying an x-axis and a y-axis with a rather crude rectangle drawn on it. Jake remembered Douglas' lack of attention to detail whenever he wrote or drew on the board. Often Douglas would ridicule a student's incorrect answer, even though the inaccuracies were often rooted in Douglas' poor representations. He considered the diagram for a few more moments, and then shrugged his shoulders.

"Offhand, I don't know."

Douglas leaned towards Jake, his hands on the edge of the desk. "Well, you would know if you were paying attention. Go see the principal, I told you I do not tolerate inattention," Douglas said with a smirk.

Jake also smiled as he rose in silence. He did not pick up his books and, instead of heading for the door, he moved with confidence towards the blackboard, holding the rest of his coffee in his hand.

"What I meant, Mister Douglas, is that the way you have drawn this function, it is impossible to determine any sort of equation to describe the area under the curve. Now, for accuracy this should be a rectangle. In that case, the answer is quite simply the delta x multiplied by the delta y."

Douglas frowned and several students leaned forward as Jake continued. "However, as you have drawn an imperfect rectangle, we have to resort to an approximation. The trapezoidal method would suffice quite well here," Jake postulated as he grabbed a piece of chalk and divided the figure into several smaller rectangular shapes.

"Here, you could compute the area of each of the rectangles, and add them to get an approximation of the overall area. The finer the mesh you use, the more accurate the solution you get. The most accurate solution would of course be formed by taking the limit of delta x as delta x approaches zero."

He returned the chalk to the blackboard's rail and sauntered back to his chair, grinning as he reveled in the silence in the classroom. The other students did not have a clue as to the meaning of what he had said. Douglas had a stunned look on his face, because he knew Jake was right.

"I've always wanted to do that," Jake thought as he sat down.

*   *   *

"Hey, Jake, loved what you did in Douglas' class!" a voice behind him greeted as Jake began to eat his sandwich.

Jake turned to the source of the compliment. "Mark," he thought as he continued the "naming the face" game.

"Thanks. I've wanted to do that for a long time," he replied with honesty. "I was a bit surprised though that Douglas still didn't send me to Blanchard's office."

Mark sat down in the vacant seat to the right of Jake. "What'd you do, stay up all night studying calculus just to pull that whammy? It was great! He was speechless!"

"Uh, nah. Just learned the stuff fast, I guess," Jake responded. He did not want to get in an extended conversation about the incident in Douglas' class or anything else, and turned his attention back to his sandwich, hoping Mark would get the hint.

Mark continued, "And what was that deal in Social Studies? Suggesting the Soviet Union was near its end and that war would break out with Iraq? You had some pretty good arguments but Mr. Brookes didn't come close to agreeing with you."

Jake had resisted referencing future events but deviated from the strategy when the topic had turned to the global balance of power in Social Studies class. Still intent on not engaging in the current discussion, he only nodded and opened his chemistry notebook, hoping for success with this indication of wishing for solitude. Scheduled to report to Mrs. Thomas in half an hour to take the make-up chemistry exam, he wanted to focus on his immediate task.

"They gonna give you the chemistry makeup today? Hey, where'd you go yesterday, anyway?" Mark asked, not biting on the second suggestion.

Jake sighed inwardly as he closed the notebook, not able to escape the moment. "I, uh, stayed home. Felt sick."

"So why'd you stop in before? Jeez, you were a zombie."

"You saw me yesterday?" Jake looked up, surprised. The entire school seemed almost deserted when he had strayed into the building searching for a pay phone. "When?"

"Right before lunch. You were getting a drink and I was late for my music theory class so I couldn't stop. Man you must've really been out of it! I figured that you just zoned out from cramming for that test."

Jake understood. Mark had seen him right before "hall monitor lady" had stopped him. "Yeah. I was really out of it. Had to get out, though."

"Where'd you go? Marla said she saw you walking down Riverside Drive a few minutes earlier, like you were drunk or something." Mark leaned forward. "Hey, did you guys ditch school and party at the bridge without inviting me?"

Jake took the chance at an alibi. "Yeah. A couple of friends of mine from Seton had a bottle of Captain Morgan. We got shit faced. I figured I'd come up with some excuse to get out of that test."

"Probably a good call, it was a bitch. Why are they making you take it today? Did they know?" Mark asked.

"No, I don't think so."

An announcement over the school's public address system interrupted the conversation. "Jake Stockman, please report to the main office."

"You sure they don't know?" Mark said in response to the page.

Jake rose and gathered his garbage. "Guess I'll find out."

*　　*　　*

Seeing the interior of Principal Gene Blanchard's paneled office brought back a flood of memories for Jake, all bad. Jake remembered Blanchard as a reasonable person, but he had taken advantage of Blanchard's sensibleness too many times. Eventually Blanchard had reached his breaking point and had almost expelled Jake sometime during the latter part of his senior year. Jake could not remember exactly when, but surmised it had been around this time.

"Jake, you had another unexcused absence yesterday." Blanchard started after walking in and sitting down behind his desk. "Why?"

Jake shifted as he fidgeted in his chair. "I had some, uh, personal problems to attend to."

"Did this include drinking?"

Jake's stomach turned at the principal's mention at his alibi. He remembered the last, and only, time he had left school to drink with friends had been during his junior year. "No, sir," he steadfastly objected.

Blanchard picked up the telephone and pushed a button marked "INT." "Please send in Miss Teale," Blanchard said into the receiver, then placed it back in its cradle.

A moment later an older woman with glasses walked in. Jake's demeanor took a turn for the worse when he recognized her as the "hall monitor lady" from his escapade at the school the day before.

"Sit down, Margaret. Is this the young man you saw yesterday?"

Margaret Teale studied Jake for only a moment. "Yes. He just ran off out the back courtyard. We couldn't catch him."

"Had he been drinking?"

"I smelled alcohol, and he did not seem entirely 'with it.'"

Blanchard leaned in his chair towards Jake, seated at the desk directly across from Blanchard. "Can you explain this, Jake?"

Jake swallowed, understanding telling Blanchard the truth about 1992 would never fly. Denying being on school grounds reeking of alcohol was out as well, since Margaret Teale had talked to him, he had been absent without an excuse, and others had seen him leaving the building earlier. There was only one answer.

"No."

"Then you had been drinking?"

"Not yesterday, the night before," Jake responded truthfully. "I had a bit too much to drink, passed out, and woke up too late for school. I had come back to take my chemistry exam, but I got sick, and threw up in the men's room."

The story gained momentum as he continued. He turned to "hall monitor lady." "That's when you saw me, Miss Teale. I still had felt incredibly sick. I couldn't take the test. So I left, hoping that I could take it today."

Jake had learned a long time ago that the most convincing lie contained as much truth as possible. He hung his head. "I know it wasn't the right thing to do," he said, his speech trailing off.

"You know I spoke with your mother yesterday," Blanchard said.

"I know. I know I'm on thin ice, but, really, I've changed," Jake replied.

"Well, we've given you enough second chances, Jake. You knew expulsion was the next alternative. You did this to yourself."

Blanchard had come close but had not expelled Jake from school before, yet Teale had not caught him with alcohol on his breath last time, either.

"This isn't supposed to happen," he told himself.

Jake stared at the principal, realizing his precipice. "Mr. Blanchard, please, let me stay. I know my future depends on this, and I really need this. It's too close to graduation," he said, exasperated.

"Jake, you're failing English and chemistry. The chances of you graduating even if you do stay are remote at best."

Jake remembered that in 1985 he had barely managed to pass both. "Wait. I've been studying very hard for the chemistry exam, and I can prove it, if you let me take the exam."

Blanchard held up his left hand, negating Jake's proposal. "No, Jake, you've already proven to me that you can squeak by. I don't doubt that you'll pass, but just passing does not show a commitment. You should be getting As."

"But Mr. Blanchard, I want to take it. I can do it," Jake protested. "I've been accepted at Buffalo but need to graduate. I've got dreams, you know, dreams of my future."

"Jake, dreams are the seeds of the future. You've got to plant them right, in good soil, and give them a lot of sun and nourishment. If you cultivate your dreams, they will grow into reality, but dreams, like seeds, are not enough. You have the talent. You have the intelligence. But you don't the drive to push yourself. Like I said, you should have an A in that class," Blanchard responded.

"A reasonable man," Jake thought, recalling his memories of Blanchard. "He always wanted to help, and I just pushed the wrong buttons. Not this time. He liked the straight approach."

Jake stood up after the moment of reflection and decision, looked Blanchard directly in the eye, and made the offer. "Fine. An A, no problem. If I get an A on the test, and continue to do my best and stay out of trouble, then I stay. If I don't, I leave, no more discussion."

He sat back down with confidence as he folded his arms. "I'll take the exam now."

Blanchard shifted his weight in his chair. He did not want to let Jake get away with another halfhearted excuse for returning to school, yet he was aware of what Jake was capable of achieving. The newfound sincerity and determination in Jake's voice swayed Blanchard into agreement.

"Alright, you'll get one more shot. Mrs. Thomas is off today, though, so I don't have the test and you'll have to wait until Monday to take it. Until then, you are suspended."

Objecting the suspension would not be productive. He softly replied, "Ok, I understand. I'll come in Monday morning to take the test."

Blanchard checked his schedule. "Stop back at ten thirty Monday and I'll administer the exam here."

*　　*　　*

His fixed his gaze on the building across the street as he filled the Pacer's tank with gas. The Box Score bar resembled The Oasis, and he again thought of the night less than forty-eight hours ago and years in the future. He continued to draw a blank as to what happened to him after "shot for shot."

Certain he would have no problem earning an A on the chemistry test without any more preparation since he was a subject matter expert in alloys, he decided not to waste precious time over the weekend studying for the exam. He needed to figure out why he was reliving his past, now, and there was only one answer to accomplish his objective.

He must go to Buffalo.

Convinced a logical explanation for his perceived transferal across space and time existed, Jake reasoned he would find answers in Buffalo, where the experience started about two days ago. His engineering mind, looking for a clear answer, demanded no less.

After withdrawing money from his 1985 savings account and a brief visit home to pack an overnight bag and write a note, he merged the Pacer on to Route 17 west towards Buffalo. The funds would cover all trip expenses if he was frugal and the note should alleviate Julie Stockman's concerns, he hoped. As he traveled through Johnson City, he experienced a measure of confidence he would find those reasons.

He did not consider the possible ramifications of learning the truth.

Seven
Miss

Buffalo, New York
Saturday, April 27, 1985

Jake drew in a deep breath through his nose. He welcomed the distinctive, familiar smell of fresh growth in the Buffalo morning air proclaiming the long western New York winter over. After months of hibernation, all set their sights on numerous outdoor activities.

He soaked in the visual scene as he munched on a convenience store burrito while again pondering his predicament. He smiled as two boys ran through one of Delaware Park's grassy fields in an attempt to fly kites in the brisk April breeze coming off Lake Erie. To his left, behind the kite children, adults in their mid-twenties engaged in a softball game as several joggers meandered along the path in front of him. In all aspects this day was not much different from when he jogged there himself last Saturday, except to Jake that Saturday was years ahead.

He postulated a huge vodka-induced hallucination or perhaps an LSD tab slipped in his drink unnoticed explained his perceived transferal back through time. He had never tripped, and wondered if this was what it was like, on an extreme scale. Completely awake, cleansed from the toxins administered at The Oasis two and a half days earlier and refreshed after the drive thanks to a three-hour rest stop, he dismissed the drug angle.

A second option was he had actually travelled back to 1985. Science fiction aside, an amateur's fascination with Einstein, Sagan, and Hawking had instilled in him the belief of possibility of time travel, at least theoretically if not practically. He found it difficult to accept such an absurd notion, though.

A third theory, crazier than the second, had entered his mind while trying to coax the Pacer above sixty miles per hour driving the night before. Strangely, the prospect that he had died did not occur to him until the road trip.

"Well, if I'm dead, I don't think this is heaven or hell, maybe purgatory," he thought.

He discounted all three theories. Dead or not, he enjoyed the spring day in Delaware Park. He deliberated a quick jog but decided against doing so, though he did experience a pang of guilt at not continuing his Saturday morning routine. Then again, his habit would not start for a few years anyway, he rationalized.

An hour strolling through the park produced nothing in the realm of meaningful revelations, matching his honest expectations. He accepted the fact no answers burst forth and no messages from God came leaping out of a burning bush. He tossed the burrito wrapper in a trashcan ("two points!") and returned to his car, hoping he would have more luck at the next location.

He drove up Delaware Avenue to the northern loop and headed east. Navigating on autopilot, he forgot the highway he planned to take was still a blip on the New York State Department of Transportation's upcoming project schedule in 1985. After a brief disorientation, he corrected his error and shortly thereafter arrived at Flint Loop, the main entrance of the "new" campus of the University at Buffalo.

Compared to 1992, the site lacked several buildings, although two where he would attend classes were under construction. He strolled through the main plaza, looking, searching, and marveling at its beauty. The scene was not too much different from how he remembered it, the absence of a few structures notwithstanding. He stopped walking when he reached the library.

He stared up at the modern brick facade, bold and plain, a feature of architecture of the early eighties. Something about the structure tugged at him, and he entered the library, open for students to prepare for final exams the following week. Jake rode the elevator up to the fourth floor, not knowing what he was looking for.

The lift doors squeaked as they closed behind him, but he was too amazed at the newness of the old scene to notice. Study cubes lined the inner wall surrounding the courtyard. He strolled a few feet and then stopped at one not far from the stairwell. He smiled as he recalled the day when he had used those stairs to smuggle in a bagel with cream cheese and a coffee for Nina when she was deep into researching her paper on early childhood development. It was a minor violation of library rules and a simple moment in life to convey a multitude of love.

He froze at the cubicle as a realization hit him hard. "Nina. This has something to do with Nina."

Though he did not recognize its relevance at the time, he had learned another rule governing his situation.

His hunger returned, as the burrito had not completely satisfied his appetite. With no concrete answers or further revelations forthcoming, he decided to leave the library, and the campus, and go to Sal's. Less than a mile away, Sal's had the best wings in the area, and Jake craved some good, hot chicken wings.

*   *   *

Jake ordered the special, ten hot wings with bleu cheese and celery and a Labatt's draft for only two ninety-nine, a bargain even in 1985. He produced three one-dollar bills from his wallet, noting the"1990" date on one. He still possessed dollar bills and coins with dates from the late eighties and early nineties from before "The Transferal" began, as he started to refer mentally to his situation. He chuckled to himself, thinking someone will examine the "future" money and wonder how an expert counterfeiter who had perfected their craft to the point of having created an otherwise exact replica of American currency had screwed up something as simple as the date.

As he dove into the wings, he surmised the apparent lack of luck thus far at gaining useful information likely in itself was a valuable clue. Perhaps he should have paid more attention to the humanities while in school, he thought, considering the answers he sought may reside within the discipline of philosophy instead of the physical sciences or logic.

Still, he had an inkling of what direction to take. He realized it when he stood in the library. He did not want to do it, but he had to. Just the sight of her may trigger some philosophical or emotional response within him and reveal an answer.

He also knew no matter what happened, he could not interact with her. "I've seen enough science fiction movies that warned of the possibility of a 'disruption of the space and time continuum with disastrous consequences' and all associated techno-babble bullshit," he concluded. "Not gonna be responsible for the implosion of the universe."

Interacting with those in his past in Binghamton violated no law or rule, he deduced, because he was supposed to be in Binghamton in 1985. However, he had never been to Buffalo before the fall of 1985, nor met Nina until after starting classes at the university. No, interaction was out, but seeing her was worth a try, he decided.

After the wings and single beer, he drove down Niagara Falls Boulevard to the street where she had grown up. He pulled his car off to the side of the road, across from the house, about seventy feet away. Not sure what to do next, he lit a cigarette, rolled down the driver's window a third of the way for ventilation, and sat in the Pacer in silence. Small and unassuming, the Thater's ranch type structure appeared as he remembered.

Jake leaned back and took a long drag on his cigarette. He struggled to repress the memories and the pain of his previous encounter with Nina. Being in the apartment they had lived in their entire marriage had evoked strong feelings within Jake. That apartment had been the last place where they had shared happy times.

That apartment was where he found out about the affair.

That apartment was where only days ago he last argued with her.

That apartment still to this day held the bitterest, and the sweetest, of memories.

And this house, the only home she knew before Jake, is where he had picked her up for their first date.

He dropped all resistance and let his memories drift to the happy days with Nina. Everything had seemed so right, so perfect, and yet did not last. How something so faultless ended so disastrously Jake never comprehended.

The Catholic Church, firm in conviction of the sanctity of the vow before God he and Nina made, mandated they both had to honor that commitment, whatever the cost. One alone could not sustain the marriage, but Jake found himself filling that role. In his mind, he toiled in vain to preserve the union, while she cheated on him.

The Church said he must stay and suffer.

The Church demanded he, or she, or both be the martyr.

The Church was not married to Nina Thater.

In the year Jake took to arrive at that conclusion he drifted from his faith. With seemingly no forgiveness without participation in offerings of guilt for not trying harder, or not praying more, or not confessing often, or not being good enough, Jake left Catholicism. He never reconciled the presentation of life as one huge balance sheet weighed down by the guiltiness of sins.

While he left the Church, the guilt never left him. He never understood why God had abandoned him, and why he had ended up so alone, and so lost.

At least in 1992 he had family and friends to help him deal with his drifting. Due to "The Transferal," he was now truly isolated in time.

He had no home.

*　　*　　*

He had spent over an hour waiting in the 1977 Pacer, several times fighting the urge to take a quick nap, before she finally emerged from the house. Jake sat up straight and stared at Nina, younger, but still the same Nina, eighteen and a senior in high school at this time.

"God, she's beautiful."

She walked directly to her car parked in the driveway and started the 1979 yellow Toyota Corolla's engine. Jake had already made the decision to follow her as she backed her vehicle into the street, not far from Jake's Pacer. He hoped doing so might trigger an awareness of an answer as to why "The Transferal" had happened.

The same moment he turned the ignition key, a tap on the driver side window interrupted his plan. Jake turned his head to the left and found himself face to face with one of Amherst's finest.

"Yes, officer?" he said as he rolled down the window the rest of the way, while watching Nina's car turn a corner and travel out of sight.

"Turn off the engine."

Jake swallowed and complied.

"License and registration."

Jake retrieved the paper from the glove compartment and produced the New York State Driver's License from his wallet. The officer was already closely examining both documents when Jake realized his mistake.

"What the hell is this?" the officer said as he thrust the license issued in 1990 at Jake. The document's configuration was far different from the mid-eighties version. Jake had no other option but to state the obvious.

"Uh, it's a fake."

The officer grew impatient. "I know it's a fake, genius. You'd better have a real one instead of this garbage."

"Uh, I don't have it with me, but I do have a license," Jake said, hoping that the police could access the DMV records from their patrol cars and thereby verify the validity of his 1985 license.

"Uh huh. What are you doing in this neck of the woods, if you're from Binghamton?"

Jake stammered to try to project himself as a confused teenager. "Officer, I'm up here checking out the university. I want to attend UB after high school. I got a bit lost, and somehow ended up here. Honestly, all I did was stop the car, and I was going to ask for directions, but I put my head back and the next thing I knew I was asleep. It was a long drive from Binghamton. I just woke up when you tapped on the window."

"Yeah, well this is a pretty close neighborhood, and the residents get a bit uneasy when someone is sitting in a car looking like they're stalking someone."

"Stalking? I wasn't stalking! I don't even know anyone here!" he said, truthfully, given the year.

"Uh huh. Stay in the car." Jake followed the officer's movement to the police sedan through the side view mirror, then turned his attention down the street where Nina's Toyota had disappeared. He sighed, put his head in his hands, and massaged his right temple in an attempt to ward off another encroaching migraine, conceding his effort would likely be in vain.

The officer returned after a few minutes and spoke with a more humanitarian and less authoritarian tone. "Well, Jake, everything looks ok, but you should have your license with you at all times," he said as he handed the registration and the "fake" certificate to Jake. "And, in the future, don't give the police a phony license. The only reason I'm giving this one back is because it is so bad. Son, the least you could do is get the color right!"

"Thanks," Jake weakly said as he took the documents, then rolled up the window as the officer returned to his patrol car. The brief altercation with the Amherst police had come at the worst time. Nina's destination was unknown but he had an idea. He turned the ignition key, put the Pacer in gear, eased up on the clutch, and checked his watch.

"Five fifteen. She's probably heading to JCPenney in the Twin Pines Mall for her Saturday night shift," he thought to himself as he guided the car back to Niagara Falls Boulevard.

As he drove, he remembered something the officer said. "Maybe in a way I am stalking her. Even stuck in the past, you're obsessed," he thought, remembering Tom's words from the night at The Oasis.

He cleared the notion from his head. He needed to focus and find the reason for his trip back in time, convinced "The Transferal" involved Nina in some way.

She had landed a part time job in the men's department at JCPenney while a senior in high school, and continued working there well into her college years. Jake recalled she used to hate her schedule because she often had to work until nine thirty on Saturday nights, infringing upon weekend activities. Jake, a freshman at the University at Buffalo, had inadvertently bumped into her at JCPenney a few days after meeting her at a party.

He remembered that second chance encounter in December of 1985 had led to their first date.

Eight
First

Amherst, New York
Saturday, December 14, 1985

"Come on Jasen, let's check out Merry Go Round."

"What kind of a jacket are you looking for, Jake?"

"Um, I want to get one of those brown suede deals," Jake replied.

"Why not go for the leather?" asked Jasen as he tossed his empty McDonald's soda cup behind his back and into a waste receptacle without hitting the rim. "Two points!" he proclaimed.

"Sure, I'd love to, if I could ever afford it. I can't blow a hundred and fifty dollars on a jacket, not now. I have to save up for tuition for the spring semester," Jake countered.

"I thought you were getting financial aid."

"I am, but the way they go about things in the Financial Aid office I may not see that money until I graduate. I just got the check for the fall, and I paid the tuition over two months ago." He turned his attention to a pretty women walking by before continuing. "Besides, aid doesn't cover all my needs."

Jake had made up his mind to pay his own way through college, somehow. In his view, he needed to make up for his propensity to avoid responsibility in his high school years. Either he funded the portion of the tuition, supplies, and living expenses not covered by financial aid through his meager wages, or he did not pursue his degree.

"They didn't refund your fall tuition? I mean, it sucked that you got food poisoning so bad you had to take incompletes in all your classes. They should have given you a pass."

"Yeah, especially since it was probably due to the crap they served in the cafeteria. So unless I figure out how to make a good buck fast, an expensive leather jacket is out."

"Well, why don't you go back to writing? There's big money in books, right?"

"Yeah, especially at the bookstore," Jake agreed with sarcasm. "Cost me fifty bucks for the Chem 101 book alone."

"Whatever happened to that book you were writing in high school you talked about?"

"Oh, that, it was a piece of shit," Jake said as he tossed his empty soda cup into a garbage can fifteen feet away. "Three points! Nah, it just never turned out right. I hate it. I'm not cut out to be a writer, I guess."

Jasen stopped and focused his attention about forty-five degrees off center of the mall's vast midsection. "Whoa look at that!"

"Huh? Where?"

"Next to Cavages."

"Uh. Ok, I see them. Man, Jasen, you're sick. They've got to be fifteen, if that old!"

"No way. Bet they're at least eighteen. But you've gotta admit, they're pretty damn hot!"

"Sure, for preschoolers!" Jake replied. "Come on, Romeo, I've got a jacket to buy."

"Alright. But first I've got to check on something at JCPenney."

"What?" Jake asked.

"I just got my JCPenney credit card, and I want to check out the stereos. I may even end up buying one."

"Ok, but I'm going to see what Merry Go Round has."

"Man, I'll only be a few minutes, come with me," Jasen protested. "You can help me decide."

Jake reluctantly agreed, but Jasen's "few minutes" soon turned into a half hour as he engaged in an in depth conversation with one of the salesmen on the finer points of the advantages of a system with a CD player. Jake could not imagine CDs replacing cassette tapes or vinyl records and quickly lost interest in the discussion.

"Jasen, I'm gonna head down to the men's department and check out jackets. Come down when you've decided what you're going to do," Jake said as he walked away.

Jake delved deep into inspecting leather jackets, comparing quality and price, oblivious to the small display of sock and handkerchief stocking stuffer gifts behind him until too late. A moment after his foot caught on a leg of the table everything came crashing to the floor. Red faced with embarrassment, he scurried to replace the sale items to their original configuration, hoping his clumsiness did not alert anyone. As he grabbed several sock packages, the giggling from behind him offered testament otherwise.

He sighed and closed his eyes. "Maybe, just maybe, I can leave here with just a hint of dignity intact," he thought.

"Here, let me help you," a sweet voice offered from in front of him.

With exaggerated slowness, Jake moved his head upward, his gaze following long thin legs to where they disappeared beneath a gray skirt. He swallowed as his attention progressed to the light sage fuzzy sweater, past the nice, rounded breasts, finally stopping at the source of the words. He marveled at the beautiful, full lips, slightly parted and magnificently red. He blinked and stared into her piercing blue eyes.

Dumbfounded and speechless for the second time in less than a minute, Jake recognized the girl he had met at the party Thursday night. He found his speech and tried to cover up his humiliation, aware his face was probably as red as her lips.

"Uh, thanks. My foot got caught."

"Sure, it happens all the time," Nina Thater said in a polite attempt to ease Jake's obvious embarrassment. "Hey, didn't we meet at the Phi Delta Epsilon party?" she asked as she helped gather the rest of the handkerchiefs.

"Yeah. Nina, right?" he said, not attempting to hide the sheepishness in his voice.

She nodded and grinned at him. "Hi Jake!"

"Thanks for helping," he said as together they worked to return the display to its previous condition. When finished, he grabbed one of the jackets he had inspected moments before and held the black nylon garment up in front of him, desperate to change the subject. "What do you think?"

"I think it's not quite you. Perhaps a dark gray would work better," Nina said as Jake returned the jacket to the rack.

He bent over to dust his pants off. "I was thinking the brown one may work," he said when he rose, but she had already left. He sighed, and began walking towards the escalator, still stinging from embarrassment. "Jasen should be ready now so we can get out of here," he hoped.

"Wait, try this on, Jake," the sweet voice called from behind. Jake turned as Nina walked towards him, carrying a dark gray suede coat. Jake removed his denim jacket, and Nina slipped the garment over his shoulders. Her soft touch excited Jake.

"It's perfect!"

The attraction was instant, and mutual.

Nine

Hit

Amherst, New York
Saturday, April 27, 1985

Jake replayed the memory of talking to Nina at JCPenney, eight months in the future in this timeline, as he drove the Pacer into the Twin Pines Mall's parking lot. Not since Courtney had he experienced such an intense attraction for a woman.

He passed her car and parked several rows away. "She's here," he confirmed.

Nervousness enveloped him as he walked into the mall. Part of him did not want to go forward, unsure of what scared him. "You gotta do it, Stock," he reassured himself. "Don't talk to her, just see her."

Still, hesitation ruled, so he stopped for a coffee at McDonald's in the food court, only partially for alertness. The beverage bought him a bit more time to ponder his insecurities.

"Why are you afraid, Jake? You're here to find out why you're here," he thought, aware a part of him longed to encounter Nina in this past.

He stopped before going in to JCPenney. "No use in delaying this any longer," he commanded himself as he finished the coffee. He tossed the empty cup into a garbage can near the entrance to the store. "Two points!" he exclaimed with a smirk as he entered the store and walked towards the men's department.

He feigned interest in a patterned cardigan sweater, taking extra care to avoid table displays, while he surveyed the area. Shortly he spotted her, dressed in a black skirt and a white blouse. Jake's jaw dropped. Nina appeared every bit as beautiful as the day he met her. As he stared over the tops of the clothing racks at her standing next to the cash register, warm feelings flowed within.

"When I return to 1992, maybe we could try one more time. Maybe we have one more second chance left," he thought.

He peered closer. She was talking to a man, taller than he was, and somewhat thinner. He did not make out the face, though his mannerisms and appearance suggested he was in his late teens or early twenties.

His mouth slightly parted as his eyes followed them as they walked to a small alcove in the men's coats section. They embraced and kissed.

Instantly consumed with jealousy, Jake tried unsuccessfully to remember if Nina had said anything about dating a coworker from JCPenney.

He drew in a deep breath. "Calm down, Jake. This is way before you met her."

He continued to stare as they broke the embrace. They both turned, and Jake recognized the man's face.

He dropped the sweater.

The man was Lucas.

"No, it can't be!" he thought, his stomach turning over. There was no mistaking that evil grin.

For a moment, Lucas' eyes met Jake's, and the smirk grew wider.

Jake had to throw up.

*   *   *

"Jake? Jake are you home?" Julie Stockman called out as she entered the front door. She had hoped Jake would be at the apartment preparing for the chemistry exam when she returned from working the Saturday day shift. "Jake, you don't have to go get drunk every time something upsetting happens," she thought as she reread the note she found the previous night.

Mom,

I'll be back midday Sunday. Don't worry, everything is fine.

Love, Jake.

She shook her head as she put the paper down, tired from working two shifts in twenty-four hours. "He may really be studying," she tried to convince herself. Wary of his cons, she wondered if he had taken his study materials with him.

She climbed the stairs and peered in though Jake's partially open bedroom door. The scene of a made up bed, a clean desk, and a chemistry book nowhere in sight comforted her, somewhat. Julie sighed and turned to leave the room when the phone rang. She picked up the extension in Jake's room.

"Hello?"

"Hi, Mom, it's me."

"Jake, where are you?" she asked in relief and anger.

"I'm taking a break from studying, Mom, and went to the mall with a couple of friends to unwind."

"He is studying," his mother thought. "Where are you?" she repeated.

Jake sighed and tried to divert the topic. "I just wanted to call to let you know I'm ok, and that I just need some time away to concentrate on studying for this."

He paused. "I take it Principal Blanchard already informed you of what happened?"

"Yes, Jake, and to tell you the truth, I'm not surprised. So, where are you?" she asked for the third time.

Jake realized he was not going to deflect the question. "I'm in Buffalo. Remember I had said I wanted to take a trip up here to actually see the university before orientation this summer? I figured since Principal Blanchard sent me home early I'd do the trip this weekend."

"But Jake, the test . . ." Julie began to protest.

"I know, and that's part of it. By being here it is providing me the motivation to do well Monday." He lowered his voice a notch. "Mom, please trust me," he said with sincerity.

She paused and nodded her head, not fully understanding, but accepting the response. "Ok, Jake.

Just remember you don't have any second chances left."

"I know, Mom. Bye," Jake said and hung up the phone.

*   *   *

The acidic residue of bile still present in his mouth, his head throbbing, Jake hung up the pay phone at the Twin Pines Mall. The call home was necessary, but studying for the chemistry exam was the last thing on his mind.

"Why didn't she ever tell me?" he wondered, overcome with bitterness and distrust. Quite evident Nina had at least known Lucas a lot longer than she had led him to believe, he concluded they probably had been dating long before Jake had met her at the party.

"She never said a word that entire time we were bowling in the league," he thought as he reached his car. "Why didn't she say a single word?"

He leaned against the door of the Pacer, not wanting to drive away yet, and lit a cigarette. "'I thought I recognized her' is what he said," Jake recalled with disgust. "Now I understand what he meant."

The popular mixed couples' league at Lockport Bowl-O-Rama had required use of about half of the lanes on Friday nights for a couple of hours, he recalled. They had met many people then, including Lucas Robinson.

At least the summer bowling league was when *he* had first met Lucas.

Ten
Strike

Amherst, New York
Friday, June 9, 1989

"Jake and Nina Stockman, you'll be bowling with Lucas Robinson and Becky Harrison. They're already out at lanes twenty-five and twenty-six."

Nina and Jake grabbed their rental shoes from the counter and meandered through the crowd of people towards the designated lanes. Neither was an outstanding bowler yet both enjoyed the sport, though Nina sometimes argued that bowling hardly qualified as a sport.

"I wonder what the other couple is like," Nina questioned in her usual inquisitive manner.

"Well, we know that they probably aren't married, given the last names."

They approached the lanes as the ten pins on lane twenty-five shook and fell thanks to a well-placed pocket shot. The figure who had delivered the crushing blow, a man who appeared slightly older, taller, and thinner than Jake came forward and extended his right hand. "Hi, I'm Lucas, and this is my girlfriend Becky."

"Seems nice enough," Jake thought as he received the greeting, noticing Lucas' Yankees cap. "You see that article about Winfield? He's not gonna play this year at all."

"He's too old, the Yankees are better off getting rid of him," Lucas opined.

"If he can come back from his back issues, I think he still has a few good years left," Jake countered as he cleaned his ball with a towel out of habit. He approached the foul line to take a practice roll and released the finger tipped fourteen-pound ball. It hit the pocket light, leaving only the ten-pin standing.

"I've been having a problem with lift recently," he complained as he sat down.

"Try following through with the release a bit more," Lucas offered as he made an upward motion with his right arm. "You'll get the extra action on the ball if you just bring the hand up a bit," Lucas said as he grabbed the pitcher, filled a plastic cup, and handed it to Jake.

"Bud Light ok?" Lucas asked.

"Sure, thanks," Jake said as he took the beer. I think my hand's just tired," said Jake as he adjusted his wrist brace.

"So, Jake, what do you do?"

Jake took a sip of beer before responding. "I'm a full time student, working on my Mechanical Engineering degree at UB and Nina's finishing her undergrad in psychology. She manages the men's clothing department at JCPenney at night but I think she's gonna go back for her Master's degree in psychology full time once I finish next year. You?"

"JCPenney, huh? I thought I recognized her. I'm working the dock at Grappone Lumber, but I'm planning to get into the Marines."

"Marines? Cool! I'm in the Air National Guard at Buffalo. 'Weekend warrior,' but it helps with the bills. I work in the avionics shop."

"My dad just retired as a DI at Parris Island," Lucas responded, seemingly excited to have found a military connection with Jake.

Eleven
Resignation

Amherst, New York
Saturday, April 27, 1985

No action or behavior had betrayed a hint of any sort of a prior relationship, outside of Lucas mentioning Nina "looked familiar." In fact, Nina and Lucas hardly even spoke to each other the first few weeks of bowling.

Some discomfort in his stomach remained after he had regurgitated most of the wings lunch in the JCPenney bathroom, but Jake shook off the nausea. He needed to think.

"Maybe this was why I'm here, to find out about the past affair," he postulated. "Certainly if in fact she had been seeing Lucas all that time, she hid it well during the league, and I never suspected anything."

He shook his head, struggling to accept what appeared to be the truth presented to him. Yet if learning about Nina's prior relationship with Lucas was the reason for "The Transferal," should he now magically to his own time, he wondered? "Just like Sam in 'Quantum Leap' isn't it time to leap?" he thought, only half-jokingly.

He sighed. "Six eighteen. Nothing else to learn here, time to leave" he resigned, overcome with heartache.

He decided, with conviction, if he was destined to relive the late 1980s and early 1990s he would not make the same mistake he did before. He would not meet Nina Thater.

He dropped his cigarette, and with more force than necessary, he pulverized the butt against the parking lot asphalt with the heel of his right boot. Buffalo held no more revelations for him.

Or so he thought.

Twelve
Homecoming

Buffalo, New York
Wednesday, May 22, 1991

The Boeing 737 descended to three thousand feet, and the knot in Jake's stomach tightened in anticipation of seeing her again. Nina had been his rock during the deployment, and the thought of being back with her was the singular meaning of heaven to him now.

The aircraft gently arched over the western New York sky on approach to Buffalo International Airport. Niagara Falls, where he had asked Nina to marry him, came into view. He smiled as the plane completed its arch and intercepted the glideslope for the runway. "We'll be back soon," he thought.

The next moments after landing seemed to last forever, the skewed perception of time the result of the increasing anticipation of reunion. Aware of his now rapid pulse, he took a deep breath as the ground crew marshaled Delta Flight 1007 to a stop at gate four. He and a few others in his unit were ordered stateside early from the Middle East to prepare for the arrival of the four C-141 aircraft stationed in Buffalo. He never asked why he drew the lucky straw.

Through the aircraft window, Jake located the small crowd of family members and friends of the returning Buffalo Air National Guard personnel. He fought to locate Nina Thater Stockman among those waving American flags with yellow ribbons tied to them.

"Come on Jake, time to go home," Harold Murphy said as he rose and retrieved his A-3 bag from the overhead bin after the plane had stopped at the gate.

Jake broke his gaze out the window then did the same. "Yeah, finally. It was a hell of a time, Murph."

Jake opened his bag and took out a single rose he had picked up during their layover in New York City a few hours earlier, then sauntered up the jetway to the indoor gate. He heard her scream with joy before he saw her. He turned and she embraced him tightly.

"Easy, easy!" Jake said as he took the rose from behind his back and presented the flower to Nina.

"Oh, my God, is it really you?" Nina asked, laughing and crying at the same time.

"Yes, it's really me. I love you!"

"I love you too!"

Thirteen
Reality

Binghamton, New York
Sunday, April 28, 1985

His return from the war, when he stepped off the plane and into her arms after many months of separation and uncertainty, was at one time the happiest moment in Jake's short life. The knowledge she had engaged in an affair while he served overseas, however, had forever marred the homecoming memory.

Regardless of whether her relationship with Lucas began during the deployment or back in her JCPenney days, the effect on Jake was the same. He resolved to put the bad parts of his past behind him and to focus solely on the future.

He vowed never to visit that memory again.

He strove to make as little noise as possible as he unlocked the apartment door, not wanting to wake his mother up at three thirty in the morning. Stoley's sensitive ears heard him and he slowly walked to greet Jake, not uttering a sound.

"Good boy! Shh, keep quiet," he whispered as he scratched behind Stoley's ears.

He removed his shoes and tiptoed up the stairs to his room. He closed the bedroom door, gently set his overnight bag next to the dresser, and placed his chemistry book on his desk. Without taking off his clothes, he fell into the bed, exhausted.

$$* \quad * \quad *$$

A knock on the door woke him up at seven in the morning. Jake opened his eyes and realized with a sigh he was still in 1985.

"Jake, are you in there?"

The headache from the Twin Pines Mall had never quite ebbed, and he massaged his temples. "Yes, Mom. I came home last night after you went to sleep."

Julie Stockman let go a long breath of relief. "Well, I'm going to work. I have to put in four hours at the clinic this morning and after I'm going grocery shopping. Is there anything you want?"

"Yeah, a twelve pack of Sam Adams," he thought. "No. Well, maybe some Frosted Flakes. I think we're out."

"Already got it on the list. Crack those books, tomorrow's the big day," she reminded Jake.

"Yes, Mom, I will."

Jake rose from bed a few minutes later and dragged himself into the shower. He stayed under the spray for an extended time, enjoying the soothing effect the warm water had on his muscles and headache. His tension eased with each drop. He knew though he would need a large coffee or two to start the day.

On most Sunday mornings during his high school years, he and his mother attended the eight thirty service at The Church of the Holy Trinity. With her at work, however, he opted to relax with the Sunday paper and review material for the exam tomorrow. Besides, years had passed since he had last attended Mass, or cared to.

He donned a pair of sweats and a t-shirt and grabbed his chemistry textbook. As he descended the staircase while concentrating on a quantum state diagram in the book, his foot slipped. The last thing he remembered was tumbling down.

Fourteen
White

Buffalo, New York
Saturday, May 9, 1992

He was lying on a bed, unsure of what had happened, in an unfamiliar room with white walls and a large bright fluorescent light above. He discerned a sort of beeping sound in the distance. His vision cleared, and he surveyed his environment. Shiny metal pipes and strange equipment surrounded him, some with tubes, and others with wires. He followed one tube from a blue and gray box on a chrome pole to his right arm, the end disappearing under a bandage.

He recognized his location as a hospital room.

He groggily tried to lift himself up, but decided not to when dizziness nearly extinguished his consciousness. His head ached, and he forced himself to scrutinize further the space, moving only his eyes. He focused on a display screen as two people dressed in white, a male and a female, entered the room.

"How long since he's shown signs of consciousness, nurse?" he heard the woman say.

"He began to move his extremities about fifteen minutes ago, but he's only now coming out of it."

The doctor leaned closer to the man lying in the bed. Holding the patient's eyelids open and using a small pocket flashlight, she examined the pupil's reaction to the light. Satisfied, she addressed the patient. "How do you feel?"

"Uh, a bit groggy. Pretty confused, actually."

"Do you know where you are?"

"Seems like some sort of hospital."

"Good. Nurse, what are the vitals?"

"Pressure is one-oh-two over seventy-three, pulse is sixty-two."

"Very good. I want you to continue to lay back and rest. You've had a rough accident, but you're going to be fine," the doctor said.

"How long, uh, how long have I been laid up here?"

"A few hours."

"What happened?"

"You suffered head and chest injuries in an accident," the physician replied.

"Am I going to be ok?"

"Yes. Tell me, what is the last thing you remember?"

The man propped himself up with his elbows, and no vertigo remained. "Hmmm. I was at this bar called The Oasis. It's on Main." He paused to collect his thoughts, staring at the wall behind the two figures in white.

"We were shooting pool, me and a friend, betting with shots," he continued. "Sink a shot, drink a shot. Kind of a stupid idea I know, but we were just blowing off steam."

"And that's it?"

He nodded. "Pretty much. At some point I remember the game being over and that I had won, but also that I had drank way too much. I guess I must've passed out, or come close, sometime after. Should have laid off earlier."

He paused. "I shouldn't have drank so much," he repeated.

The doctor brought one finger to her lips and frowned. "Do you remember the truck?" she asked.

"A truck? What truck?"

"The one that struck you. A black pickup."

"I was hit by a truck? Wow," he replied, taking a deep breath before continuing. "No, no truck that I can recall."

"Hmm. Ok, well, Tom, just rest up and take it easy. Outside of light alcohol poisoning and some bruises, I think you're going to be fine. If all goes well, we'll likely release you tomorrow. Your parents are waiting to see you."

Tom Schultz watched the doctor and nurse as they left the room. He pondered what the truck strike must have felt like.

Fifteen
Test

Binghamton, New York
Monday, April 29, 1985

Jake visited Ernie's Deli across the street from Binghamton High School for a much needed and desired large black coffee before heading for homeroom, still cursing himself for his act of clumsiness. The fall damaged his pride and gave his recurring headache a high-octane boost. He popped a couple Extra Strength Tylenols in a bid to force the pain out of his head.

He had not been a fan of coffee in high school before. The long all-nighters early in his college career cramming for exams had produced a love affair with the beverage's attention-enhancing effects. Not until his junior year at the University at Buffalo had Jake realized the fallacies of putting off preparing for tests until the previous night. Despite downing a healthy quantity of coffee, he had bombed his first Differential Equations midterm. Going forward, he prepared for exams by studying a small amount most days over the course of the semester, and getting a good night's sleep prior.

But he kept the coffee habit.

He adjusted one of the zippered mesh sections on his muscle shirt as he entered the school, not quite comfortable in the current fashion attire. He fumbled with the Velcro fastener of the parachute pants, still not confident he had gotten the look right. "Man, what was I thinking when I bought this outfit?" he mumbled to himself as he studied his eighties clothes in the mirror of the restroom nearest to his homeroom.

He rehashed in his mind the same conclusion he had come to in Buffalo as the morning announcements came over the speaker. If finding out about the prior relationship between Lucas and Nina was not a trigger for returning to his time, he was probably destined to stay caught up in his past.

He accepted the fact he would return to 1992 only by reliving the next seven years, and recognized his second chance constituted an opportunity to sidestep his previous mistakes. He found the prospect intriguing. He could avoid meeting Nina, and the accompanying heartache and guilt. He wondered how many other errors and situations he could alter.

"Maybe even change the world," he thought.

The tap on his shoulder shook him from his preoccupations, and he turned around to face the student seated at the desk behind him. "Yeah?"

"Jake, they just called your name on the PA."

"Really? What for?"

"You have to go see Blanchard. Little out of it today, huh?"

Jake got up and rubbed his head. He had experienced headaches before, but not one ebbing and flowing for days. "C'mon, Tylenol, work," he said to himself as he picked up his chemistry textbook and binder.

After turning a corner in the hall, an arm grabbed his jacket and flung him into a locker. He lost his grip on his books and they fell to the floor.

"What the fuck?" Jake turned to face two male students, the larger one dressed in a plaid flannel shirt and a denim jacket, the other in a "Who" concert jersey.

"Listen, asswipe, I bet you think you're real funny," the larger one said as he motioned towards Jake again. "Forgot I was coming back today, huh?" He shoved Jake backwards, and Jake's shoulder crashed into the metal door behind him.

"Man, I am having one hell of a bad week, and it's only Monday," he thought. "What the fuck are you talking about?" he said, agitated.

"Why'd you lie, peckerhead?" the tall teen asked as he leaned closer. Jake grimaced, smelling his attacker's putrid breath.

"Lie? Lie about what?" Jake replied, drawing a blank. "Look, I don't have time for this."

"Denim Man" slapped his open left hand against the locker behind Jake about eight inches from his head. "Don't play games, ass."

The "Who Fan" spoke up. "Me and Conner were suspended for a fucking week because of you, shithead. My old man threw a fit!"

Jake tried to think, but could not register how he was connected to these "kids." "I do not the time for this shit," Jake reiterated as he bent over to pick up his materials. As he gathered his books the "Who Fan" clocked his skull from behind, sending him to the floor.

"No teachers around to save your sorry ass this time," "Denim Man" said as he kicked a rising Jake in the ribs, knocking Jake back down. "I didn't steal nothing from the bookstore."

The words triggered Jake's memory. "Stealing from the bookstore? Whoa, Conner Griffin," Jake recalled as he rubbed the back of his head. Conner and Larry Janik, the "Who Fan," had received a week suspension during Jake's senior year because Jake had reported seeing the two stealing sweats from the school's bookstore.

"Got my ass kicked for it too. Well, perhaps here's a chance to test the 'Avoid Major Mistakes' theory," he decided as he jumped up and took a defensive posture.

"Whoa, weenie boy's gonna fight?" Larry snickered with glee as he also assumed a fighting stance, not quite as sophisticated as Jake's. "Come on, take a punch. I fuckin' dare you."

Jake shook his head. "Nah. Women and children go first."

Larry grunted as he launched his right fist. Jake blocked the attack with his left arm while landing his right knee to Larry's midsection. Jake slammed his right arm into his opponent's back, knocking him to the ground and leaving him gasping for air.

Jake turned to Conner and extended a hand. "Hey, let's forget this whole thing, and let bygones be bygones."

"Fuck off," Conner countered as he threw a left at Jake. The punch was slow, and Jake stepped to the side as his attacker's fist smashed into a locker. He landed a right cross squarely on Conner's jaw, sending "Denim Man" sprawling into the lockers.

"Damn, I always wanted to do that," he thought as he adjusted his jacket, picked up his books, and resumed his trip to the principal's office. "Maybe this 'living in the past' deal isn't so bad after all."

Confident of having broken no other rules, Jake strolled into Blanchard's office, confident the call was solely about the chemistry exam. "I haven't been here long enough to get into trouble," he concluded.

"Good morning, Mr. Blanchard," Jake greeted the middle aged, short, rounded man from the office entrance.

"Hi, Jake, come on in, ok?" Blanchard signaled for Jake to enter the wood paneled room as he sat down behind his desk. He motioned at the chair in front for Jake to do the same.

"Jake, I'm glad you're in today. When you didn't show in the in house suspension room this morning I got worried."

"I thought I was supposed to go straight to homeroom?" Jake protested.

Blanchard held up his left hand to cut off Jake. "That's ok. I wanted to inform you we've reserved room 113 for the exam, whenever you're ready." Blanchard leaned forward and examined Jake closer. "How'd you get that bump on your head?"

Jake touched his left temple, still tender to the touch from contacting the banister the previous day. "I slipped and fell down the stairs yesterday morning. It's ok, though. Just a bump, and a bruised pride. And a wallop of a headache."

Blanchard smiled. "Ok. Well, we've got room 113 reserved whenever you want to start the exam," he repeated.

"I'm ready now," Jake responded with confidence.

Blanchard nodded. "Good. Good. Ok, well, then report to 113. Ms. Tannenbaum will be the proctor. And Jake, I don't have to tell you this is a very important test for you."

Jake nodded as he rose to leave the office. "I know," he said. The test was not solely about chemistry.

*　　*　　*

Forty-five minutes later Blanchard compared Jake's answers to the solution key in his office. After a few moments, he laid down his red pen after reaching the end of the exam answer sheet. He took off his black horn rimmed reading glasses.

"Well Jake, congratulations. You earned a perfect score."

"As if there was any doubt," Jake thought, but only nodded.

Blanchard leaned back in the olive cloth upholstered office chair. "Well, if I recall, our agreement was a week suspension if you earned an A, and expulsion if not. Well, maybe the weekend has tempered me a bit, but I think a suspension may be a bit harsh particularly considering you made a perfect score on what Mrs. Thomas told me was a very difficult exam. Actually, Jake, I have seen a positive change in you over the past few days."

"Thank you, sir. I have been trying."

"I can tell," Blanchard said as he tilted forward again. "From what I've heard you're also excelling in Calculus, eh?"

Jake sat motionless as the blood rushed to his face. He managed to find his voice, knowing Blanchard was referring to his explanation of integrals. "Well, I've been studying more for all of my classes." Douglas going straight to Blanchard did not surprise Jake, as Douglas had often complained to the principal about Jake's attitude.

Blanchard gave Jake a sideways smile. "Son, tactfulness is a primary key to winning friends and not making enemies. But you'll never be punished here for answering a question correctly. Keep the sarcasm down, but since you, as one student put it, 'blew Mr. Douglas out of the water' with your answer, we'll let it slide," he said with a knowing nod. "Now, get out of here. You have a class to go to, don't you, Mister?"

"Yes, sir! Thanks!" Jake stood up and walked out of the office, energized and relieved no more punishment was forthcoming. Even the constant throbbing in his head had eased.

"That's him! That's the guy who kicked our ass for no reason!"

Jake whirled around to face the source of the words in the principal's reception area. Conner

Griffin sat next to Larry Janik, his "Who" shirt stained with a few drops of blood. Blanchard emerged from his office, the accusation loud enough to alert him.

Jake's euphoric demeanor dropped like an anvil on the coyote.

"What's going on, Margaret?"

"I found these two sitting near the lockers in the North wing, second floor," Margaret Teale responded. "I asked them for a hall pass and then noticed the bruise on Conner's face and Larry's bloody nose. When I asked them what had happened, they said Jake Stockman had beaten them up without provocation." She glared at Jake.

Jake stood motionless and silent, staring at "hall monitor lady." "Damn, does she have it in for me or what?" he thought.

Jake saw his future crashing down around him. He feared Blanchard would not care if he excelled in academics or not. Jake's reputation as a chronic troublemaker would be enough for expulsion, which to Jake meant a life-long sentence of mediocre food service industry jobs.

"Well, maybe I'll one day manage my own McDonald's," he considered as Blanchard stared at him.

Blanchard turned his eyes from the five foot eight inch Jake to the six foot two inch and five foot eleven inch frames of Conner and Larry. Both of the injured youths had been in trouble before for fighting. He scrutinized Jake again and then returned his attention to the two larger teens.

Blanchard put his hands on his waist. "Boys, I'm not dumb. Do you seriously expect me to believe Jake beat the crap out of both of you? Hell, Jake probably would have a hard time defending himself from a girl his size." He turned to Jake. "No offense, Jake. Go ahead to your class."

"None taken," Jake replied as he realized what was happening. For whatever reason, Blanchard had chosen Jake's side, and Jake was not about to question it. He walked quickly out the office vestibule door before the window of opportunity for vacating shut. But he made sure to flash a cocky sideways smile, hidden from Blanchard and Teale, to his two adversaries.

"I am digging this second chance!" he thought as he climbed the stairs to gym class.

PART III
Mistake

Sixteen
Choice

Binghamton, New York
Friday, June 21, 1985

"Graduation is tomorrow, and I am excited to again shake Blanchard's hand and receive the diploma! While last time I only worked enough to get by, the last couple of months I've enjoyed applying myself to the fullest of my abilities. Every exam, including finals, I aced, several with perfect scores."

He stretched his arms out in front of him before continuing to write. "Even Blake Douglas admitted a remarkable change in my demeanor and approach to academics. I took Blanchard's advice, and over the past two months, I actually formed a positive relationship with Douglas. He's really not a bad guy, just sort of, well, different. I think we have a high level of mutual respect now that we never had before."

He laid the notebook down on his desk and stared out his bedroom window into the pitch-dark night. Exhausted and unsure why he had begun chronicling events of "The Transferal," he closed his eyes for a moment to regain focus. He did not wish to miss the opportunity to record his experience, realizing on some level doing so had rekindled his passion for writing. "A few more thoughts to go," he encouraged himself.

"It's been fun reliving things. I absolutely enjoyed taking the discovery flight again at TriCities Airport last week! If I join the Air National Guard again, I'll have to take advantage of the military discount the Buffalo Flying Club offers."

"What's interesting is while most events have played out not much different than before, I see great benefits to having the opportunity to make other choices. Yet, it seems more often than not I end up following the same path as I did before."

Stoley interrupted Jake's composing, demanding attention in the form of a head scratch. Jake complied before continuing. "One example is deciding where to attend college. I'd been accepted by the University of Buffalo earlier in the year, and deadlines for fall acceptance and entry have long past for other universities. So why change direction? Besides, I'm familiar with the school and area, and actually am looking forward to meeting old friends again. I can't imagine a life without Tom, Shane, Hector, Jasen, and everybody else."

He stopped for a moment. "Well, not everyone. I'm not going to meet Nina again."

He set the pen down, recognizing he had reached a good end for the night. He closed the notebook, and climbed into bed. He stared at the photo of him and Courtney taken on their prom date the previous month. "So many things I can do differently," he thought as he turned off the light. "So many landmines I might avoid."

He did not consider taking a different path to circumvent one land mine could lead to a field full of mines.

*   *   *

In addition to graduation, Saturday marked Bob Goode's birthday, and his parents organized a combination party to mark both occasions. Bob planned to attend Cornell in the fall and was certain his mother and father were going to present him with a car at the celebration for gaining entrance to the Ivy League school. He hoped for a new black Trans Am.

Coming from a lower middle class background and raised by a single working parent, Jake was somewhat incredulous of Bob's wish for such an extravagant gift. The 1977 Pacer might be a jalopy but he took pride of ownership after buying the auto with money earned from the hospital job. Assuming responsibility of all aspects of maintaining a vehicle gave Jake the ability to appreciate the Pacer. Bob's parents may give him the gift of a pricy Trans Am but would miss, again, an opportunity to educate about the sacrifices necessary to achieve what one wants.

Jake arrived at Bob's house not long after the graduation ceremony ended to help load up the Goode's Blazer with food and other necessities for the celebration at Chenango Valley State Park. Although his parents had wanted the party at the house, ostensibly to flaunt their wealth, Bob insisted the location be where he had spent much of his free time with friends, comrades he would not see nearly as often once he began pre-med studies at Cornell.

Jake's desire for attending the gathering went beyond Bob's friendship, however. He remembered almost every detail when he and Courtney lost their virginity together, on this day. Still, although Jake enjoyed replaying the memory, he was unsure if he wanted to relive the experience. He had over seven additional years of life under his belt then the eighteen-year-old Courtney, and recognized the significant differences in perspectives, philosophies, and many other areas between the late teens and mid-twenties.

Even more so, Jake struggled with the morality of sleeping with Courtney. "What am I supposed to say if we did it? I can't tell her I've done it before and that she was, uh, is my first," he thought. He did not want to lie, but could not explain the truth of "The Transferal" to her, not yet at least.

His uncertainty of his feelings for Courtney compounded his dilemma. When they had met in the previous timeline, he had fallen in love with her almost at first sight. His affection for her had stayed with him for a while after leaving Binghamton for Buffalo but eventually faded, as he never received a single letter from her.

Now, still stinging from the pain from his failed marriage to Nina, he was not sure if he would ever experience love again, or want to. And although attracted to Courtney, almost to the point of irresistibility, he did not desire sex without devotion and commitment.

"It's a confusing mix," he concluded as he shook his head while loading the Blazer.

Previously, Jake had been more concerned with fitting in and had adopted his peers' casual attitude towards sex. Everything changed, however, when he and Nina aborted their child. Consumed with guilt, he became bitter. Eventually he had dealt with the pain by "manning up," burying the hurt under superficial layers of false attitudes and expressions.

He vowed never to abort a child of his again, and to treat sex with dignity and respect. He reminded himself of his pledge as he finished loading the Blazer.

He had yet to learn running away does not solve a problem, and attempting to control one's destiny is not often possible, in spite of second chances.

*　　*　　*

He made the decision during the short drive to the park. He would enjoy the day with her but avoid taking the walk by the lake. The deviation had led to their time at the shore together. To Jake, no other better alternative presented itself.

"Hey, sweetie, where ya been? Congratulations!" she gave him a long, extended hug coupled with a kiss for the ages.

Jake sighed after he released the lip lock. "Hi, Courtney, you too. How was the movie last night?"

"I think Karen drooled the entire time. She's crazy about Michael J. Fox. Too bad you couldn't come, though, it was pretty good. You would have liked it, since you're into all that sci-fi stuff."

"Now that's what I need - a Delorean converted into a time machine so I can return to 1992," he thought.

"How's Stoley?"

"He's ok, just getting old. Probably just a touch of arthritis. I wanted to bring him down here today but the vet said he really needed to rest."

"I'm glad he's ok. Maybe we can go for a walk alone together later, and I'll take your mind off of him," she said, seductively.

Jake grimaced to himself. "This is not going to be easy," he thought.

*   *   *

After the mid-afternoon lunch, Bob, Courtney, and several other guests changed into swim gear and went for a dip in the park pool, contrary to parental warnings about swimming on a full stomach. Jake could not help but notice how Courtney's one-piece bathing suit showed off her near perfect form.

Dave's suggestion of a game of Frisbee football after lunch provided the excuse to fight the temptation to join her. Before, he and Courtney had taken their walk immediately after drying off. Jake figured if he avoided the pool he would sidestep their ensuing stroll, and thus their moment.

"Why haven't you changed?" Courtney asked, noticing Jake had not swapped his shirt and jeans for swimming trunks.

"Court, I'm gonna play Frisbee football for a bit."

Her seductive eyes melted him as she playfully grabbed at his hands. "Mmm. I was hoping maybe we'd blow off the pool early and go for a walk."

"Uh, sure, we can do it, later."

"Come on Jake, let's take a walk now. Down by the lake is really romantic," she said while tugging at his shirt.

"Hey, Jake, head's up!"

Jake spun around in time to catch a red Frisbee before it struck him. "Later, sweetheart." Jake said as he tossed the disc to Liam, thankful for the easy escape.

Courtney reached out, grabbed Jake's shoulders, and pulled him back. "I think that it'd be fun," she said coyly as she started to kiss Jake intensely.

Jake's passions began to well up, and for a moment he considered taking the walk and accepting the consequences. Memories and guilt painfully squelched his contemplation.

"No! What part of 'no' didn't you understand?" he shouted, angry at almost succumbing to his hormones as he broke the embrace.

Courtney's face betrayed her abrupt mood change from flirtatious and romantic to upset and hurt. "Fine!" she said and stormed away.

Jake listlessly jogged to the field, having left his passion with Courtney. He hoped the friendly competition would provide adequate relief from both the pain of his decision and yet another growing headache.

*   *   *

Jake sat on a bench, dejected, ten minutes after the contest ended and about an hour since he spoke with Courtney. Despite trying to stick to his convictions, he could not ignore the growing sense he had made the wrong decision, or at least had executed it poorly.

"It's not her fault. She doesn't understand. I'm an ass."

He stood up and walked toward the pool, intent on finding Courtney to apologize to her. He hoped that he would find the right words, even telling her the truth about "The Transferal" if necessary. But she was not there, nor at the pavilion.

He started in the direction of the lake.

Jake found her sitting on a rock beside the trail where the field ends and the brush begins. He slowly, approached her.

"Hey, how are you doing?" he said, gently, not expecting a warm reception.

She stared straight ahead. "Fine," she said, her tone cold.

Jake sat down next to her and took a deep breath, quite aware her anger remained, and rightfully so. He gently put his arm around her.

"I'm sorry."

She did not answer, but also did not push him away.

"Court, I'm sorry," he repeated. "I didn't mean to be so short with you."

She cut him off as she turned to face him. "Jake, do you care about me?"

"Yes, of course I do, very much," he replied, taken aback by the question.

"Then what's been wrong recently?" she asked, exasperated.

"Wrong? How?"

"With you. With us. With everything," she said. "Look. I know you're worried about Stoley but there's something else going on. Sometimes I think you're the man of my dreams, but other times, you seem so, well so distant. Sometimes it's almost as if you were somewhere else."

Jake nodded in agreement. Her perception was not far from the truth. "It's not just Stoley. I've had a lot on my mind," he muttered.

"So have I. Jake. I need to know, now, what's going to happen to us when you leave?"

"Well, you'll to stop writing me, and it'll break my heart," he thought.

"I don't know," he finally said.

"Jake, I've never felt closer to anyone else in my life. I'm scared of losing that feeling, but I don't want to hold you down. You've got your life waiting for you in Buffalo, and soon you'll forget me." Her eyes became misty.

"That's not true!" he said with honest conviction. "I won't forget you. I'll wait. Buffalo's only four hours away, we can handle the long distance relationship." Jake heard himself say the words, and realized he meant every one.

"Jake, while you were playing with the guys, I had a chance to sit and think. Actually, I've been thinking for a long time. Karen thinks that we should just end it now, but I can't. It's not that cut and dry for me."

"Why'd she say that we should end it?" Jake asked, confused.

"Because then we would avoid the hurt. She went through the same deal with Billy when he left last fall, and it tore her apart. She thought it could last, but after a while she had to stop writing him. Not because she didn't want to, but because she wanted to let him go free. She didn't want to hold him back. She said though that it'd be easier to stop it now before it gets to that point. She really loved Billy."

A feeling of warmth from understanding surrounded him, and he held Courtney closely in silence. She never told this to him before. He now understood why letters from Courtney never came. Communication ceased not for falling out of love with him, rather because her love was great enough to let him go.

He cursed himself. In a small and deep recess of his heart, he had never gotten over losing Courtney.

He hugged her again, and she snuggled closer.

He sensed the genuineness of her love, and his. Tired of trying to swim upstream against the current, he spiritually released the firm grip of control, letting the river of circumstance take him to his destiny.

Thoughts raced through his mind almost as fast as his heart beat. "Maybe Courtney is the current, the reason it all happened. It does seem to make perfect sense. Maybe I returned a few months before I left for school to have a second chance with Courtney. Maybe I'm supposed to do this," he rationalized as he brushed her hair with his fingers.

The narcissistic Jake never considered the purpose of the "The Transferal" might not involve him alone.

She looked up at him. Accepting his newfound revelation of clarity, he let himself experience an emotional intimacy with Courtney as never before.

He let go further. Love took over.

They stared into each other's eyes as they leaned in, together, to join lips. The passion increased, as did the intensity of the kissing, as she slowly moved her fingers between Jake's legs and started to rub.

They stopped. Without a word, Courtney stood up and took Jake's hand. He followed, and together they walked into the woods.

The birds sang and the stream to the lake echoed a faint gurgling as Jake and Courtney made love.

Seventeen
Mist

The Shore
Some Time

He walked down to the shore, and stepped into the old, weather-beaten wooden rowboat. The early morning sun, still minutes from rising, provided ample light to highlight the gentle puffs of steam rolling off the water's surface. Not too wide even at its maximum girth, he confidentially rowed to the opposite side where answers awaited him.

Two doves circled above in a pattern resembling a sideways figure eight. Below the birds and straight ahead, two people laughed on top of a large flat rock. He rubbed his eyes as he removed the oars from the water and let the boat drift closer to the shore. The two naked figures embraced. He strained to improve his view. Although he was embarrassed watching the pair have sex, he had to know who they were.

He recognized the woman's face through the mist. "Courtney," he whispered. She turned her head towards Jake after he said her name and smiled. Jake also identified the male. He was looking at himself.

The boat hit the rock hard and spun around uncontrollably, jarring Jake from his trance. The other occupant, an elderly man, grabbed one oar from Jake and began to paddle. Jake had not noticed the gentleman before but thought nothing of his oversight.

"Where are we going, Albert?" he asked of the old man.

There was no answer.

Jake returned his attention to the two on the shore, but saw only one. He stared at Nina's face.

Eighteen
Consequence

Binghamton, New York
Sunday, June 23, 1985

He awoke with a jolt, and tried to clear is head with a good shake. The dream had appeared so real in all senses and experience. He squinted, then surveyed his bedroom to verify his situation, awake and in his mother's apartment in Binghamton.

He sat on the edge of the bed, letting out a muffled groan as he read the clock.

He rubbed his neck and closed his eyes. In crystal clarity the images of the lake, the rock, the boat, Courtney and then Nina remained. He opened his eyes, and without a second thought grabbed a pad and pen and scribbled words describing the nocturnal trip.

He had several more hours to sleep. He turned over and hoped he would return to the dream.

*   *   *

Jake woke up later in the morning, refreshed from several hours of deep sleep undisturbed by further dreams. He yawned and stretched, and then remembered the notepad.

He had not written much, only "lake, boat, Courtney, Nina, Albert, contentment," the last capitalized and underlined several times. He struggled to try to remember the details behind the words, particularly the identity of "Albert."

Jake found most dreams were easy to recall, but a few remained quite difficult. He wondered if those that remained locked contained clues to the meaning of "The Transferal." By keeping a pad and pen near the bed, he hoped he might record enough to extract those clues.

The significance of the lake and Courtney seemed clear enough to Jake. No doubt lingered about his love for Courtney. Yesterday had been every bit as inspiring and fulfilling as the first time, even more so in some ways. In that aspect, all seemed perfect in Jake Stockman's world.

Thoughts of his visions stayed with him throughout the morning and into the early afternoon until midway through a ride along the meandering paths of Chenango Valley State Park.

Everything stopped for Jake Stockman.

He jumped off the bike, overcome with panic.

"Not all's perfect, not at all!" he grasped. The horror on Jake's face betrayed his sunken soul.

Unlike before when he and Courtney first made love, yesterday Jake had intended not to have sex. Without his hopeful thinking in the previous timeline, the need to remember to stop at CVS on the way to the park to buy condoms had been non-existent. And Courtney never used oral contraceptives because of negative side effects.

*   *   *

"Jake, I'm sure it's fine, don't worry."

Jake paced up and down the hallway in his apartment. "Court, how can you be sure? And how could we - how could I have been so stupid? I should have had a rubber."

"It's not like you had time to get anything, it just happened," Courtney said in a tone that changed from soothing to concerned. "You don't regret it, do you, Jake?"

"No, no, that's not it," he protested. "Look, we have to get you checked. I mean, I have to know."

"Jake, look. I just had my period last week. This is the safest time to do it. Why are you so worried?"

Jake drew a long breath. "We have to be more responsible, Court. Are you ready for a baby? I'm not."

"Well, if I am pregnant, I'd still have it, and I'm sure we'd find a way. You would stay with me, wouldn't you?" she said with hopeful, piercing eyes, searching for a truthful answer.

He turned and hugged her. "Yes, absolutely!"

"Of course, there's always an abortion option."

Jake stood up as memories of him waiting for Nina at the clinic came flooding back. "No! No way! No abortion, ever!"

"Jake, Jake, I wasn't serious!" Courtney said to calm him. "I'd never, ever consider doing something like that, especially to a child that was conceived from our love!"

Courtney's response did nothing to relieve Jake's uneasiness. "Well, I still have to know. Let's go get one of those home pregnancy test kits."

Courtney sighed. "Well, ok, Jake, but I really don't think it's necessary. Besides, we couldn't do it now anyway. I have to wait a couple weeks after I miss my period, if I miss it, I think. At least that's the way it was with the test that Karen had used."

*   *   *

If the previous night had been the happiest in Jake's life, this one was the antithesis.

Jake tossed and turned in his bed, unable to sleep. The instructions on the side panel of the home pregnancy kit's packaging confirmed Courtney's assessment. He faced several weeks of anxious waiting.

Jake spent the sleeplessness mentally kicking himself for his slip up.

He had been down this road before.

He thought he had learned to be more careful.

He was twenty-six. She was eighteen.

He had the experiences, the heartache, the guilt. She did not.

"What good is a second chance if the same grave mistakes are repeated, even in different circumstances?" he thought in anguish. His guilt brought back the pounding headache.

"What if she is pregnant?"

He then returned to the one question that had fueled his guilt for years.

"If Nina and I hadn't aborted, what would our child have been like?"

*   *   *

Sleep came almost an hour later, and he again found himself in the land of vivid dreams. Confusing images of bright geometric patterns swirled around his head until they coalesced into a street scene. Jake studied the road, drawn to run across the Court Street Bridge over the Chenango River to find his home. When he reached the woods on the other side, he turned on to the path that led to where he and Courtney had made love on the shore of the lake. A fog had rolled in, partially obscuring his vision.

He thought he heard a girl giggle.

"Stop mocking me!" he shouted to the unknown source of the sound.

The laughter ceased and a figure emerged from the mist. Jake squinted and barely made out a naked and pregnant Courtney. The moment their eyes met Courtney's face morphed into Nina's, again.

He shot up, awake, covered in sweat, the wetness not due to the warmth of the summer night. He stared at the pad by the side of the bed. No need to write, as he understood the meaning of the dream, burned into his soul to guarantee recollection.

PART IV
Regret

Nineteen
Goodbye

Binghamton, New York
Tuesday, August 20, 1985

"So, are you ready for Buffalo?"

"Yeah, I think so, Steve," Jake replied, knowing full well his brother had no idea of the scope of his question.

"You know, in a way, we're in the same boat. You're starting college, and I'm starting law school."

Jake took a drag on his cigarette. "Yeah. It would have been cool if you accepted Buffalo's offer, though. We'd be there at the same time."

Steve shifted his weight. "UB's got a good law school, but Albany's better. I like Albany. My undergrad time there was awesome, and I'm looking forward to going back. It seems that for me all roads lead to Albany, you know. Besides, you don't want your older brother hanging around your first year of college."

"Yeah, you're right, I suppose," Jake agreed. "Listen, let me ask you something, ok? Are you happy with the way your life is going?"

Steve shrugged his shoulders. "I dunno. I like where I'm at, but I decided a long time ago that I don't need a roadmap, just an idea of a general direction. Life is like a river, Jake. Sometimes it's best not to force where you want to go and just let the currents carry you."

"Yeah, that kinda sounds familiar."

"C'mon, little brother. Let's go to S and S and get a couple of spiedie subs, I'm starving. Stop being so serious all the time, and have some fun!"

*   *   *

"I haven't been able to shake the need to be serious all summer," he wrote, referencing what Steve had said earlier. "Some days living in "The Transferal" are filled with fun, such as the last bash before heading off to college or even just working at the hospital, enjoying the experience, not just the small but useful paycheck. But other days I have been acutely aware just how out of place I've been here. I came close to telling Steve about the experience, but as close as we are, I couldn't bring myself to open up to him."

He rubbed his chin and continued to write in the notebook that he had been recording his thoughts about "The Transferal." "I don't understand what seems like the only constant this summer, the recurrence of a headache that has never completely left me. I never had a problem with headaches before. When it comes it is persistent and invasive, not deep like a migraine but rather seemingly located on the peripheral of the skull, almost as if my brain was struggling to move in two different directions, and smashing against a brick wall each time."

The human mind is not meant to comprehend two lifetimes simultaneously.

"I thought getting back together with Courtney was the best explanation for this second chance at life," he continued to write. "The shining point of this summer without a doubt was reliving old times and experiencing new ones with her. Yet while being with Courtney is great, it doesn't feel right. And I think she feels the same. I care for her, but as painful as it is to admit I don't think we're supposed to be together. I can't put a finger on why. It's just a feeling."

He still had no clue as to "The Transferal's" real meaning or purpose.

*   *   *

"What are you thinking about, Jake?"

Jake leaned against Courtney's shoulder. "Oh, earlier this summer, when I thought you may have been pregnant."

"You were really scared, I could tell, based on how relieved you looked when the test came back negative!" she responded.

"I know. It was tough, though. I would have stayed, you know."

"What, and give up your fabulous engineering career? I wouldn't have stood for it. I would have gone to Buffalo."

"Well, no, you would have had to give up acting."

"I know. We would have figured something out."

There was silence before her mood turned more serious. "Jake, I know we've talked about it, but you're leaving in a couple of days. Have you thought more about it?"

Jake nodded. He and she both agreed that sometimes people needed space to pursue their own objectives and goals, unencumbered by the bonds of a long distance relationship.

"I think that we should do it, I mean, not commit to each other."

"Jake, this summer has been wonderful. I don't want you to think I don't care."

"Court, you were right last week when you said we're both young and we deserve a chance. I guess that means seeing others," he said, for her benefit only.

Courtney swallowed, trying to accept the situation, but she shared Jake's sentiment. "Well, you know, if it's meant to be . . ."

"Then it'll work out," Jake finished. "Court, I know this is hard, but for us we can't be under the pressure of a long distance relationship. I don't want that for you or for us."

"But I'm worried."

"About what?"

Courtney sighed. "Is this the Karen and Billy story again? I mean, I really do love you, and it was the same with them."

"I don't know. I suppose that only time will tell, Court."

"Jake, I'll always love you."

"Me too."

They held each other tight as they sat under the stars, sometimes looking up and pondering their respective futures. Jake appreciated the lesson. Second chances were only worthwhile if you avoided the mistakes and subsequent hurt from the first time around.

But he was hurting, again.

Twenty
Direction

Binghamton, New York
Friday, August 23, 1985

Accepting breaking up with Courtney as the best action did not diminish his pain. Yet he took some comfort in the fact this time they followed their relationship full circle. Courtney would likely remain as a close friend in his life but, as before, he would leave her for Buffalo, and she would focus all of her energy on acting.

Perhaps sometime in the future they may reconnect, he thought. Still, he would not long for romantic letters from her.

Despite his knowledge of forthcoming events, the past few months more or less played out the same the second time around, a revelation he found both interesting and disturbing. Even when he altered situations based on his experiences, his overall direction did not deviate much from before.

An exception was the recurrence of his headaches. He did not remember having such an issue with chronic head pain, always lurking, ready to strike, emerging whenever he attempted to force a change in his destiny. Tylenol and coffee offered only minimal relief.

But he did plan one major divergence, regardless of the migraines. Nina Thater would never meet him.

"The Transferal" offered him a chance to avoid the betrayal, the hurt, and the resulting loss of his basic innocence of trust. He did not want to relive those feelings from the lowest point in his life, when the thought of ending it all had crossed his mind more than once. Suicide would kill the stabbing agony, he had considered. Yet the desire to move forward, bolstered by faith, friendships, and purpose, had won.

"Headaches be damned, I'm not going to meet her," he reassured himself. Confident of his control over his future, he would make all changes necessary to preserve his sanity and his soul.

He pondered if, with his knowledge of impending events, he had a moral obligation to change the world and try to prevent events such as the Gulf War or the Israeli Buenos Aires Embassy bombing from occurring. However, the possibility of altering world events when he could not change his own direction seemed absurd to him.

"Besides, with the 'New World Order' coming about, terrorism is a dying breed, and hopefully the Gulf War was the last war for the United States," he optimistically thought.

In fact, he more often questioned the reality of his life before "The Transferal," entertaining the idea that he had not experienced the war, Buffalo, Nina, or any other future events he seemed to recall in amazing detail. Perhaps the perceived knowledge of things to come was simply an illusion, the result of finding a key to unlock a psychic ability within his soul.

Perhaps this was his reality, and he was eighteen years old.

He recognized a major hole in the intriguing theory, though. "If I'm psychic and have only seen elements of a future, then why do all my memories end at such a distinct point in time, at the 'shot for shot' game?"

"Maybe I am dead, and I died after the game," he again contemplated. "Maybe reliving one's worst mistakes is purgatory, or hell. Certainly the headaches sometimes feel like hell."

He was not comfortable with entertaining the death angle, not at all. He felt alive, so he must be alive. Dead or alive, he must continue on, moving forward each day at a time.

He turned off the bedroom light and drew the covers up around his shoulders, leaving only his head exposed to the air. He shivered, though not cold. He closed his eyes and thought of how his first week in Buffalo had unfolded before, characterized by the unpacking, the mad rush to find the classrooms, and the uneasiness of being alone in a sea of others in the exact same predicament.

He had made friends in short order before, erasing the loneliness. He recalled when he had met Tom, also a freshman, the first night at the dorm. Tom and his roommate Karl had consumed a substantial amount of a liter of Absolut vodka and had attempted to tag along with Jake and a few others from the floor to a fraternity rush party. As the door to the elevator of the high-rise student residence started to close, Jake pushed a very intoxicated Tom out of the lift.

They had often chuckled about the elevator incident in the months following. Tom promised one day he would repay the "favor," though he later admitted going to the party would have been a bad idea, given the amount he had consumed and the intensity of his hangover the next day.

If the "shot for shot" game did in fact mark when he will die, then he still had many experiences to live, he figured. Perhaps with luck he could leverage the premonitions or memories or whatever they are of the first time through to his advantage and avoid his personal finality brought on by the pool drinking game, thereby cheating death for a while.

Jake yawned and turned on his side. Within minutes, he settled into a deep sleep with images of The Oasis, the pool table and a row of vodka gimlets playing in his mind.

*   *   *

A voice to his right prompted Jake to turn his head to the source. As he tried to move faster, his surroundings appeared to move in distorted slow motion, though the words were clear. "Hey, Jake, I thought we were going to do 'shot for shot.' Are you ready?" Tom asked.

The words "shot for shot" resonated with Jake. He turned his bloodshot gaze to the row of plastic shot glasses lined up on the oak bar to his left. Fifteen balls demanded fifteen shots of vodka gimlets, plus the honorary sixteenth. Vodka gimlets were not potent, but mass quantities of any mixed alcoholic drink had the potential of producing a strong intoxicating effect. Jake winced but nodded in agreement, as he continued to stare at the shots.

"Let's roll."

An audible crack pierced the silence in the bar as the cue ball struck the triangular formation of balls. The result of Tom's break, three stripes sunk, mandated Jake drink three shots. He paused between each, struggling to swallow the liquid. After Tom missed the next shot, Jake sauntered from the bar and to the pool table and dropped two before missing the four ball in the side.

After downing two vodka gimlet shots, Tom sank another ball but scratched. Jake still had to drink the shot. He thought the gimlets tasted odd, almost acidic.

Jake took aim and knocked in the seven in the far left corner, bringing the cue around for the four in the side per plan. But the eight ball fell in the process. The remainder of the shots, ten, he had to drink.

He did agree to "shot for shot," including the standing base rule of the game. If you sink the eight ball prematurely, you have to drink the remainder.

He fought to get the thirteenth shot down, suppressing the urge to vomit. He laid his head on the oak bar, relishing in the wonderful coolness against his forehead.

Several moments later, a hand landed on his shoulder with a slap.

"Hey, Jake, wake up!"

Jake groggily turned to the voice, but he did not come face to face with Tom. The hand belonged to an elderly man. Jake did not recognize him.

"Wake up, Jake."

"Uhh. Do I know you?"

The man did not acknowledge the question. "Wake up, Jake. Ye dinnae see th' big picture, do ye?" He spoke with a slight Scottish accent, an inflection Jake thought he had heard before.

Jake tried to shake the cobwebs out of his head, without success. He looked at the man's face, and though some familiarity in the features existed, he could not identify the Scotsman. He rubbed his temple with his right palm and tried to clear his blurred vision. The alcohol and the returning headache were altering his perceptions.

The Scotsman was not a regular at The Oasis. "Big picture? What the hell are you talking about?" Jake finally muttered.

"Th' big picture, mah friend," he repeated. "Ye really don't remember me, do ye, laddie?"

"Oh boy, I have met this guy before," Jake thought, but did not say anything. The gimlets took firm control of his eyes, and he barely focused on the man.

"Ah told ye, ye would be making a mistake, Jake. What has it gotten ye?" he continued.

Jake did not answer, with his nausea and dizziness increasing in intensity.

"How heavy is yer heart, laddie?" the old man said, softly. "Ye must guard yer heart."

Suddenly Jake's blurred vision registered a flash to his right, accompanied by a sharp crack. He turned to face the light and the sound. As he stared into the extraordinarily bright hues of endless colors, the intensity of the radiance faded to reveal a mist, then a lake.

Jake found himself on the boat, drifting across the calm water near the shore. The early morning sun bathed the scene in a rich orange, and a flute played in the distance.

He was not confused, nor in any discomfort. He was content, but he did not know why.

Nor did he care.

*　　*　　*

Jake enjoyed a hearty egg and bacon breakfast expertly prepared by the elder Stockman. Afterward, he took a long, warm shower to help physically and mentally prepare him for the four-hour drive to Buffalo.

While dressing, he noticed what he mentally referred to as the "dream pad" protruding from under the bed. He stopped buttoning his short-sleeved shirt, picked up the notepad, and attempted to decipher the scribbling with a certain curiosity and uneasiness. As in the case of the other nocturnal journeys, he had no more than vague shadow recollections of the experience, and no memory of writing. His writings told him those dreams about

The Oasis always ended with the "shot for shot" game, an understandable outcome if that is when his life ends.

This time, however, the words on the paper told more. Jake read them aloud. "Oasis, shot for shot, Tom, old man, mistake, light, lake, contentment."

He closed his eyes to try to recall. "There was a lake afterwards," he thought, though he could not visualize the body of water through his hazy memory. "And an old man."

An uneasy sensation formed at the base of his stomach, a collage of fear and anticipation.

"I've met him before," he realized.

He flipped backwards through the "dream pad" and found the entry from June. He said the name.

"Albert."

He shook his head in resignation. He had no idea who "Albert" was.

Twenty-One
Buffalo

Buffalo, New York
Saturday, August 24, 1985

Jake arrived at Clement Hall on the University at Buffalo's south campus at approximately two in the afternoon, an hour earlier than the first time. Perhaps he could not cause major changes in the direction of his life, but gaining an hour by avoiding a previous navigational error was a plus.

He shared few common interests beyond engineering classes with his assigned roommate, Arnav, and they never became more than casual acquaintances. He recalled Arnav had not arrived on campus until the second day of classes, so Jake looked forward to three full days of solitude in the room.

He stretched out on his bed, turned on his small black and white television, and tuned in the news. He contemplated an evening jog when the station reported overnight temperatures expected in the sixties under clear skies.

A knock forced him to peel his attention away from the television. He opened the door and was mildly surprised to see a pretty girl wearing little makeup, with features of a natural beauty not requiring augmentation. "Yes?" he said, self-conscious about his disheveled appearance from lying on the bunk watching the news.

"Hi, I'm Cheryl from Campus Ministries. Are you Jake?"

"Uh huh."

"Jake, I'm here to inform you about our services schedule. We have Catholic Masses in the Newman Chapel on the North Campus. Do you regularly attend Mass?"

"I try to," he lied. He did not recall this particular event but had come to accept the fact he had not committed to long-term memory many experiences, or could not predict all future happenings.

"Good. Well, here's our Mass schedule, and our phone number is at the top. If you have any questions, or if you just want to talk to a priest, give us a call."

"I will," Jake said halfheartedly as he accepted the document, then he gently closed the door. He studied the service times for a moment before tossing the pamphlet on his desk.

He slowly sat down on the edge of his bed. Reflecting on one's religious upbringing and faith as part of a coherent self-examination of the basic fiber of one's being is an exercise that most adults undertake at least once if not often in their life. Jake had ample reasons to do such the past several months.

Brought up as a Catholic, the adult Jake did not attend Mass regularly during his college years. As he progressed along his own journey of faith, he grew less and less comfortable with the Church's focus more on tradition and less, in his eyes, on the central messages of Jesus. Still, he managed to hold true to most of the Church's societal teachings, but not with regard to birth control. He always practiced safe sex, except for that one time.

"That one time," he thought again. Like Courtney in this timeline, Nina had not been on the pill and Jake had forgotten a condom, that one time. During that one time, Jake had told Nina not to worry.

All it takes is one time to conceive a child.

The resulting guilt from agreeing to abort his offspring scorched his soul. Because of his selfishness, he had said no to a life.

"Maybe this is purgatory, payback for a crap ass decision," he again thought, with strong bitterness.

Another knock interrupted his self-loathing. He closed his eyes, then opened them and approached the entrance. This time, he knew who was calling.

"Hey, how ya doin?" a younger Tom announced as Jake opened the door, a half-consumed bottle of Absolut vodka in one hand and a lit cigarette in the other. "I'm Tom, and we're, me and my good friend Karl here, are trying to pump some life into this floor. Have a shot!" Tom offered as he thrust the bottle at Jake.

Jake slowly managed a sideways smile. "Uh, ok." He took a long swig of the vodka, something he had not done the first time. "Maybe if I drink some he won't have as much and feel so horrible the next day," he thought. Premature friendship may have

been a rationalization, but in reality Jake strongly
wanted, no, needed a drink after reliving the
memories of the abortion.

"Hey, do me a favor," Jake said to Tom.

"Yeah?" asked Tom between cigarette puffs.

"Don't get pissed if I throw you out of an
elevator someday."

PART V
Again

Twenty-Two
Water

Buffalo, New York
Thursday, October 3, 1985

He grabbed the yellow legal pad and, using his Fortran-77 manual as a lap desk, steadied the paper on the book, clicked his pen, and began to write.

"The first month of the fall semester unfolded as it did last time, just as I had expected. In some instances I was able to change minor details, but the general direction of my life proceeded as before. I have grown accustomed to this and to life in "The Transferal." I'm not dead. I don't understand yet why I'm reliving life, but I've come to accept this 'new normal' as my life."

He contemplated the Fortran book under the legal pad. The first exam of the Introduction to Fortran programming course this semester had been difficult for him. All undergraduate engineering students learned to program in Fortran-77, but Jake had not coded using the language in practice as an engineer with Buffalo Steel.

"The first rounds of examinations are over, thankfully," he continued to write. "I earned four As and a C. The C was in Fortran, and honestly I'm glad I did that well. Overall it's an improvement over my four Bs and a D from the first round before."

He knew he should have spent more time studying Fortran, but he was enjoying pledging the

Phi Delta Epsilon social fraternity again. In the previous timeline he had met a girl at a rush party he had liked but had not pursued because of his relationship with Courtney. This time he had allowed a connection with the "party girl" to develop.

"I am enjoying spending time with Sue, with no promises, no ties to bind, no commitment. I'm actually thoroughly enjoying the second run through. Sue is a deviation from before. I don't think this is a long term deal, but, well you never know."

He finished the last bite of his rye toast at Jack's Place, a small diner on Main Street, which served an excellent two eggs, hash brown, toast, and unlimited coffee breakfast for $1.99. Often, before, he would complete homework at the diner prior to class, but with the second chance, he opted to be more proactive in completing his assignments. Having a clean slate at the beginning of the day allowed for stress free time during breakfast for writing in his journal or reading The Buffalo News.

"I view 1985 as the present, not the past now. While I still think often about my previous life, I'm not obsessed anymore about why "The Transferal" happened or how to get back to 1992. I am enjoying the experience, one day at a time."

He took his last sip of coffee and left three dollars on the counter, offering a generous tip. He began to place the pad in his backpack but stopped halfway and removed the log to record one more thought.

"The dreams, and more importantly the headaches, have not occurred since I returned to Buffalo. I think that is chiefly due to my resolve to never meet Nina."

He put his journal back in the bag and gave his customary goodbye wave to Amy, the proprietor of Jack's Place. The snow outside had picked up in intensity and had accumulated on the sidewalks and streets, cold from a night of temperatures below freezing. He pulled the collar of his jacket up to protect his neck against the wind and the early lake effect snowstorm as he walked the block to his car.

He thought about the last line he had penned before leaving the restaurant. He acknowledged a chance they may run into each other. But she would not recognize him, and he would simply walk away.

He had the power to do so, or so he hoped.

As he started the Pacer and pulled out on to Main Street, fate shattered his new normalcy. The Pacer suddenly accelerated on its own, and slid out of control across the street. Jake slammed both feet on the brakes, but they were only marginally useful on the slick pavement.

After the swift, intense, and jarring impact which resulted in his car wedged between another and a telephone pole, he drew in a couple of deep breaths to calm himself and performed a quick self-assessment. Blood trickled down the left side of his face, and he determined he had a head injury. He did not feel dizzy and subsequently underestimated its severity.

Glancing out through the cracked windshield, he looked for movement from the driver of the vehicle he had collided with a few seconds before. He detected none.

He violently forced open his driver's side door, unable to operate as designed with the left front fender crunched against the hinges. Through the heavy falling and blowing snow, he still did not detect any movement from inside the other vehicle. As he stepped on to the curb and approached the driver's door of the yellow car, he perceived a woman behind the wheel. She appeared unconscious, with blood covering a portion of of her blond hair.

He did not realize the identity of the occupant until he opened the door. Her head rolled forward, revealing Nina's bloodied face.

"Oh, my God, no. *No!*" He recoiled in shock. "Please, let this be a dream!" he shouted.

The sight of her immobile, damaged body caused Jake to slump in despair to the ground next to her open door. Sirens blared as Nina's hand dangled against his head. He realized the blood on her fingers came from him. His vision became weak, and darkness surrounded him before the first responder arrived.

*　　*　　*

This time, it was not a dream. He knew it, somehow, or felt it.

He surveyed the calm and serene lake from inside the rowboat, no different from the dream in

August. The flute again played in the distance. While before the melody complimented the scene as background music, Jake now took great care to listen to the familiar soothing twists and turns through the piece. He recognized the work as "Amazing Grace."

He leaned to concentrate on the hypnotic tune, the shifting of his weight nearly tipping the boat. Instinct kicked in, and he redistributed his balance to steady the wooden vessel.

"Easy laddie, ye dinnae want to end up in th' water, do ye?"

Jake whirled to the speaker of the words and found himself again face to face with the elderly Scottish gentleman of dreams before, standing behind him in the boat. Jake remembered. He paused as he gathered his thoughts, licking his lips in the process. "You. You're the key to this, aren't you?"

The Scotsman took a drag on his pipe as he grinned. "Aye, I suppose ye kin say that, in a manner o' speak'n." He removed the pipe from his mouth and gazed across the water.

Jake studied him for a few moments, expecting an answer with more substance. When no additional words came forth, frustration got the best of Jake. "So, 'Albert' is it? Is that all?"

"I'm here to answer, but ye have to ask th' questions."

Jake thought for a moment, once again licking his dry lips. "Alright, I'll bite. First, is this real?"

"Th' only thing real lad is within yer heart."

"Dammit, stop it with these mysterious allusions!" Jake shot back. "There's too much going on here to play games! Just be straight with me! Geez, I think I'm losing my mind."

"Na, Jake, yer just starting to find yer soul."

Albert's statement caught Jake off guard. "My soul?" he muttered. He hesitated before asking the next question, fearful of the response.

"What, am I, am I dead?"

The man sighed. "In th' soul, ye carry a burden that ye haven't yit resolved."

"Am I dead?" Jake reiterated, with more force.

"Life is transitory wi' time, Jake. Ye learn, ye grow, ye move on. That is how yer soul grows. Ye have not moved on. So yes, in that sense, yer soul is dying."

Jake stared out over the calm water and realized the flute music had ceased. He sat still, transfixed by the brilliant colors of the changing leaves on the shoreline. "Why are you here?"

"To help ye. Nothing more."

"Who sent you?"

Albert held up his left hand. "Jake, stop play'n th' engineer. Stop this constant analysis. These are not questions I kin answer, th' answers ur in yer heart."

"Then why all this?"

Albert stared intently at Jake with deep, dark, understanding eyes. "Because ye have a choice to make. Don't let this chance pass by again. Do what yer heart tells ye, Jake."

Gray clouds built up to the west and a stiff wind blew as the sky darkened. The flute music started again, a different tune unrecognizable to Jake. The boat rubbed against the dock as Albert flung a rope around a pylon. As Albert disembarked, the craft secured, he turned back and said, "Jake, listen. Listen to th' flute. It echoes yer heart."

Darkness again enveloped Jake.

*   *   *

The beeping, loud and intrusive, grated on Jake's nerves. He struggled without success to will himself to open his eyes. He heard voices, again, becoming stronger as the time passed. Jake discerned some words through his confusion.

"Recovery. Support. Improving."

"Fracture. Crash. Paramedics."

"Love. Left."

The odd, regular, mechanical sounds drowned out the voices as Jake again lost consciousness.

*   *   *

The next time the annoying beeping sound prompted Jake to alertness, and he found success in his efforts to open his eyes. He studied his surroundings. Jake observed monitors, chrome bars, and rubber tubes in abundant supply. No other souls occupied the space.

"I'm lying down, in a bed," he realized.

He focused on the horizontal shiny metal rails close to his right side. "Bed rails. Hospital bed rails. I'm definitely in a hospital bed."

He tried to raise his head without success, and sighed in despair. He noticed a cord against his side. With his eyes, the only part of his body he had control over, he followed the cord to where it ended in a small control device cradled in his right hand. He struggled, but his thumb would not move to the call button. He recognized with a certain sense of trepidation his paralysis.

Jake sighed again as he attempted to gather his strength. He hated hospitals, and he wanted to get out.

"This is my body. I own it."

The button presented his only hope. If he pushed the switch, he would escape. He stared at his thumb and tried in vain to assert control. Nothing moved.

Exhausted and frustrated, he shouted in desolation, overpowered with the desire to survive. He needed to live, yet he had power over absolutely nothing.

Again, he stared at the button. With all the effort he had ever been able to muster in his life, he tried one more to move his thumb. He needed to own it. He had to press it.

He saw his thumb twitch.

The room took on an eerie red glow as he applied the minutest pressure to the button. Jake barely acknowledged the change in ambient lighting as he slipped back into unconsciousness.

    *   *   *

He stared at the bright white light, devoid of hues of red or other brilliant colors. As before in the dreams, it subsided and gave way to an image of water, but he did not see a lake. He studied the clear liquid in a strange transparent container.

"An IV," he thought.

He fell into a mild trance watching the slow, rhythmic dripping of the fluid from the bag into a tube, closely matching the frequency of the constant beeping. He heard voices, and he moved his eyes to the origin of the sound of the human speech.

"Jake, follow my finger with your eyes," the bearded man in a white coat commanded.

"What a stupid thing to ask," Jake thought of the request by "white coat guy." But he attempted to comply, and focused intently on the man's extended index finger. He had to get out of the hospital and perhaps if he complied with the instructions maybe they would let him escape. He had failed to push the button hard enough as he was still there, maybe someone else's finger could free him.

He tracked the movement, and stopped as the finger brought into view another face. Nina stood beside the "white coat guy," her beautiful cheeks marred by tears. He searched her eyes staring at his. He tried to speak, but nothing came out.

His sight, followed by all other senses, faded again.

*   *   *

This time, the excruciatingly annoying beeping woke Jake up like an alarm clock announcing he had overslept for work. He sat up, with no impediment from paralysis. The speed of the ascent caused the IV tube inserted in a vein in the back of his right hand to shift, stinging Jake sharply.

But Jake welcomed the pain signifying he was alive. His eyes again fell on the control on the end of the cord near his bed. He grabbed the device and pressed the button with firmness and purpose. The room took on a red hue from the attention light above the door. Within a minute, a nurse entered. Jake smiled as she approached the bed.

"Jake, well hello! How are you feeling?" the nurse asked.

"Uh, well, actually thirsty. My mouth's so dry. Could I have a drink of water?"

The nurse shook her head. "Not until Dr. Epstein has had a chance to look at you. He's on his way." She gently grabbed his wrist and proceeded to take his pulse.

"You know, I could really go for a pizza," he said weakly.

*   *   *

"That was quite some crash, Jake. We were really worried," Tom said as Jake finished his last chicken wing.

"Yeah, I really don't remember too much."

"Well, good thing you were wearing your seat belt. The cops said it saved you from going through the windshield," Tom replied. "Oh, here," he continued as he turned to grab an object from behind his chair.

"The Sigmas wanted you to initial this," he said as he laid a wooden object on the hospital bed next to Jake.

"The pledge paddle?" Jake said as Tom nodded his head.

The wooden paddle, a symbolic representation of unity of the Sigma pledge class, had a large Greek letter Sigma inscribed at the top above "Phi Delta Epsilon." Black marker signatures of his pledge classmates in two columns ran the length of the paddle below the fraternity name.

"Sign on the top, Jake."

Jake blankly looked at the blank space reserved dead center at the top of the signatures. "You and the guys want me to take the pole position?" he asked. A majority vote of the pledge class determined who the class leader was, and that person had the honor of signing on the top of the paddle, at the "pole position."

Tom, Pete, and Hector nodded. "It was unanimous, Jake," Hector said.

Jake studied the paddle further. He was not alone. "I don't know what to say."

"Well, don't say anything, just sign. And get out of here soon. We have a mixer with Delta

Omega in five days." Hector gave Jake a black marker, and Jake signed in the top spot.

"Hope I can make it," Jake said as he wrote. "It's been four weeks. I pretty much shot this semester to hell, I guess."

*   *   *

Later in the evening, alone in his room and lying in bed, Jake thought about those words he said after signing the paddle. He recognized yet another example of how he could change minor details of his life but the overall course of events continued to unfold as before.

Last time, food poisoning had kept him from completing his first semester. Now, under different circumstances, the outcome was the same. He would have to repeat those classes, again.

He had thought at first that one detail had changed, recalling Nina's face, but he learned there were no occupants in the other vehicle. A blown tire had caused Jake's car to crash into a parked black pickup truck.

He had imagined Nina in her yellow Corolla and at his side in the hospital room, and he did not know why. He wanted her with him, yet needed to avoid her at the same time.

His head ached from the paradox.

Twenty-Three
Revelation

With no realistic opportunity, again, of catching up and finishing his class work before the end of the term, Jake decided to return to Binghamton after his release from the hospital. He had lost his first semester prior due to food poisoning, and this time because of the accident and subsequent convalescence. The result, as always, was the same.

Going home provided an opportunity to recover from the lingering injuries suffered in the crash. He also wanted to see Courtney again. Leaving Buffalo would prevent Nina from meeting him at the party as well.

Courtney's experience in the drama program at the State University of New York at Binghamton had exceeded her expectations, according to her last letter. Jake had understood her passion for acting but never realized the depth of her talent until she auditioned for and won the female lead in "The Salem Massacres." While he missed the play's two-weekend run due to recuperating, he hoped he would have an opportunity to catch her perform in a different role in the second fall production.

He often thought about rekindling the romance with Courtney, having ended his association with Sue before the accident. Sue had yearned for the false comfort of instant love, bred from her insecurity from enduring several abusive men. While the relationship had its moments, Jake had grown disenchanted by its shallowness. She had not taken the breakup well, and vowed to get him back at all costs. Leaving Buffalo also distanced himself from the possible danger from an obsessed, scorned partner.

Courtney, while the same age as Sue, had an aura of elegance and maturity far beyond her years, and possessed the sensibility and stability Jake desired in a woman. The phone calls with Courtney over the past few months helped him realize she offered that and more, much more. Her surprise visit to his hospital room while he was laid up served to confirm his assessment.

But he did not know what he really wanted, deep down inside.

He sighed as he rubbed Stoley's head. The German Shepard had curled up next to him in the lower bunk bed as he had done so many nights before. "Stoley, what am I gonna say when I see Courtney tomorrow?" Jake was not sure how to interpret Stoley's playful lick of his nose in response.

*   *   *

"So then Tom and I finally pull over. We do the obligatory 'look under the hood' thing but we couldn't figure out what was wrong. It was a bit past midnight, and we're still an hour outside of Buffalo.

We figured that we'd have to get a tow to somewhere. Hell, with his car breaking down so often he was used to it by now. So I said I could walk to a rest stop that was a couple miles or so back, and we agreed that I'd go and he'd watch the car."

"You left Tom alone?" Courtney asked.

Jake took a drag on his cigarette. "Yeah, but he was ok. He had plenty of beer and cigarettes to keep him happy. Well, I walked for about a half mile, right? I realized that at that rate it'd take me forever to get to the rest stop. So I decide to try hitching. A few thousand cars later one car finally stops and backs up towards me. Only thing, though, the driver, he's shitfaced."

"No!"

"Uh huh. I should've realized it when he backed over one of those mile marker signs when he stopped and backed up towards me. Scratched up his shiny Trans Am, but he didn't notice, or care. Anyway, I was grateful to have a ride, but, Court, I shit you not, this guy's doing 80, 85, and he's blown out of his mind. He tells me he's going back to Syracuse after attending a wedding in Buffalo, and he kept on saying that he'd never done so much coke in his life!"

"Holy crap. You must've been shitting your pants!"

"I was. I kept on praying, 'Please Lord, get me to the rest stop safely!' Anyway, we do get there and I dove out of the car as fast as I could. Didn't even say goodbye or thanks. I asked the gas station attendant call for a tow, and he goes to dial someone.

A few minutes later an older tow truck arrives and now I'm finally feeling relieved. By this time it had to be something like 40, 45 minutes since I left Tom."

"He's probably sucking down those beers."

"Uh huh. But it's ok 'cause he wasn't going to be driving anymore that night. Anyway, we get in the tow truck and I swear we're not a half mile outside of the rest area when, get this, the tow truck runs out of gas!"

"You're kidding?!"

"Yup. The freaking tow truck ran out of gas! He had a can with like a couple of gallons or so with him, so it was ok. He said that his truck's fuel gauge was fucked and that he was afraid that this'd happen sometime. Honestly, I think he may have been fucked up, too. Anyway, he put the gas into the truck's tank and went back to the service area. We get a full tank of gas and leave and finally we get to Tom."

Jake paused for another drag on the cigarette. "So we finally get back to Tom, beer in his hand. The tow truck driver couldn't start the car, which was good, 'cause Tom was fucked by now and I still was buzzing from getting wrecked at the Phi Delta Epsilon convention in Utica."

"I remember you mentioning the convention. It was just a few days before your accident, right?"

"Yup, about a week. We had the car towed to a garage in some back ass country town, and the tow driver dropped us off at a motel about a half mile away. By this time, it's after two in the morning, and checkout time at the motel is at 9AM. You'd think the motel would give us a break on the rate but the bastard charged us the full 40 bucks for the night."

Courtney rubbed her neck and took a sip of beer. "You guys made it back ok, though?"

"Uh huh. We figured the fuel pump was fucked, so we walked to an auto parts store the next morning as soon as it opened. Really, it was amazing that the store opened at 9 on a Sunday. It was right next to the motel, what luck, right? So Tom bought a new fuel pump. Well, we installed it, still a no go. It was Sunday and the mechanics at the garage down the street wouldn't be in until Monday, so we decided that we had to find another way to Buffalo that night."

"Didn't you guys have a big test coming up?"

"Yeah, but it wasn't still for a couple days. Still we had to get back. Tom called Hector and Hector drove out from Buffalo to get us. So Tom and I have absolutely nothing to do but just hang out by the car for an hour waiting for Hector. Of course, we still had a couple of beers left, warm beers, but drinkable. So we drank and shot the shit. It was only a few minutes before Hector showed up that I noticed a wire just lying on the top of the engine block. Tom didn't know what it was for but we saw a receptacle near it so we plugged it in. Sure enough, the car started up fine."

"So that was all that was wrong? A loose wire?"

Jake nodded his head. "Yup, one freaking loose wire! Man, Hector was so pissed that he had to drive all that way for nothing!"

After finishing the story, Jake inwardly smiled at yet another example of how he could not alter the general course of events. Before, they had taken Jake's Pacer on the trip to Utica, and had blown a tire around the same location on the New York State Thruway where Tom's car had broken down. Taking a different vehicle did not prevent an unplanned overnight trip near Rochester.

Courtney finished her beer and Jake poured her another one from the pitcher at the Cobblestone, a small pub off the Vestal Parkway around the corner from Courtney's apartment and a stone's throw from SUNY Binghamton. A popular hangout among the college students, the warm early November evening beckoned for enjoying a few beers on the bar's back patio.

"So, Court, how'd that play go?"

"Oh, it was good," she replied with a sigh. "We got good reviews and everything. The opening night, I totally messed up one scene, though. One of the other actors, though, he covered."

"What happened?"

She hesitated for a moment. "Well, I had skipped ahead a few lines in a courtroom scene. Jake, the audience couldn't see my face, since I had my back to them, but Brian could. He knew by my expression that I was absolutely mortified and of course he knew that I'd skipped ahead. I had never forgotten a line before."

She paused, and her face lost most emotion, retaining hints of sullenness. "Thank God I was facing away from the audience."

"So what'd Brian do?"

She paused for a moment, as if distracted, and her gaze focused behind Jake. "He picked up immediately on what had happened, responded to my line and then backed up a few lines to where we were supposed to be," she said, her voice slightly lower. "I realized what he was doing at that time and I had remembered the correct lines, and just recited them from there."

"And it still went over well?"

She paused again, and Jake suspected something was not quite right. "Uh huh," she said weakly. "Not even the director noticed that we had messed up."

Courtney nervously lit a cigarette. She mindlessly fumbled with the matches.

Jake detected her discomfort, and decided on the direct approach. "Court, ever since we got here you've been, well, different."

"Different how?" Courtney said, offering a hint of defensiveness in her voice.

Jake shrugged his shoulders. "I don't know. You just seem different from when I last saw you. It's almost like your mind is elsewhere."

She gave Jake an icy stare. "Well, it isn't."

Her uncharacteristic cold response added to his suspicions that there was more to the story. "Well, if there's anything wrong . . ." he started.

"What? What? What do you mean, 'if there's anything wrong?' What the fuck kind of statement is that, Jake? I can take care of myself!" she said defiantly.

Jake retreated in shock from the leaning position he had subconsciously adopted. "Sorry. Just trying to help," he said as he held up both hands, palms outward.

"Well, I don't need your damn help, Jake," Courtney said, then abruptly stood up and briskly walked from the back deck into the bar.

After a few moments, he took his dumfounded gaze off the bar entrance where he had followed Courtney's departure with his eyes, incredulous at what had happened "Something is definitely fucked," he thought as he rose to follow her.

He searched the bar but did not locate her. Through the front window of the Cobblestone he spotted her leaning against her car, crying. He took a deep breath and walked out the front door.

"Court?" Jake said with concern as he approached her slowly. "Hey, Court, I just . . ." He stopped talking, finding no other words.

Courtney turned to Jake and silently wrapped her arms around him. They hugged, in peace and confusion, for over a minute.

"Jake, Jake I'm sorry, I'm sorry," she said as she gently released the embrace.

Jake stroked her hair with compassion and care. "It's ok. What's wrong?"

"Jake, it's not you," Courtney said.

"Court, what's wrong? What happened?"

"Please don't hate me. Please promise me you won't hate me."

"Courtney, what? I won't hate you. What's wrong? Court, I won't hate you, I care so much for you, you know that," Jake responded with honesty and love while holding Courtney's hand.

She drew a deep breath.

Jake focused all attention on her, about to find out the details of the reason behind her uncharacteristic behavior.

"Well, Brian and I went out after the last performance," she started.

"Uh huh. I remember you talking about him. That you liked him." Learning about Brian had evoked jealousy in Jake, but he reminded himself he agreed their breaking up had been the right thing to do.

"We went to this one place for a beer, a bunch of us from the play. Later he said he wanted to talk to me alone, so we left and drove to his apartment."

She sighed, and Jake kept silent. "Both of his roommates were out and we started to kiss, alone in his apartment. But it didn't feel right, and I told him that it was late and I should go."

She looked down, avoiding eye contact with Jake. "He started to fondle me. We had gone a bit further than I wanted. I told him no and I got up off the couch, but then he threw me back down."

Jake feared where the story was going. He stayed completely still, hoping he could control his reaction.

"The son of a bitch raped me," she said, her voice barely above a whisper, saturated with bitterness.

Jake silently held her tight as he searched for something to say, but there were no words, nothing he could do to fix the situation. He felt helpless, and anger, and sadness for her.

"Court, it'll be alright," he eventually said, aware that he had to offer something.

"No, no it won't" she responded with the same sullenness Jake detected earlier.

He rocked her slowly, still in the embrace, but did not say a word.

"Jake, I'm pregnant."

Twenty-Four
Lesson

Binghamton, New York
Tuesday, November 5, 1985

"I never learned of Courtney's rape before. How ironic that the second production of the semester she had earned a small part in the beginning, but playing the role of the pregnant teen 'Sandy' in 'The Outsiders' was too real for her. She quit the play."

Jake stared at the notebook for a moment. He resumed writing, stopped, and then scribbled out the three new sentences. He missed the word processing power of his computer, as he could simply delete imperfect thoughts in WordPerfect. It was not so easy with ink on paper, or in real life.

"Since our talk at The Cobblestone a couple days ago Courtney has withdrawn more and I feel increasingly powerless to help her. She had vehemently decided not to press charges against her attacker, contrary to my strong objections. In my eyes, not prosecuting meant allowing someone who had done such a heinous act to walk away to possibly do the same thing again to someone else."

Fear of constantly having to relive her personal nightmare fueled Courtney's decision. Jake realized the battle and choice were hers, and reluctantly did not push the topic out of respect for her feelings. The best he could do was offer support.

He now understood why her letters never came before, and that understanding brought strong guilt. If he had overcome his own insecurities and contacted Courtney before, she likely would have told him about the rape. With that knowledge, he could have intervened and prevented the attack from happening in this timeline.

"Once again, events had played out pretty much as they had before, an apparent primary rule of 'The Transferal,'" he wrote.

The thought of Brian getting off sickened Jake. No justice existed when someone callously mars another's life with no retribution, no payback.

He was not sure whom he harbored more loathing for, Brian or Lucas.

He would not let go of the hatred for either, a slow cancer overtaking his soul. He threw the pad down. Often, writing had helped him work through pain. This night, doing so only induced more hurting.

*   *   *

Perspiration rolled down Jake's face as he rapidly unloaded the conveyor belt dishwasher in the hospital kitchen. Fortunate for the opportunity to pick up some hours at Tri Cities Regional Hospital, he welcomed the additional income.

As he stacked clean plates and placed them in their specialized carts, the dinner shift assistant supervisor appeared and hit the button to stop the large dishwasher conveyer belt. "Uh oh," he thought,

"Pat never gets off her lazy ass to come back to the dish room unless she's gonna bitch about something or somebody." He braced himself for a lecture as she strolled towards him.

"Jake, you've got a phone call," was all she said.

Jake was a bit surprised, as no one ever called him at work. "This can't be good," he thought.

"I do?" he replied.

"Yes. It sounds important. You can take it at my desk." Pat showed a hint of uncharacteristic concern on her face.

As Pat led Jake back to her office, his stomach turned as he anticipated bad news. He sat down in Pat's chair as she closed the glass door and remained outside, giving him some measure of privacy. "Hello?" Jake nervously sputtered into the receiver.

"Jake, it's Courtney," she said without hesitation. "I need your help."

"Uh, sure, Court, what's up?"

She breathed heavily. "I need to, uh, I need to borrow some money."

"What for?"

"Jake, I've done a lot of thinking, and I can't do it."

"Do what?"

"I can't have this baby. My parents would disown me," she explained in a quivering voice.

Jake sighed. "Sure you can, Court, you . . ."

"Look, Jake, I've made up my mind," she said, cutting him off. "I'm getting an abortion tonight, and I'm about fifty dollars short. Can you lend it to me?"

Memories of Nina and their decision permeated Jake's conscience. He could not be a party to another abortion, no matter what the circumstances. "Courtney, can we talk about it first?"

She recognized the tone in Jake's voice. "Damn it, Jake, I've made up my mind," she repeated. "Please don't try to talk me out of it. If you won't help me I'll find someone who will."

He hung his head in resignation. He would have no success in trying to sway her resolve over the phone. "Oh, okay, Court, it's fine," he said as he tried to suppress his memories. "Look I'm here for you, you know that. I'll help you. When do you need it?"

"The clinic is open until nine tonight. Can you meet me there at seven?"

"I get off work at seven thirty."

"Please, Jake, can you get off earlier? I don't know if they'll take me past seven thirty."

"Alright, I'll leave early. I'm pretty sure Pat will let me go. She's the one who answered the phone and she seemed concerned something was up. But let me pick you up at your place instead of meeting you at the clinic. You shouldn't be driving now, you're too upset."

"Ok, ok, I'll be waiting," Courtney halfheartedly agreed.

*　　*　　*

"I can't help her do it," he thought as he drove past St. Gregory the Great church.

He recalled the religion classes given there by Father Charley Horse. Father Charles Valentine had a hoarse raspy type of voice, thus the nickname "Father Charley Horse," a term of endearment the priest thought humorous. Father Charles had passed away almost two years earlier, but his teachings about abortion as murder, and therefore a serious sin, echoed in his mind, as if he heard them yesterday.

He had so often wished he had taken those words to heart.

He respected Courtney's choice, and hoped she would venerate his. He wanted to understand her deep, raw emotional wounds, but ached to convey to her, somehow, the guilt he still carried. There are always alternatives, and all ensuing consequences must be recognized and considered.

He needed to find a way to get Courtney to understand those consequences, even if doing so meant jeopardizing his friendship with her.

*   *   *

Jake observed after Courtney opened the apartment door she had tried to wipe off the streaks of mascara but had not been completely successful. She silently let him in.

"Do you want a beer?" she asked, and Jake nodded his head. He watched her walk in to the kitchen, and spied two Budweiser cans on the countertop, presumably empty. Jake surmised the alcohol probably had already affected her judgment. Her slightly glassy eyes told Jake she was in no condition to go through with the abortion.

"That alone may be the best angle to pitch at least to not do it tonight," he thought.

"Your roommate isn't here?"

"No, there's a track meet in Scranton so Sharon's gone for the night," she weakly replied as she passed one beer to Jake and opened the other for herself. They both sat down on the couch in the living room and remained in an awkward silence for several moments.

Jake sighed heavily, breaking the quietness. "Courtney, I want to say I'm sorry, but you know I'm here for you, and will always be here for you. And I want to help you through this the best I can."

Courtney stared out into space as she took a long drink of her beer, slowly setting the can on the coffee table in front of her. "I know. I know, Jake. I just don't know what the right thing is."

"She hasn't made up her mind. Maybe I did get through to her," he hoped. "Courtney, there are alternatives, you know," he said.

She shook her head and looked straight at Jake. "I don't know, Jake. I can't raise a child. I can't even tell my parents." A small tear formed in her right eye and ran down her cheek. "I mean, what are they going to think of me?"

Jake put his hand on her shoulder. "Court, they're going to think the same that they've always thought of you. You have to understand it wasn't your fault. Look, you're still their little girl, the artist, the actress, and they love you very much. We all do. It wasn't your fault," he repeated.

"But Jake . . ."

"Courtney, listen," Jake started. He took a hearty gulp of beer and thought hard before proceeding. He stopped trying to suppress his feelings and allowed himself to recollect his own painful struggles with Nina's pregnancy and the abortion. He had wished someone had spoken to him then as he was about to talk to her.

This was his chance. He knew now what he was going to say.

"Court, we both grew up in the Catholic faith. It's a cornerstone to who we are, what we are. Abortion, it's a sin."

"I know Jake, but I'm lost. That's why I'm struggling. I'm losing perspective. It seems like I don't have a choice. I'm too young! I'm really, really scared." Her voice trailed off, the emotional drain showing through.

Jake empathized with Courtney all too well, and continued with resolve. "Courtney, I want to tell you a story. A story about a friend of mine, a good friend, well actually a friend of my brother Steve. But we've all been friends for years. He's a little older than me, about Steve's age." He had to tell her his story, his hurt, and his guilt, in the best way possible without sounding like a nutcase.

"This happened when Matt, Steve's friend, was a junior in college. He was really depressed one night, because he had gotten his girlfriend pregnant.

That's such a shit ass way to say it, I know, but that's how he described it."

He paused for another long drink from the can. "One night he, Steve, and I were going to meet up at Thunderbirds. This was last year before Thunderbirds shut down for serving minors, but back then it was trivial to get in, remember? A halfway decent fake job on the license did it."

Courtney nodded and Jake continued. "As it turned out Steve had to take over a closing shift at Micky D's so he never made it to Thunderbirds. Kinda wish he had because he was a lot closer to Matt than I was. Anyway, after we finished the first beer he opened up more about it. He said he couldn't afford to have a child, that he was in school and was afraid that it would destroy his entire life. He wasn't going to abandon his girlfriend, which I thought was great. But I was young at the time and beyond that I really didn't know what to say to him."

Jake stared at his nearly empty can of beer, transfixed as he walked through his own story of a lost chance slowly and carefully. "So we talked about it for a bit, shot a couple of games of pool, and then I had to go somewhere for some reason. I don't remember what, maybe I had to go feed Stoley, I think, since Steve was stuck at McDonald's. So we decided to call it a very early evening – it was only about seven at this point – and we had left the bar together. I figured Matt was going to go home."

Jake finished his beer, and grabbed another. Reliving the story was tough, and reimaging it was tougher. "After feeding Stoley I drove to Micky Ds to let Steve know and to get something to eat. I was really into McNuggets at the time. On the way back home though I saw Matt's car again parked in front of Thunderbirds. I figured that can't be good, so I stopped and parked my car and went back inside. Well, he was there and must've had a couple of shots of something, 'cause there were two empty shot glasses and a full one in front of him. He was definitely more buzzed than when we had left, no more than forty minutes ago."

He had Courtney's undivided attention. "He was leaning his head against his right hand, elbow propped on the bar. I said, 'You know, Matt, it's gonna be alright.' He said, 'No, no, not this time, not this time, things are all fucked up, man, they're all fucked. There no fucking thing I can do.' I didn't really know what to say. I'd never seen him like that."

"I remember there was this older gentleman at the bar also. We were at the corner of the bar and there was this older man across, well, kind of kitty-corner from us, you know how Thunderbirds was laid out, how the one end of the bar near the window was shaped like an 'L.' So he's sitting down kinda across from us and he had just finished eating something. It was weird, he had this accent to him, Scottish or Irish or something like that. So he looks up and says to Matt, 'Ah told ye, ye dinnae want to do it, laddie.' Just like that, like, like he's just come over on the boat or something."

Courtney leaned a bit closer as Jake continued. "It was obvious there had been some discussion before I got there. Well, Matt got on the defensive, sort of. He said 'I can't do anything else.' The old man replied 'So ye'v made up yer mind, then?'"

"Matt just kinda stared at the bottles on the shelf behind the bar and shook his head slowly side to side. He said in a low voice 'We're gonna have the abortion.' And the man looked at him and told Matt that he didn't want to do it, that having the abortion was the worst that he could do, that he'd regret it. At that point, Matt had finished his last shot and I ordered two beers. Maybe I shouldn't have, because Matt likely had had plenty by this point, but I it did anyway, just to keep him there talking a bit longer."

Courtney still listened, her head tilted down again. "So anyway, Court, here's Matt, sitting at the bar, and he's shaking his head, and he keeps on saying 'I can't. I can't believe it. I feel so fucking stupid.' Well I wasn't so sure why he was saying this and neither was the old man, and he asked Matt why. The old man said 'These things are wunnderful, laddie, it's what life is a' about.'"

"Matt glared at him and angrily told him that she had gotten pregnant the first time they had done it, that he had said not to worry that they didn't have protection, that they could always get an abortion if she got pregnant."

Jake again paused as he said this, remembering with bitter regret what he had said to the old gentleman himself, and the response, after he had found out Nina was pregnant. His stomach churned a bit before he continued.

"The man looked at Matt, pointed his finger, and said, 'This is a gift. It's gift from God! Look, if ye dae nae want the baby I'll take care o' it.'"

"Matt looked kinda sideways at him and chuckled, 'Yeah right,' sort of like 'yeah, you're sixty years old, how the hell can you raise a kid,' mentality."

Jake closed his eyes for a moment, seeing the man's face clearly. "The man was adamant about it. He kept on insisting that he'd take care of the child, that it was God's gift, and that we all are here to help each other. But Matt wouldn't hear anything of it. The man then looked at him straight in the eye and said, 'My friend, if ye go through wi' this, you'll regret it fur th' rest o' yer life.'"

"It was clear Matt wasn't going to finish his beer, which was good. He had had enough. We left the bar, and as we were leaving I turned to look back at the old man. I remember him staring at me, at Matt, and he almost looked like he had a tear in his eye. I helped Matt home. I was fine enough to drive. And I found out two weeks later that he and his girlfriend had gone through with the abortion."

He stared straight ahead, hoping Courtney did not realize he was sharing his own story. "The thing about it, Court, that happened last year, but he struggles with it still today. I saw him just before heading to Buffalo a couple months ago. You can almost tell that something is missing from his soul. He said that it was the biggest mistake of his life and that he didn't think that he could ever get over the guilt."

Courtney gazed up at him, eyes still moist. "It bothers him? To this day?"

Jake nodded his head. "To this day, deeply," he whispered.

She sat up. "Oh my God. That's why you were so worried I was pregnant after the lake. The same situation."

Jake only nodded in agreement.

She flopped back against the couch. "Only difference is, Jake, is I was raped," she said with a defensive tone. "Was it 'God's gift' that I was raped? "Am I going to see his face – I don't even want to say his name – every time I look at my child? Can I love my own child when it came from that experience?"

Jake had no answer for her.

Courtney slapped her hands on her thighs. "Damned if I do, damned if I don't. I guess I need to decide which is more painful – living with a constant reminder of what was or what could have been."

Jake put his arm around her and drew her next to him on the couch. "Throughout it all, I'm here. Don't ever forget that."

"I'm just gonna need help, Jake. I'm just gonna need help."

"Don't worry, Courtney, I guarantee you'll have all the help that you need."

In the ensuing silence, the two of them alone on the couch, Jake thought of dreams, the lake, and the old man. His eyes grew wider with realization.

"Albert. His name is Albert," he thought to himself.

He remembered how he knew the name of the Scotsman in the boat. He had met him at Spanky's several years ago.

Twenty-Five
Bridge

Binghamton, New York
Friday, November 22, 1985

Grasping that the old man in the dreams of this time was the same person at the bar before was a clue to the meaning of "The Transferal" Jake had been searching for. Only a couple of months earlier he had feared Courtney was pregnant with his child. The anxiety had brought his guilt back to the forefront again, spawned by memories of a regretted decision.

The old man connected the two situations.

He figured his subconscious attempted to tell him something. "Maybe I was supposed to carry my guilt lesson to Courtney, to tell her about my experience, my aching. Maybe that's the reason for "The Transferal."

Courtney had choices, and pain accompanied each of them. She learned she did not need to endure the distress in isolation, however. With Jake's encouragement, Courtney told her parents about the rape and pregnancy, and Jack and Elaine Wilson stood by their daughter. Courtney decided to keep and raise the child once she realized she had the support of many.

Jake made sure Courtney understood he would support her, as a friend, unconditionally. However, he did not tell her his assistance would have to come from a distance.

The more she leaned on him, the more he hurt, guilt-laden pains striking at every opportunity. Yet as much as he wanted to, he could not bring himself to reveal the truth to her. Jake saw no choice but to suffer alone in his private hell.

He found himself in his selfishness growing increasingly jealous of Courtney, as she would eventually experience what he threw away, the joy of parenthood. Her pregnancy could be a bridge between a future happiness with her child and his emptiness and culpability, if he wished. But he did not share in her forthcoming bliss. Even if he avoided meeting Nina, he still harbored the inescapable memories of before.

At nights, he searched for the dreams and for the old man, believing the place of the lake held the answers. Yet no images came forth, only abandoned darkness.

He had no power to change his own past, and the haunting of what might have been crushed his soul. He decided he would rather spend Thanksgiving alone in Buffalo than be reminded of his mistakes.

He rationalized his choice by convincing himself he had a decent chance of landing a paid intern position at Buffalo Steel, seven months earlier than before. The knowledge and experience of six years at the plant, four part-time and two full-time, would trump any other applicant, he predicted.

"Beats working the kitchen at the hospital, anyway," he surmised.

He loaded up the Pacer, said goodbye to his mother and Stoley, and was on the road back to Buffalo before noon, running away from one situation and hoping to sidestep another. But as he struggled with a newfound internal conflict, Courtney's pregnancy produced a surprising revelation.

He desperately wanted to be the father of Nina's child.

Twenty-Six
Steel

Buffalo, New York
Monday, December 2, 1985

Jake did not care that he had leveraged the unfair advantage of knowledge gained from his previous life. Securing the interview at Buffalo Steel on short notice was a direct result of knowing what questions to ask which people. His extensive experience at the plant had enabled him to nail the answer to each question and steer every conversation in his desired direction. He would end up filling the internship position anyway, whether in December of 1985 or June of 1986. He had feigned surprise when offered the job on the spot with a starting date of the following Monday.

Going back to the place and career he loved would make a lonely Christmas somewhat easier to endure. He wanted to return to Buffalo Steel as he had enjoyed working with the top-notch engineering team before. The politics would not touch him as an intern, so his position presented the perfect way to return to his passion.

It also provided an ideal situation to run away to.

In the time before, he had earned a reputation as a workaholic from his dedication and his drive to discover better, more efficient methods and processes to create products. Pressures with the massive "17 Roll" retrofit project, however, had drained his love for engineering. He eagerly approached the second chance to rekindle the enjoyment of his profession.

"Maybe I can get in some comments to Jeremy on the front end of the planning for '17 Roll' in a couple of years. At least I could save myself a bit of grief down the road," he thought.

But this time, through the early years of his career, he decided he would also pause to smell the roses more often.

He enjoyed repeating his first day at Buffalo Steel for orientation purposes, centered on personal safety on the operations floor. Physical protection remained an important topic, as many opportunities existed to lose one's limbs or life where machines transformed raw metal into workable materials. He remembered all of the procedures and codes of the plant, having served his six-month rotation as safety engineer during his initial year full-time, but he did not mind the review.

The end of orientation came fast, and he looked forward to a jog after learning what his primary duties would be over the next few weeks before the spring semester started. He walked into Chief Preventative Maintenance Engineer Jeremy Winterburn's office to receive his project assignment, and immediately sensed tension when Jeremy instructed him to close the door.

"What's up?" Jake asked, then reminded himself not to be so informal with his supervisor yet.

"Uh, Jake, have a seat. I know you're a student, and this is an opportunity to learn about a lot of things, not all just scientific."

"I know, and I'm glad I have such a great opportunity to do so," Jake replied with honesty, slightly fidgeting in his chair from the feeling that he had done something wrong, but had no idea what.

Jeremy drew in a deep breath. "Well, there are certain professional, uh, appearances that a successful engineer needs to project. I'll be honest, a polo shirt and jeans just doesn't cut it."

Jeremy's admonition surprised Jake. Jeremy wore a button down shirt, a tie, and pressed pants, yet had been the one who first suggested to Chuck Vorsicht that the engineers deserved some latitude on the dress code. "Well, we were out on the plant floor for much of the safety briefing, and I thought we needed to dress like the floor personnel," Jake responded to the reprimand.

"Well, we need to dress as engineers. That's what Mr. Vorsicht wants."

"As engineers? Come on, Jeremy, you feel the same way, hell you led the change in policy!" Jake wanted to say, but opted against doing so. He still wanted to make his point, but had to remember his relationship with Jeremy as it existed in this "now."

"Yes, I know. But how can you do a thorough safety inspection without getting dirty?"

"You can, you just sidestep the grease," Jeremy replied with a slight smile, indicating to Jake the conversation was over.

"Ok, shirt and tie it is for tomorrow," Jake agreed.

Jeremy leaned forward and lowered his voice. "Jake, personally I'm with you, but the higher ups are really strict about this. Chuck - Mr. Vorsicht - already approached me about your dress this morning, and he is the boss. You can probably get away with it but I wouldn't want to piss off Chuck if I were hoping for a full-time position here someday. You've got the knowledge. Hell, you blew a couple engineers away during your interview, me included. But you have to learn to play politics."

Jake grudgingly conceded he had to walk the walk to reach the success he wanted, again. He wondered how much of his relatively meager intern wages would go to pay for shirts, ties, dress pants, and dry cleaning.

He drove out of the Buffalo Steel parking lot and turned the Pacer towards JCPenney, then changed his mind. Not only were clothes at Kmart cheaper, Nina Thater did not work there.

Twenty-Seven
Avoidance

Buffalo, New York
Friday, December 6, 1985

As the day when he had met Nina originally approached – Friday, December 6, 1985 – Jake's obsession with avoiding any situation that presented a chance of encountering her grew into mild paranoia. Every decision he made, including where to purchase clothes, factored in the chance of running into Nina.

He stared with a blank expression at the cinderblock wall of his dorm room. He now regretted returning to Buffalo so soon. Time compressed, and he had worked himself into a corner, but he found no physical place to run to this time. He eyed the Jack Daniel's on his dresser, again.

"This was the night we met last time, at the party," he thought for the umpteenth time while pondering the golden liquid.

If he could not escape to a place, he would find refuge another way. Without further reservation, he grabbed the full bottle of Jack, forcefully opened it, and took one swig, then another. He did not want to be a part of the party but he had agreed to tend the bar. He had to honor his commitment.

"If I see her, I'll ignore her," he said to himself with the courage the second swig of Jack

Daniel's provided. The warmth of the alcohol surrounded him like a comforting blanket. He tucked the bottle under his arm and left the dorm room.

"Hector will help me."

"Where you going, Jake?" Arnav asked after looking up from his books and seeing his roommate hustling down the hall towards him. Jake said nothing to Arnav as he passed the dorm's common area. Arnav shrugged his shoulders and returned to the study of integrals.

*　　*　　*

"Hey, Jake, wanna fill me up sometime tonight?"

Jake stared into the crowd, looking for Nina, and then glanced at Hector working the door, who shook his head. Jake had given Hector a general description of Nina and asked him to signal if she showed up, but did not tell him why. He dreaded catching a glimpse of her but if he did, he would leave. He would run, regardless of his bar commitment.

"Jake, about my beer?" the voice repeated.

Jake shook himself out of his private world, once again conscious of the fraternity party around him and his duties as bartender. He hastily grabbed the cup out of Tom's hands, pumped the keg subconsciously with his foot while opening the tap and releasing the brew into the plastic container. As he filled Tom's beer, he decided he wanted, no needed another one too. The Jack was out of his reach.

"Jake, what's up? You've been a bit out of it since you came back from Binghamton."

"I'm ok," Jake responded to Tom in a raspy whisper after taking a large swig of beer. His eyes scanned the basement of the fraternity house, searching. He was intoxicated, he was tired, and his all too familiar headache had returned.

"Nah, you're not. You just seem, well, ate up inside."

"I really don't want to talk about it," Jake replied, tension rising in his voice.

"That's what I mean – usually I can't get you to shut up!" Tom joked.

Jake guzzled the rest of his beer and started to pour another for himself, ignoring several underage university students requesting a refill of cheap swill. "Real fucking funny, man," Jake said with intended sarcasm.

Mike, the fraternity's social chairman, approached Jake after noticing the growing line for beer refills. "Hey, Jake, you're gonna serve these people, or what?"

Something snapped within Jake. He turned to a girl to his right, her hand outstretched holding a party cup. "Oh, sure, yeah, hey, you, sexy blond, you wanna beer? Yeah, get you drunk so some over hormoned ape can fuck the shit outta you, get you in trouble, ruin yer life! Here, slut, here's one on me." He shoved the beer into her hand.

The girl took the cup, speechless. "Hey, Jake, calm down," Mike said, glad the girl had not thrown the drink in Jake's face.

"No, man, you calm the fuck down!" Jake yelled. "You think I'm doin' such a shitty job here? You think that I suck here? Fine, you take this, and you do this shit!" Jake flung the empty plastic beer pitcher next to him forcefully against the back basement wall, grabbed his bottle of Jack Daniel's from behind the bar, and ran out of the fraternity house's cellar.

Jake liked running, and he ran to feel alive, because doing so left stress behind. He sprinted down the street and across the railroad tracks, and finally stopped in a small park unfamiliar to him. The waves of paranoia of possibly meeting Nina, mixed with regret and guilt and enhanced by his throbbing headache, were uncontrollable now, and he had no idea how to fight them. He groaned.

He did not understand where they came from or why they haunted him. An unseen enemy is always the hardest to defend against attack.

He shouted a sort of primordial wail, reflecting the conflict in his heart and the alcohol affecting his mind.

He sat on a short stone wall and took a hearty drink from the bottle, gulping down the whiskey.

His lips were numb.

His balance was unsteady.

He stared at nothing in particular in the distance, vaguely aware he had to urinate, but not caring.

He was alone. He had no home, there.

No matter how many people he kept around, he remained alone. To be unable to share his problems tore at him. No one understood.

"Damn this!" he screamed to no one in particular. "I didn't ask for this!"

"Jake."

Jake, shocked to hear his name, still did not turn around at the sound of Tom's voice. Tom sat next to Jake, and did not say another word.

The close friends from the future and the past stayed quiet for several minutes in the present.

Men do not enjoy awkward silence. Both understood Jake had created a scene. Somehow, Tom's presence calmed him.

"I really fucked up, didn't I?" he finally said after a couple of minutes.

Tom pulled out a cigarette. "Want one?" Jake nodded as he took the Camel.

"Nah, you're upset, that's all." Tom lit his cigarette and took a long, deep drag. He blew the smoke out, and watched the particles hang in the still air. "Hey, man, I'm sorry if I touched a nerve back there. But it would help to talk, you know."

Jake was glad for the company, yet telling Tom the truth was out of the question. Still, the beer and the whiskey fought for control of him, and he struggled. "Thanks, but no. Can't do it."

"Come on, Jake, I can understand. It's the whole issue with Courtney, right? Hell, I know pain. Holly just dumped me last week, remember? 'Let it out', you told me. Well, who are you to not live up to your own standards? Pretty fucking arrogant of you, I'd say."

Tom always had a way of enticing Jake to talk by putting Jake on the defensive. The tactic usually worked, and this incident proved to be no exception.

He could not deal with "The Transferal" by himself anymore.

He sighed in resignation, and gave up control, if only momentarily.

"All right, yeah, I've got a problem."

"And?"

"And it's not Courtney."

"Aw, this is gonna be deep. Gimme a swig," Tom said as he took the bottle of Jack from Jake. "If it ain't Courtney, the love of your life, then what?"

Jake shook his head. The pounding from the ever-persistent headache, and the sheer loneliness of holding on to a secret he had struggled with daily for months, had worn him down. He did not care if the alcohol severely clouded his judgment.

"It was alcohol, those damned vodka gimlets, that started this whole mess," he reminded himself.

His only release, the sole way to find some relief, was to tell someone. Tom was his best friend in the previous life and a comrade already in this one. If anyone could be open to the idea, it would be Tom, he thought.

Jake took a final puff on his cigarette before crushing it under the heel of his boot as he completely gave up the false control of holding on to his secret. "Ok, Tom, here it is. Ever consider time travel?"

*   *   *

"And, so, here I am, hammered, confused, and stuck in time," Jake said with a measure of relief. He took a drink form the bottle of whiskey, more a sip, this time not as long or deep as previously. Both were quite intoxicated, possibly dangerously so.

Tom broke his long silence. "So," he simply said.

"So, what?"

"So what do you do now? Continue to avoid her and hope?"

"You mean you believe it?"

Tom paused for a moment, not sure of his answer. "I dunno," he finally responded. "You're either telling the truth or are fucking crazy. I know you're not making it up. You're not a good enough bullshitter to make such a story sound so damn convincing if it wasn't true."

Jake chuckled, and then sighed. "Well, it feels good to tell someone, finally."

"I agree that you shouldn't see her. Paradoxes and all. Hell, you probably shouldn't have told me."

"I've kept this damn thing bottled up for eight months now, Tom. I had to tell. I feel better about it, and to hell with any paradox."

Tom's demeanor became more cerebral, and he raised his right hand. "Ok, let's test this. Who is president in, say, '91?"

"George Bush."

"Well, that's an easy guess, seeing as how he's veep now. Let me think of something else. When will I get laid next?"

"You don't wanna know!" Jake laughed.

"Now I know you're telling the truth!"

Jake became more subdued as he asked the question again. "So, seriously, do you believe me?"

"Yeah. Yeah, Jake, I think I do," Tom said as he leaned back and gazed at the stars.

"I think I do."

Twenty-Eight
Interception

Buffalo, New York
Thursday, December 12, 1985

"I really don't remember anything after that. I don't know how Tom and I got back to the dorm. I'm pretty sure we didn't return to the party. I sort of remember us getting subs at Alfonso's on the way, but not eating them."

Jake gazed out through the fourth floor window of the University of Buffalo's undergraduate library to the courtyard. A light snow was falling, possibly the prelude to a major squall or bright sunshine in a matter of minutes, given the unpredictability of lake effect precipitation.

"I don't think Tom remembers the conversation," Jake continued to write in his journal. "He had killed more of the Jack than I had. I remember he was doing shots behind the bar before I grabbed the bottle and left. I'd only had the two shots in the dorm room before, but I did have a shit load of beer at the party. But he hasn't said anything about what we talked about, at least not yet."

"Hector told me the next day that Nina had come but only stayed about an hour. We figured she had arrived about ten minutes after I left. I'm kinda glad Hector didn't ask me why I was looking for her, but that's the kind of guy he is. He's just very mellow and unassuming and willing to do a favor whenever asked."

"The important thing is that I successfully avoided meeting Nina."

Jake clicked the pen closed and stuffed the notepad into his knapsack. His stomach growled, and getting wings at Sal's after his appointment sounded inviting to him.

*   *   *

After a short meeting with his advisor to decide what courses to take in the spring 1986 semester to make up for lost time in the fall, he sauntered towards his 1977 Pacer, eager to grab some chicken wings and a beer. He often walked the mile to Sal's from campus, but even though the snow had stopped, he opted to forgo the walk in favor of the quickness of a drive.

As he approached his vehicle, a sound from the opposite side of the mostly deserted parking lot pulled his attention away from his hunger. A woman and a man were arguing next to a yellow car. Jake paid little thought to the situation and fumbled with his keys, lost in thoughts of hot sauce and hops.

A shout, not of danger but dripping with anger and intermingled with fear, drew Jake's gaze again to the verbal commotion. He sensed a certain familiarity in the woman's voice. She struggled to get into the car before the man grabbed her and pushed her against the hood.

He saw her face.

No thought, only instinct, drove him as the need to intervene and protect her from harm overshadowed his recent motivations and insecurities. "Leave her alone!" Jake shouted as he sprinted towards the yellow car.

The man spotted Jake and bolted in the opposite direction, leaving Nina leaning on the side of her Toyota.

"Are you all right?" Jake asked, genuine concern filling his voice.

Nina composed herself and nodded. "Uh huh. Thank you," she said as she hugged Jake.

Jake returned the hug, only vaguely aware both the dread of meeting her, built up over the past several months, and his chronic headache were no longer present. He let himself enjoy the embrace.

He could have, should have, and possibly subconsciously did surmise the inevitability of encountering Nina. Every time he had tried to influence his future, the result still followed the general path as before. The meeting did take him by surprise, but he did not care.

He spoke from the heart, not the mind. "I was on my way to Sal's for some wings. Want to join me?"

*   *   *

"Thanks again for intervening," Nina said as Jake returned with a basket of medium wings and two coffees. "You said your name is Jake?"

He nodded. "No problem. You just gotta watch out for the assholes."

He could not help but stare into her eyes. Seeing the kindness within conveying closeness and warmth pushed all fear from Jake. His past vows, to her and himself, held no meaning now at the table in Sal's.

"So you're a freshman, too? What are you studying?"

"Business" Nina replied, "But I'm thinking of changing to Psychology. You?"

"Mechanical Engineering, although I lost this semester because of an accident," Jake responded with a certain tone of pride mixed with regret in his voice.

"Oh my gosh, what happened?"

"Ah, it was pretty silly," Jake said. "My left front tire blew out and it pulled the car to the left and into a pickup truck and a telephone pole. It was slick that night, the first snow of the season, you know. I was laid up for a few weeks in the hospital, concussion, punctured lung, couple broken ribs. Was actually in a coma for a bit."

"Wow. But you seem ok now. You raced pretty fast across the parking lot," she said as she smiled and took a sip of her coffee.

"Yeah. I think the running helped with my recovery. I try to run regularly, but honestly, I'm not as dedicated as I should be. Smoking doesn't help either. I picked it up last year, but need to put it back down."

"I completely understand." She paused as if deciding whether to continue. "And I like the fact that you're so open," she finished with a slight, shy grin.

Unsure of what to say next, Jake nervously grabbed a chicken wing.

Nina broke the short silence. "Do we know each other?"

The question shocked Jake, and he put the half-eaten wing down on his plate. "Huh?"

"The way you looked at me before, when we sat down, it seemed, well, do we know each other?" she repeated.

Jake shook his head, afraid of showing too much emotion. "No, I don't think so. Why?"

"Because," Nina started, then stopped.

"Why?" Jake pressed.

"Because," Nina began again as she stared straight at Jake and smiled. "Because when I look at you, it feels like I have known you for a long, long time."

And that was how it started, again.

Twenty-Nine
Convergence

Buffalo, New York
Friday, December 13, 1985

All he had promised himself he would not do did not matter anymore to him.

He had spent the better part of the past eight months determined not to meet Nina Thater. For Jake, "The Transferal" provided a second chance at life, an opportunity to circumvent the hurt, loss, guilt, and everything else that contributed to what he perceived as an incredible waste. Rational consideration had resulted in the simple conclusion that not meeting her was the best method to avoid pain.

But something had happened. Fate would not allow him to alter his direction by sidestepping his encounter with her at the party. When he saw Nina in possible danger, evading her no longer mattered. He had to help her.

He ran away from running away.

Tomorrow, December 14, 1985, marked the day he originally bumped into her at JCPenney. The encounter had led to her invite to her sorority's end of semester celebration. He understood the decision point. "We could be more responsible, and avoid the mistake," he considered. "We could put each other ahead of ourselves. We could have a child when we're ready."

The apparent primary rule of "The Transferal" disturbed him, however. "Or, we could go through it all over again. I can't seem to change anything."

He ordered his third Samuel Adams from Al, the bartender at The Oasis, to try to lubricate his brain and determine the right decision. Reason, emotion, and fear struggled for superiority. His headache had returned full force, and the beer did not help. Sobriety yielded to mild intoxicated analysis paralysis, played on a field he had visited countless times over the past few months.

The notion he had control over his destiny had been wrong, he accepted with trepidation. Still, he held hope avoiding the surprise pregnancy remained a possibility. His faith rested somewhat in his instrumental role in Courtney successfully navigating through her ordeal and deciding not to abort her child, the one change from before.

Perhaps the same would hold true for him and Nina.

He rubbed his head with both hands. The throbbing had intensified just beneath his forehead.

He studied the third beer, almost finished, and motioned to Al for a fourth. He had avoided The Oasis because of the remote possibility of running into Nina. No longer a danger, he returned to the place where "The Transferal" began. He hoped the familiar confines might prompt some revelation.

He surveyed the surroundings after the fourth beer arrived, and his gaze again fell on the pool table. His two quarters sat on the edge closest to him, marking his spot next in line to play the winner of the current match. He considered a game might jar some repressed memories about his last night here. Still, not having the answer did not matter to a part of him. He accepted he would never return to his prime timeline.

The eight ball rolled in on a well-executed bank shot, ending the game. Jake hopped off the stool, nodded to Oscar, a regular who was present the night "The Transferal" began, and put his quarters in the slot to retrieve the balls.

Money breaks at The Oasis according to the house rules, and Jake's attempt did little more than to displace the balls from their initial triangular formation. Jake had hoped Oscar's skills were less mature than as he remembered, but constant observation the last half hour as Oscar outplayed his three opponents told him otherwise.

Eight months had passed since he had last shot eight ball, but little rust inhibited his skills. Jake sank all of his balls in only a few minutes. He stared down at the cue to line up a tough but doable bank shot on the eight to the corner to his right.

"Good thing I didn't do 'shot for shot.'"

"What?!" Jake stopped his back draw, shocked at the words.

"I said, 'little man,' good thing I didn't do 'shot for shot.' I'd get wasted!" Oscar replied.

Jake sensed his face turning pale and flustered at the same time, and odd combination that likely cancelled each other out. He thought he and

Tom had invented the "shot for shot" game late their freshman year.

"'Shot for shot,' what's that?" he asked, stifling his reaction as best he could.

"Ya never did 'shot for shot'? Hey, it's when you call the eight clean, no banks, you make it, I have to do a shot, your choice. If you bank one rail, two shots for me, two rails, three shots. 'Course, I'd have to buy, and get you whatever also. Darrin usually bets double shots and he'd make this on three rails, so that's six shots I'd have to drink. Hell, he'd do six also, so I'd be plastered and broke too!"

Jake sighed, understanding the different game had the same name. He positioned himself, lined the shot up, drew back the stick, and struck the cue ball. The eight bounced off two rails, as called, but stopped an inch from the corner. Jake hung his head in defeat. Two of Oscars' balls remained, both easy shots, as well as the eight. Oscar chuckled to himself before sinking each ball in a methodical progression.

"Good game, man. I thought you had me."

"So did I, Oscar," Jake said, before realizing he had not been introduced to Oscar in this time frame. Fortunately, Oscar had already turned his attention to his next opponent.

Jake returned to the bar to order his fifth Sam Adams. The beer had a firm grip on his senses, and he did not care. Hector had once said running to alcohol constituted "standard Jake" whenever he waffled on a big decision or tried to deflect emotional pain.

"Hector's right. I need to face this," he tried to convince himself.

He did enjoy her company yesterday at Sal's. He saw in her for the first time in ages qualities he had fallen in love with originally. "She had always been so straightforward with expressing her feelings," he ruminated as he recalled her saying she felt like she had known Jake for a long time.

Maybe backing off and not going to JCPenney was not the best thing to do, he thought. Maybe a future in this past existed with her.

"Maybe I have to stop running."

He made the decision, and took his money for the fifth beer off the bar. He briskly exited The Oasis, not pausing to look back.

The crisp December air made him shiver and he pulled up the collar of his denim jacket, but the coolness also stimulated Jake's rational side as he walked back to the dorm. Even though he had attained an "Incomplete" status in all of his classes, the room was still his to occupy as a registered student, paid in full thanks to finally receiving his loan check.

He stopped at a Coke machine in the lobby and selected a Classic Coke, and placed the refrigerated can against his forehead as the elevator doors closed for the trip to the sixth floor. He welcomed the coldness, worried he might be tired and a bit hung over tomorrow. Such would not be the best way to talk with Nina for what to her would be only the second time.

*　　*　　*

He walked into the store, vaguely aware of the Christmas music playing from speakers overhead. He made his way to the men's department, where winter jackets and coats dominated the displays. His denim jacket had some lining, but he needed something heftier, as the walk home from The Oasis the previous night showed him

But he was honest with himself. His purpose at JCPenney was to see Nina. He looked around, but did not spot her. A Christmas display caught his eye, however.

"Not this time," he said to himself as he smiled.

He paused to study a rack of leather coats. He selected a light tan one and removed his denim, dropping the other in the process. As he bent down to pick up the jacket, he heard the sweet voice behind him.

Her voice.

"I think it's just not quite you. Maybe a dark gray would work better."

He turned and looked up at Nina smiling at him. She held a gray suede jacket, the same one he had bought before. His returned his attention to picking up the leather. As he rose, his gaze followed the long thin legs to where they disappeared beneath the blue skirt, then to the lighter blue fuzzy sweater past the nice, rounded breasts to the beautiful, full lips, slightly parted and magnificently red. Her lovely long blond hair and the blue piercing eyes completed the scene.

"That's perfect, Nina," he said, grinning ear to ear.

*　　　*　　　*

They arranged to meet at the sorority house for Sigma Tau's "End of Semester Bash." All newly inducted members had to work the party, so Nina arrived early to assist with setting up the bar. Jake enjoyed the short walk in the crisp early evening air from the dorm to the party.

He heard the music a block away and, as he approached the source of the music, he wondered about the neighborhood's opinion of the noise, a thought that had rarely crossed his mind before. Many but not all of the old houses were rented out to students. Without official university Greek housing, several fraternities and sororities held parties where some members' lived, sometimes evoking tension between the groups and families.

He preferred not to go to parties alone, but he conceded this situation should be different. He knew several of the sorority's women from the previous time. A couple even comprised part of the wedding party.

He pledged not to drink, at least not to excess, as he had done before at this event. He needed the clarity of mind to stay present, not run, and not put himself first.

"Hi, welcome to Sigma Tau's 'End of Semester Bash' wild extravaganza!" a girl with Sigma Tau written in yellow cursive on a blue jacket said as Jake walked up the house's front steps to the wooden floored porch. He gave the required two dollars for admission and entered. Charging cash for unlimited drinks was illegal on several levels, but provided a method of raising funds for Greek organizations. Heads generally turned the other way for such events unless they got out of hand.

Not many mingled outside, but inside the house was packed, and he had difficulty making his way through the crowd. Nina would be serving drinks at the makeshift bar in the basement, as she did last time. Jake grinned.

"Sometimes knowledge of the future saves time," he thought.

He shuffled down the stairs and navigated around the back of the old furnace, almost neglecting to duck for a duct.

He spied her at the bar serving some sort of punch to a couple of men with outstretched hands clutching cups, their minds probably wishing they were grabbling something else. Jake took a moment to stare at Nina in her Sigma Tau sweater. For all she was, she was incredibly beautiful. He continued to the bar, but only after regaining his composure.

"Hi."

"Hey Jake how ya doing?" Nina said as she picked up a cup and began to fill it with punch for him. He almost started to protest but did not, opting to nurse the drink instead. He worried more about getting a contact buzz, recognizing the sweet smell of burning pot. He watched a bowl passed among three stoners located at the opposite corner of the basement beyond the furnace.

"Good, thanks," he said, returning his attention to Nina. He took the cup and tasted the mixture. Jake surmised the strong, fruity, sweet taste was likely from the Kool Aid, and did not come close to masking the alcohol.

"Just the one," he reminded himself.

"Did you have any problems finding the place?"

"What, are you kidding? You can hear the music all the way down the street. It's like a beacon for partiers."

She moved out from behind the bar and joined him. "Yeah, actually we've had a bigger turnout than expected. Three kegs have already been killed, and a couple of the girls went out for more."

"Cool," Jake said, suddenly uncomfortable.

"Hey, you want to go outside?" she asked. "I could use some fresh air, and I'm done with my duty here." Jake understood she referred to the marijuana smoke, as she had never enjoyed the smell.

"Yeah, good idea."

*   *   *

A light snow had started to fall. Nina hopped up on to the hood of her car parked in the driveway, and he leaned against the driver's side door.

"Oh, it feels good to get out. That smoke was killing me."

"I know what you mean."

"My mouth gets so dry from it." She swallowed a rather large amount from her cup, and Jake wondered if she was getting drunk. He had gotten sloshed at this party, but did not recall if she had as well.

Jake took another sip, and winced. The alcohol content was high and the mixed drink did little to relieve his thirst. "This stuff doesn't do too much for a dry throat. I don't know how you can stand such a large gulp."

"Oh, it's easy, when you're drinking just Coke," she laughed.

"Coke?"

"Uh huh. Want a sip?"

Jake took the cup and took a long drink, savoring the wetness. "Why are you drinking Coke? You usually, uh, you were bartending. I'd think that you'd be drinking as much as the rest, at least," he said.

"Well, I did have a couple earlier, but I usually don't drink too much."

Jake sighed. "I wish I'd known that you had Coke back there," he said with a smile.

"Really? I thought you'd think I was weird or something. You guys all like to party. Your parties are known on campus for being some of the rowdiest."

"I know, but truth is I don't get into it too much."

"That one you guys had a couple weeks ago was a blast. Were you there? I don't remember seeing you."

"I set up and then bartended for a bit, kinda like you here. Then I split," he replied, not wanting to delve further into the events of that night.

"Do you want to go in and get a Coke?" she said as she began to slide off the hood of the car.

"No, no that's fine, not right now. I'm enjoying the talk," he replied with strong honesty. He gave himself a mental kick for thinking she had more than a Coke in her cup. Before, he had finished his punch, and coaxed her into joining him for another. Jake now realized she probably had done so to look cool in front of him. "Stupid," he said aloud.

"What?"

"Uh, I was just thinking that it is really stupid when people try to impress one another by doing things they don't want to do. Like, for instance, I wasn't going to drink much tonight, but when you passed me that drink I didn't want to reject it for fear that you'd think I was being too 'square' or something. And the funny thing is that you were drinking Coke. Isn't that stupid?"

"Yeah," she replied, and then chuckled. "You know, I've seen so many relationships that are like that, though. Take my friend Robin, for example. She's down there smoking weed with her boyfriend and some of his friends, just because they're doing it. I mean, she doesn't like the shit, in fact she hates it, but she started to do it because Stanley did it. He's a stoner with shitty grades, and probably not much of a future, and now she's starting to act like that. It's sad."

Jake nodded as she took another sip and then continued. "I think that is so important, you know? To be yourself and not try to be like you think someone wants you to be. I've gone out with my share of losers before, and I'm sick of wasting my time. If someone doesn't like me the way I am, then too bad." She jumped off the car and stretched, then turned back to Jake. "Sorry, I'm rambling."

"No, no that's fine," he said, seeing a side of her he had not before. He had assumed she had been a partier, and she had just told him otherwise, with assertiveness and confidence.

"Did I ever know her, really know her?"

So many fights between them had started or escalated because she went out with friends for a drink or two but Jake had presumed worse. He now realized he had based his insecurities and misplaced lack of trust largely on the impressions of her from this evening.

"Jake?"

"Huh?"

"Are you ok? You seemed kind of, well, distant there for a moment."

"No, just thinking," he replied, ashamed of his assumption.

"Well, if you want to go back inside, we can."

He wanted to get to know her better, as he should have this night years ago. "No, would you like to take a walk instead?"

"Sure. Like I said I helped set up, so my duty here is done," she replied with a hint of eagerness.

"A walk does not imply a commitment, a future, or anything else," he told himself. "But I have to get to know her."

He took her hand and thought of the possibilities missed and the opportunities ahead. He smiled at her touch while taking care to avoid the pile of puke left by someone who had consumed too much alcohol in a bid to escape reality.

*   *   *

"I like what you've done to the room" Nina said as Jake closed the door.

"Thanks. Want something to drink? I've got Coke, water, or some Stroh's, if you're interested."

"Oh, why not, give me a Stroh's," she said. Jake retrieved two beers from the small, cube shaped dorm refrigerator.

"I usually drink Molson, this is Tom's," he said as he handed a can to Nina. "He left it here Tuesday after poker."

"Is Tom your roommate?"

"No, he lives down the hall, but we pledged together. He's a good friend of mine. My roommate is pretty much an introvert. Smart, but I don't really know him well."

"Oh. Will he mind?" Nina asked with a hint of concern in her voice.

"Arnav? No, he's gone for the weekend."

"No, I meant Tom, drinking his beer."

"Nah, I don't think so. He owes me a six-pack from the game anyway. This just lets him off the hook easily."

"Where is he?"

"Oh, he went with a few other Phi Delts to Alabaster's in Fort Erie."

"Why didn't you go?"

"I wanted to go to your party. I wanted to see you," he said, straight from the heart.

"That's really nice, Jake," she said, sincerely. "I really appreciate it."

"No problem," he said.

"No, I really mean it. I'm not used to guys treating me well."

Jake took the cue. "You mean, like that steroid monster who was out with you in the parking lot?"

"Yeah, for one," she replied. "He seemed nice at first. I mean, I'd known him for some time, but we had never dated before. Maybe I just wanted him to be nice, I don't know. As soon as we started going out though it was like I suddenly became his possession. I couldn't do anything without him approving."

"That sucks."

"Uh huh. But most of the guys I've dated are like that it seems. I think it goes back to my father," she said, her voice dropping.

"Your father? I don't understand," he lied.

Nina took a deep breath. "My father was, well, a control freak, and hard on us. We weren't rich growing up, and we'd help out wherever we could — chores, odd jobs, that sort of thing."

"Uh huh."

"Well, no matter what we did, my sister Sheila and I, it was never good enough for him. I can't tell you how many times he just hurt me with his words. And Mom was no help. It seemed no matter what I did he either didn't approve or, as I got older, would put me down. And if he had too many beers, watch out! Mom told us never to bother him if there were three or more empty cans on the end table next to his chair."

She sighed while reflecting. "I guess it was my freshman year in high school when he really began to lose it. That's when he started hitting us," she said.

Jake remembered the story of abuse well, but hearing it again produced as much pain as the first time.

"I got out of the house before it got real bad, but he really lit into Sheila after I left. She was always a little more wild but never did anything that was so bad."

Nina looked off into the distance. "She was a good kid. She wouldn't take his crap. One night – I wasn't there but Mom told me – he hit her so hard her lip busted and a tooth flew out. That's the night she gathered some things and just left."

She sighed. "It's been about a year since I last heard from her. She's out somewhere in California working as a waitress, going to community college, last she told me."

Jake recalled another year would pass before Sheila's return to Buffalo. Nina had encouraged

Sheila to complete her Associates degree, and Sheila subsequently had landed a job as a dental assistant. She had met a decent man, gotten married, and had a beautiful baby boy together.

Jake was the godfather.

"Jake, I never told anyone else that. Please don't tell anyone."

"I won't. But it wasn't your fault, you know."

"Well I could have stopped him from going after my sister, couldn't I?" she said, a hint of bitter regret in her voice.

"How? You didn't know. And besides, you couldn't stop him from going after you, how could you have stopped him from going after your sister? Nina, 'would haves,' 'could haves,' and 'should haves' are fine, but don't dwell on them. You've gotta move on."

"'Would haves,' 'could haves,' and 'should haves' are fine, but don't dwell on them. You've gotta move on," Jake repeated to himself. "Take your own advice, Stockman."

They sat in the stillness of the dorm room for several moments, each lost in their private thoughts.

"Jake?" Nina broke the silence.

"Yes?"

"Thank you."

"For what? All I did was listen."

"And yet you minimize that. Do you know all I've ever wanted in a man was for him to listen to me?"

Funny, Jake had known that once, but somewhere along the line it became more important to him for her to listen to what he had to say, not vice versa. He could not remember when he had stopped listening to her, but it had been well before the affair.

"The lessons keep on coming," he thought.

He leaned closer to her in the stillness of the dorm room. She looked up into his eyes as he gently caressed the side of her face with his hand. She softly took his other hand in hers as he drew her to him, ever so slowly.

For the first time, again, Jake and Nina kissed.

*   *   *

"So how'd you meet her?"

"I was walking back from meeting with my advisor, to work on my class schedule for the spring. Just past Fronczak Hall I heard a commotion in the parking lot, you know, kinda near the basketball court. Well, I was parked in the overflow lot so I had to cut through there anyway, you know? Anyway, as I get closer I see this guy and he's yelling at a girl. I figured it was some sort of boyfriend-girlfriend type dispute but when he grabbed her roughly, I had to say something. Tom, he looked like he was about to hit her."

"Man. So, what'd you do? Did you get into a fight?"

"No, I yelled something like 'Hey, what's going on' and he ran. Nina said it was some guy that she had recently started dating and wanted to control her. Kinda like she couldn't do anything without his approval, and apparently he was pissed she was on campus at that time. She doesn't think he'd have hit her but I don't know. He had his arm drawn back like he was going to before I yelled."

"Did you know who he was?"

"You know, the funny thing is that he looks kinda like one of the regulars at Ford's. You know that group of Zetas that seems to almost live there? I think he was one of them, but I didn't press the issue. Anyway, I didn't ask her, wasn't my business. What court are we on?"

"Three"

"Cool. Have you been playing long?"

"Nah, I took up racquetball last spring," Tom replied. "My dad's been playing for years and he finally convinced me to give it a try and, well, I kinda liked it. I played a bit with him and some others at the gym my dad goes to. You?"

"Well, like I said before, I've played a little, but not recently, so I'm sure I'm a bit rusty." Jake spoke the truth. He recognized the irony that the last time he had played racquetball was against Tom in the past, or the future, or whatever. Jake's thought process had never come up with a suitable algorithm for describing events of both past and future.

"Well, I'll go easy on you," Tom said with a smirk as they entered court three at Alumni Arena shortly after the facility had opened Sunday at noon.

"Let's volley to warm up first," Jake suggested as he hit the ball against the far wall.

"Ok."

At first, Jake only lobbed the ball against the wall. As the warm-up progressed, he slammed well-placed low kill shots against the back wall and executed decent pinches, betraying his experience. "I should go easy on him but, hell, Tom would exploit such an edge," he smiled to himself.

Tom stepped into the server box and lobbed the ball into the corner to Jake's left, a tough serve to return. Jake's hit, more defensive in nature, provided a perfect kill opportunity for Tom. But Tom did not execute the shot, giving Jake an almost identical chance. Jake capitalized on the gift.

"Ok, so you really wanted to serve first, fine," Tom said as he flipped the ball to Jake. Jake pondered which serve he should lead off with, an easy lob or a drive. He chose the latter, and Tom watched the ball rush past.

"Boy, this feels good!" Jake thought as he moved about the court. He had loved racquetball as a means of tension relief during his stint at Buffalo Steel, but now he had no stress, just excess energy. The party the night before had been wonderful, Nina had confided in him, and they had shared the most wonderful kiss before he had walked her back to the sorority house.

He experienced an emotion he had not in years - pure, genuine happiness.

Playing racquetball, completing his recovery from the accident, getting his college career back on track for the spring semester, and reliving the early days of what would become a good friendship with Tom contributed to his contentment. However, the true cause of his ecstasy sat elsewhere.

He was falling in love with Nina, again, and did not fight against the current. He let the feelings flow. He had come back from a long journey, one started well before "The Transferal," well before the gimlets, and well before the fights.

He was coming home. Finally, home.

*　　*　　*

"You think you love her? Jake, how long have you been dating her? Wait, a better question is how many dates have you had?"

"Three."

"Three dates, in what, five whole days? You met her a week ago, and now you are head over heels in love with her? Well, at least I know how you beat me in racquetball. Never play an opponent who's in love, always challenge one who's just been dumped," he joked.

"He really doesn't remember the conversation after the party," Jake again concluded. "Tom, I know it sounds silly, but . . ."

"Silly?" Tom interrupted Jake as he leaned forward in the Burger King booth. "'Silly' doesn't do it justice. Seriously, Jake, it's ridiculous. It's impossible. You don't know her."

"Yeah, I do, don't you remember our freaking conversation?" Jake wanted to say but chose otherwise. Sometimes, though, he thought if Tom had recalled that night, he would understand and therefore offer more meaningful advice.

"Well, your timing sucks. Now you have to get her a Christmas present. You should have saved the love angle until after the New Year, or February fourteenth. She's gonna expect stuff, you know."

Jake was glad Tom backed off from the serious attitude. But he did start to think that perhaps some of what he was feeling for her could be simply reflections from the prime timeline.

"Do you think maybe you're just in love with the idea of being in love, Jake?" Tom continued after finishing the last french fry.

"No," Jake said flatly, somewhat displeased with the question. Tom had asked him the same thing several times during the divorce proceedings. Yet he pondered if the notion held any elements of truth.

"Well, maybe a bit, possibly."

"Jake, you've got your entire life in front of you," Tom said as he finished his Coke. "Don't wish for something so much that you try to make it happen. Hell, I want to be in love, too, and get married, have two point three cars and one point two kids or maybe it's the other way around, but not until I'm ready. And not until I find the right one."

He paused as he stood up and put on his coat. "You have time, Jake."

"What a beautifully, ironically truthful statement," Jake thought as he also put on his jacket, the gray suede.

Thirty
Moment

Buffalo, New York
Monday, December 23, 1985

Jake was happy, very happy.

The snow, clustered in large, wet, sticky flakes, fell steadily around him, creating a picturesque winter wonderland. He jogged through the two inches already on the ground, with more forecast. The lake effect precipitation fell in localized bands due to cold winds moving over the warm waters of Lake Erie. A well-formed band might dump a foot of snow in one location in the span of a few hours, whereas areas a couple of miles away would receive nothing but a flurry.

This particular storm was not bad at its northern edge over the city of Buffalo, but promised possible fabulous downhill conditions at the ski resorts in the southern hills. Skiing would have to wait, though. Jake had more important things on his mind.

In the eleven days since he had again crossed paths with Nina, he became firmly convinced he was indeed falling in love with her a second time. "Kindness! I forgot she could show kindness!" he thought.

He struggled to recall the first time they had started to date, the similarities and differences to now, and what they had done right and what they could have done better. Still, the past arguments and other "badness" no longer mattered to Jake. Jogging on the wet roads of the campus, he found no reasons, no debates within the mind, no intellectual arguments to back his decision.

Only "now" mattered.

The fear, the paranoia, the sweats, the odd dreams, and most importantly the headaches had all vanished shortly after they began dating again. He had vanquished the "ghosts" that had shadowed him as constant, unwanted companions since "The Transferal" began. He was free and clear to navigate his life as he desired.

He accepted the blessings from "The Transferal" with a heart full of gladness, if not a mind or soul full with understanding. And he did not care.

He no longer yearned to achieve lofty career goals or acquire material possessions. Staying in the moment only mattered. Once he focused his mind on the present, not his future or past, he found inner peace and contentment. His moment was now. His moment was his own.

His adrenaline surged, and he sprinted the last quarter mile past the fur trees with branches bending from the heavy wet snow. This jog was his moment.

Dizziness overtook him after he stopped, and he bent down to catch his breath and balance. After about a minute, he straightened up as a father pushed a stroller holding a little girl past him.

He became nauseous.

He shook off the discomfort with several deep breaths, and began to walk to prevent his muscles from cramping. Clarity returned to his mind as the dizziness evaporated. He turned his attention to the place he wanted to take Nina to later.

This night would be their moment.

*   *   *

"So then what happened?" Nina asked before taking a bite out of a chicken wing.

"Well, I found a leak. It was only a couple of drops, but it was enough. There was a leak in one of the hydraulic lines that feeds the slicer. It's kind of like a big saran wrap cutter that chops down on the metal after it's unrolled, to separate the metal into sheets that can be stamped," Jake explained as he made a cutting motion with his hands.

"Well, I reported it to Jeremy and he came out to take a look. Funny, but he couldn't believe that I had gotten so close to the line. Same old thing, the dress code keeps the preventative maintenance engineers from getting in close. You had to Nina, in order to see it."

Jake paused as he wiped some blue cheese from his chin and took yet another sip of his beer to try to wash away some of the sting from the wing's pepper sauce. Sal's was famous for a level of insane hotness even the medium wings possessed.

"I had to direct Jeremy to it, and you know what the first thing he said was? 'Oh, that's probably why we've been adding more hydraulic fluid to the number two reservoir.'"

"They knew about it?"

"Well, the maintenance crew did, and the maintenance logs they give back to engineering show the increased use of hydraulic fluid. Jeremy is the Chief PME - Preventative Maintenance Engineer - and he should have caught it."

"Did he get in trouble?"

"No, nothing like that. But we, well he shut down the line and did a further, closer inspection. As he was doing that, I ran some 'back of the napkin' stress calculations and determined that only luck prevented the line from busting. Nina, if that thing had busted the cutter probably would have fallen unexpectedly on to a worker, possibly slicing off his arm."

"Wow! So, then, in a way you saved some worker's arm."

The wings caused Jake's forehead to sweat. "Well, I wouldn't go that far, but it brought about my earlier point, that the engineers need to get in and do more hands on inspections there. There's so much waste that could be eliminated. Hell, Chuck would be amazed at the increase in productivity. I ruined a nice new shirt, though." His voice trailed off, distracted by Nina staring at him.

"What?" he said, uncomfortably.

She smiled. "I'm impressed, I mean really impressed. You've been there, what, a week, and you've already got such a handle for the place. That's incredible."

Jake blushed, and this time he did not try to fool himself by blaming it on the hot sauce. "Just observant, I guess."

Nina still stared at him. "But that's not all, is it," she said.

"What do you mean?"

Nina brushed her blonde hair back as she reached across the table and gently grabbed Jake's left hand. "Listen to you! You have such a passion for this. No one can listen to you and not be at least a bit jealous. You've found something that you love! The passion you have for engineering shows through, and you should be happy. Most people, and I include myself, don't have much more than an inkling on what they really want to do with their lives, but you're there already."

Jake sighed. "Well, Nina, really all my life all I've ever wanted to be is an engineer, but . . ." He stopped and turned his gaze downward.

"But what, Jake?"

"But I don't want it to ever take over my life."

"I don't understand."

Jake drew in a deep breath. "I don't want it, my work, to ever become the primary focus of my life, overshadowing my personal life, my family, my future wife." He looked up at her as he finished speaking.

"Jake, I honestly can't see that happening."

"Why do you say that?"

"Because you haven't put it in front of me. You've shared yourself, your career, your ideas, and although I may not understand it all, to just hear the enthusiasm in your voice makes it special to me also."

Jake studied her eyes, and could not stop asking himself the same question. "Who are you?" he wondered, but no words came to his lips. He let go of her hand and shook his head in silence.

The image of an older Nina accusing him of loving his career more than he did her played in his head. Her words from then conflicted with the reality of this conversation. He wanted, perhaps needed another beer, and refilled his glass from the pitcher, loosely conscious of the jazz band assembling on the small stage at Sal's.

"Jake, what's wrong?" Nina asked, reaching again for Jake's hand, but this time Jake pulled away.

He turned his head, not wanting to remember how things had evolved between them. He tried to suffocate his feelings, and did not respond to Nina.

"Jake, what is it?" she asked again. "Jake, did someone hurt you?"

Jake turned slowly to her. Maybe this presented an opportunity to let go of some of the truth he had been holding close, he thought. He nodded. "Yes. But it was a long time ago."

Nina put her beer down and tried to take Jake's hand, but he again pulled away. "Did you push someone away because of your dreams?"

Jake nodded. "Yes, in a way, but not intentionally. I felt that I had something to prove, I guess. I was a bit of a rebel in high school, and I guess I feared that people couldn't respect me unless

I proved that I wasn't a screw up any more. I felt, no sometimes I still feel like I'm chasing a ghost or something. Like I'm trying to prove to others that I can do it, that I can be successful."

He would not tell her the whole truth, not yet at least, but he postulated sharing some tangential thoughts might help him deal with the demons of past and future that still invaded his present. "So, I was seeing someone, we were kinda serious, but something happened. We were separated for a while, I was way too much into school and clubs, and she found someone else."

Jake tilted his head upward, the contours on his face betraying a hint of the emotional agony telling Nina aspects about their relationship's end had on him.

This time Nina found success in grabbing Jake's right hand, and she stared straight into his eyes. "Jake, did you try communicating with her?"

He looked at her beautiful blue eyes, lost in love, wondering how something so amazing had slipped away. "I tried, I tried, but it was too little too late."

"Well, maybe it wasn't completely your fault, Jake," Nina said. "Communication is a two way street, you know. I mean, you're still working hard, right? But you're not neglecting me. In fact, you're taking the time out to tell me about your work, your desires, and your dreams. Do you know how special that feels? That you trust me enough to share such intimate thoughts? Jake, it's not bad to work hard and follow your own path, so long as you share it, like now." She paused to refill her beer.

"You did share yourself with her, didn't you?"

Jake's stomach turned as the band took the stage. He had stopped sharing anything beyond an external shell with Nina long before their relationship had soured. The bitterness from his mistakes fueled uneasiness in his stomach as the band opened with a flute solo.

He would not make that or any of his other mistakes again, he swore to himself.

*   *   *

His eyes followed her the entire way as she rose and walked to the restroom until she disappeared behind the door. He held no doubts.

The situation was perfect. Everything was perfect. By opening up to Nina, he realized he now found the person he had initially fallen for. By learning to trust in himself and communicate with her, he found himself in love deeper than ever before.

The past future no longer existed to him. He reaffirmed what he had concluded earlier in the morning during the jog.

"The Transferal" was over. This was reality.

Nina was and is the love of his life. He could not, would not lose this happiness again.

"Soul mates," is how they had referred to each other in the beginning before, and tonight Jake knew the description to be true. They would have no future problems borne out of self-centeredness.

This time, things will be different, he reassured himself. This time, they will survive.

He still had yet to realize he had control over nothing.

She returned as Jake placed the tip on the table. He enjoyed the happy sparkle in her eyes, serving to reinforce his decision.

*   *   *

From Jake's perspective, the night was not yet over, not by a long shot.

They went to his room, as they had done in the other timeline on this date. The University at Buffalo's dormitories shut down for the winter break and required all residents to vacate, with some exceptions. Jake's job at Buffalo Steel warranted such, as a school sponsored paid internship.

He remembered this was *the* night, and he had made the necessary preparations for their first time together. Unlike before, callousness proclamations of lust would not overrule responsibility. He had set the stage before their date, a bottle of champagne on ice waiting.

They had each consumed less than a glass of the champagne before they allowed the passion to engulf them. Wordless expressions of love entwined them like multicolored ribbons of desire as they fell into Jake's bed. They tore at each other's clothes and were soon together.

They fell asleep in each other's arms, he still inside of her, exhausted from the intense passion fueled by deep, intimate love.

The river flowed to the lake of inevitable conclusions, as per destiny.

*   *   *

He awoke not much later, nudged by nature's call. Over the toilet, as he prepared to release, he removed the condom, the one detail he had neglected before. Not having protection was the one mistake that had led to the unbearable guilt and their end together.

He blinked his eyes, trying to clear the sleepy mist of confusion. He looked down. His eyes focused. He was initially confused, then horrified.

The evidence, illuminated by the dim twenty-five watt bulb in the dorm suite's bathroom, confirmed he again would not circumvent his destiny.

The condom, ripped and nearly reduced to a latex ring, hung off him. He removed the worthless instrument slowly, methodically, insanely.

In a moment of realization, blinded by understanding truth, Jake perceived space and time folding up on itself, creating a cosmic multidimensional full circle of repeated circumstances.

The toilet seemed surreal to him, the contents still bubbly from when the urine hit the water, the yellow mixing with the clear in the bowl.

He cleaned his hands and his penis, but they did not feel clean. He did not feel clean. He splashed water on his face, cupped his hands, filled them from the faucet, and drank. He stared at himself in the mirror.

"Damn this thing. Damn!"

In the silence of the dorm room bathroom, he hung his head in defeated resignation, understanding this night would spawn the pregnancy, the cause of the guilt, the hurt, the breakup, and his empty life. Everything would play out as before, again. In this moment, his moment, he accepted his destined existence in this, his manufactured personal hell.

He wandered back to the bed. Nina's body stayed still and peaceful and innocent, the hint of a rising and falling chest her only movement. He discerned no outward sign of what had already begun to play within. He allowed himself one more moment of fantasy, a world where everything would be all right, and he would find his home.

That moment was forever gone.

His head pounded and his stomach churned as he considered with longing love Nina silently sleeping. He closed his eyes, still standing over the bed, his mouth quite dry though he had drank from his hands at the sink only a minute earlier.

He failed a test. He added more guilt to his collection from both lifetimes. He again set in motion the events to lead to the darkest moment in his life. His chance squandered, his body weakened, and his soul dark, he yearned for the ultimate end.

He opened his eyes, and saw his future.

As before, by the end of January, on the same day of the Challenger disaster, she will take the home pregnancy test. Later in the night, she will tell Jake of her pregnancy.

They will have the same discussions. They will argue, they will fight, and they will realize and compromise.

They will decide, either together or alone.

They will drive to the clinic. Or she will. Or someone else will drive her.

All will happen again, one way or another.

He pondered his cyclical existence in his personal hell as he gazed out the dorm window, his head aching. The peacefulness of the frozen snow on the trees, several stories below, contrasted with the struggle ahead.

A click behind him broke him from his trance. With little energy and increasing lightheadedness, he turned towards the sound from the center of the room, in time to see a flash of light accompanied by a loud bang.

He fell backwards, a severe, unimaginable, excruciating pain permeating throughout his skull.

Then there was nothing.

PART VI
Heaven

Thirty-One
Guilt

Somewhere
Sometime

Jake, laying down at the edge of a field where grass met woods, smelled wet leaves as the sun beat down on his face. He gagged as he began to vomit, and he rose to avoid choking.

After the final heave, forcing up nothing more, he stood up and struggled to find his balance, the disorienting dizziness accompanying his intense headache almost knocking him back to the ground. Coughing, he fought to keep a vertical stance as new sharp pains permeated his chest and skull again, as if hit with a thousand little needles. He grimaced and groaned until the discomfort subsided somewhat after a few moments.

He inhaled a deep breath through his nose, exhaled it forcefully though his mouth, and squinted, the afternoon sun brilliantly illuminating the landscape. Psychedelic images in bright colors were swirling around his head, and he could not clear them, though he did not try all too hard.

A certain purpose seemed to envelop his person, the need to go home. The struggle was over, and he was tired. He had hoped for this end, with no more doubts and agonies. He only had the one final journey to make.

He fought the good fight, and now was his moment. Nothing else mattered.

"Home. I need to go home."

He surveyed his surroundings. Standing beside a road with sidewalks in a residential neighborhood, he stopped the movement of his gaze to stare off to his right at a deserted, almost pure green baseball field. He barely registered how everything, from the foliage to the buildings to even the sky, seemed to be colored in robust primaries, with little blending.

He spied no people or cars, and sounds were limited to birds chirping and the rustling of the leaves in the trees from the gentle, constant breeze. Yet the lack of any other audible or visual stimuli did not seem odd to him.

He rubbed his eyes, glanced towards the street again, and recognized his location. "Riverside Drive. Binghamton. I'm in Binghamton," he established, as he gazed at the hills overlooking the Vestal Parkway across the Susquehanna River. His head still throbbed, but not with the strong intensity of a couple of minutes earlier. He sensed a familiarity to this situation, without reason why. He strained to pinpoint a reference for the sensation of déjà vu.

He realized he did not recollect anything about how he got to this place, nor did he care. Logic was a tool he no longer possessed, or missed, or questioned.

Consumed with a singular purpose and destination, he had to find the bus to take him to his journey's end, his ultimate home. Nothing else mattered anymore to him. He did not need to check his watch to verify the urgency of his situation.

He had to catch the bus before time ran out.

He made his way down Oak Street pass the high school to Main Street, one foot in front of the other at a pace just above a slow jog. He halted and again doubled over in agony. Nobody heard his cries of his distress, a solitary inhabitant in a world constructed for thousands.

Nobody came to help.

The pain left rapidly, and he straightened up, stretched his arms above his head, and took in a deep breath. Sweat saturated his chest and he had an insatiable thirst. He hoped he would find water at his destination.

He resumed his walk, not concerned the normally busy streets remained completely deserted. Unfamiliar, frightening noises behind him broke the silence, and he stopped in terror. The sounds manifested themselves first as a low gurgling then rose in intensity until seemingly almost upon him from all directions. Continuing to sweat profusely, and consumed with panic, he whirled around, but the street was still empty and the echoes of conversations without meaning ended abruptly.

He continued his journey with cautiousness and slight paranoia. His aches had left him by the time he reached the halfway point of the Court Street Bridge. The Chenango River, deep blue against the uniform green countryside and flanked by buildings in bold white, black, tan, gray, and red, flowed effortlessly below him. Jake paused to gaze out over the water towards the hills.

"That is where home is. That is where I need to be."

The bus pulled into the stop at the other side of the bridge. Jake lumbered across the remainder of the span, with no need to hurry. He understood the driver would wait.

Jake entered the bus, climbed the stairs gingerly, and deposited the fare in the coin receptacle. He had his choice of any seat as the sole occupant and reason for this route. He settled into one next to a window in the front, his favorite spot. Soon he would be home, and get the deep sleep he craved.

Another wave of discomfort hit with a flash of light, followed by a sharp pain to his left temple. He moaned, took a deep breath, and tried to wish the agony away. But he had solid faith that at the other end of the ride he would find his peace and freedom from all of his suffering.

The bus pulled away from the bridge, and Jake settled into a state between sleep and unconsciousness. He experienced only blackness, devoid of everything, including love, thought, and hope.

*   *   *

He awoke to more darkness, save the wooded scene outside illuminated by the full moon. The driver had left, as had the physical discomfort and the sweats.

As he rose from the bus seat, all memories of what had happened to him – "shot for shot," "The Transferal," Courtney, Nina – returned in sharp clarity. He also recalled the emotional highs and agonies he had endured, but he did not sense any residual hurt or fear. Only peaceful contentment remained.

"Home," he said aloud. "I'm almost home."

He stood on the last step of the doorway of the bus, calm and serene, and relished the cool breeze that carried fresh air and freshly fallen leaves around him. He disembarked and marveled at the full moon hanging over the sedate lake, its reflection dancing ever so slightly on the small wavelets generated by the gentle autumn wind.

He gazed skyward at the expansive sky filled with thousands of flickering lights arranged in patterns he did not recognize. He turned his attention back to the lake. The water reminded him of how dry his mouth felt and how thirsty his soul was.

"I've always hated cottonmouth," he thought as he walked from the bus at the edge of the woods and down the sloping hill covered with grass to the shore. Kneeling down and cupping his hands, he filled them with the chilly water and eagerly drank once, twice, then a third time. He had never experienced so satisfying a drink.

He splashed water on his face and raised his head, noticing a soft yellow light across the lake, off to his right. The faint glow contrasted with the robust pale sage of the sky.

He stared for moments, long moments, at the faint yellow radiance. "Home. That is home."

He turned to look at the bus, and then back to the glow across the lake. He feared leaving the bus, as he had no directions back to where he came without its driver.

But he needed to, had to, must go to the light. He allowed himself one last longing gaze at the bus, sighed, and began to make his way along the wooded shoreline.

The woods were thick with no discernible path, but he had no problems traversing the brush. The glow was not too far, less than a half mile he estimated. As he approached the source of the light, he discerned the radiance emanated from a cabin's window lit from within. He stopped when he heard a melody from the direction of the structure. Several seconds passed before he identified the tune.

"It's a flute. A flute playing 'Amazing Grace,'" he realized. He paused to focus all of his attention on the sweet pleasing sound the instrument and the musician produced.

He resumed his walk, by this time a short journey remained to the edge of the woods not far from the front of the one story cabin.

The structure, simultaneously rustic and new, boasted a large porch across the entire width of the front. The foundation, constructed from round stones such as those produced from eons of grinding from a glacier advance, supported solid, square

timbers of considerable girth. A wood shingle roof
with a chimney on one side, also of the same round
rock construction, topped the bungalow. The front
of the cabin, bathed in the cool blue moonlight, faced
the shore, about thirty yards away.

Jake wanted a home like this.

The flute played on.

The twigs snapped under his unsteady feet,
betraying his presence.

Jake emerged from the woods as the cabin
door opened, yet he was not scared. An older,
somewhat heavyset man appeared in the doorway for
a reason other than the silence Jake broke. The
gentleman walked out slowly and methodically
closed the door behind him, all the while keeping his
gaze fixed on Jake.

Jake approached the foot of the steps leading
up to the porch, sure of his situation. His gait and
posture solid and steady, he projected a purpose.

It was time.

"I know you," Jake said with confidence as he
met the man face to face at the base of the stairs.

"You were the one at the bar, and in the
dreams."

"Aye, Jake, a've been with ye all this time" the
man said.

"Your name is Albert, right?"

"Aye, Jake. Ye remember."

"Somewhat," Jake answered as he fixed his
gaze on the cabin door behind Albert. "So, is this
home? I need to go home."

"Jake, come walk with me," Albert said as he walked slowly past Jake towards a dock on the water to a waiting rowboat. "Gonna do a wee bit o'fishen tomorrow. Interested?"

Jake nodded as he strolled with Albert to the mooring and helped him load poles and other equipment into the boat.

"Ah meant to git this done earlier, but ye'r a fighter."

Jake deposited the final container into the craft. "I didn't want to leave."

Albert nodded but said nothing in reply.

Jake stood and faced the water. "It's been almost like a dream. I've been places, seen things, lived another life. But it was my life. All the same, yet different. And I still don't understand."

"Don't understand what, lad? I'm here to answer."

"Was any of it real?"

"Jake, reality is like beauty. The significance rests in th' eye o' th' beholder."

"But, I still don't understand," Jake protested. "Where am I?"

Albert shook his head as he rose from the boat, realizing Jake had not touched the truth, yet. He produced a pipe from his coveralls and began to pack it with tobacco from a pouch he removed from his right leg pocket. "Let it go, and believe in what is around ye. It is th' most tangible experience ye will know. This . . ." Albert opened up his arms and looked skyward, "this is really how it is, lad. A mix of everythin' and more, equations and emotions and faith, all intertwined."

Jake nodded, if only from understanding he did not have to understand. He stared out over the moonlit water for a while without uttering a sound, confusion overshadowed by an overwhelming sense of content. All he had been running from, and to, existed together here. Fears and hopes, dreams and disappointments, all lived within his soul.

This place held, as Albert said, the harmonious existence of emotion, equation, and faith. The reality of the situation threatened to overwhelm him. He sensed the intoxicating presence of God.

But the completeness and meaning of the situation unfolding escaped him.

"I feel comfortable here, but not, uh, not fulfilled, not whole, well, I can't find the words," Jake said as he attempted to define his thoughts and feelings. He hesitated before he asked the next question, afraid the truth existed far below his expectations and needs.

"Is this all there is?"

Albert tightened the rope securing the boat to the dock before turning to him. "Jake, yer heart has been heavy for so long now. It has permeated yer soul, and ye have fought it for so long. Ye confronted, ye ran t' it, ye ran away from it. Ye decided, that was good, but ye decided within, t' go back, and ye did."

Jake thought about trying to avoid meeting her, then accepting fate when their lives touched again. "Nina."

"Aye, Nina."

"I should never have left her to begin with."

"But you felt ye had to."

"Why?" Jake threw his arms up in the air in despair. "Why, Albert? She was everything to me, and it was wonderful, but then it died. Why?"

"Ah think ye know th' answers Jake." Albert turned towards the cabin and looked up again at the stars in the sky. Jake did the same, thinking the individual lights shone brighter than any night he recalled.

"Ye can't be whole again, ye can't be yerself unless you let yourself explore those answers, and then you'll accept yourself for who you are. Ye've found most of the answers, but ye must not be afraid. Ye must act on them! Ye've faced it, but don't turn back now."

Albert began walking up the path from the dock to the cabin, and Jake stood still.

Albert turned to Jake. "There is no more running, Jake."

Jake nodded and did not say a word as he began to follow the old Scotsman. He understood the truth if not the meaning of Albert's words. The yearning for certainty and clarity kept him going as he caught up to Albert at the midpoint of the path.

Albert sighed. The time had come. "There's someone I'd like ye t' meet." He continued the walk up the sloping hill towards the cabin, turning only once to Jake, his eyes burning with invitation and admonishment at the same time.

Jake followed, and the melody from the flute grew in intensity as they approached the cabin. The tune he did not recognize this time, but the soulful sounds conveyed love, loss, yearning, and hope, all together at once.

While walking up the wooden stairs to the porch, Jake glanced through the window. He saw a girl with long brown hair through the sheer curtains. From her height, she appeared to be around five or six years old.

Suddenly everything stopped for Jake.

Suddenly he knew.

Right there, he faced himself.

All the misgivings of his mistakes he had clung to in his life did not compare to this. The one massive guilt overshadowed all of the others, the hidden blame for the worst of wrongs.

For all of his life he had run from it, or he had pretended to confront it, but he never had truly faced it. The running and pretending ended here, he knew now.

And he shivered uncontrollably at the fear of seeing just how dark his soul had become. Remorse, regret, and self-loathing, stronger than any emotion Jake had ever experienced, collapsed his strength.

Waves of truth washed up against his shore of distress and mistakes. He experienced the bitter coldness of pure darkness, devoid of all love.

It was her.

"Oh, God, no, no Albert, I can't!" Jake wailed as he turned and sank on the stairs, not quite sitting. His face twisted in agony, tears of fate streamed down his cheeks. "Don't make me do this. I can't. Please don't make me do this!"

He turned his attention to the woods in desperation. He had no idea how to find to the bus.

"Jake," Albert started slowly as he sat down beside him, and, as a father would a son, put a comforting hand on Jake's shoulder. "Ye have to," he said, gently.

"I can't!" Jake protested. "I can't face her."

"Ye have to, else ye will never grow. I'll be with ye. Do it, Jake. Ye must."

He often wondered how she would have turned out, the person she would have become, had they not succumbed to pure selfishness. Those thoughts were always from afar, as she had only existed in his imagination, and only when he allowed.

Until now.

He stood up and looked at her sitting inside, real flesh, as real as his. Seeing her again had an instantaneous if not expected effect on him. The guilt, fear, and self-loathing subsided. Calmness and warmth enveloped him, again.

The girl had not noticed him, yet.

He did not try to control his feelings anymore, and understood what he must do, and why.

He climbed the remaining two steps to the porch. He stopped and glanced at Albert, who smiled slightly and nodded his head in encouragement. Jake turned his attention back to the cabin, took a deep breath, and gently pushed open the door.

The structure had a rustic ambiance on the inside as well. She sat on a simple wooden bench next to the fireplace, her long wavy brown hair pushed back on the right side of her head. Facing the burning logs, she continued to play the polished silver flute with confidence, reading from a music stand situated next to the hearth.

He held back tears as he stared at the girl, struggling to remain strong. He had no idea how to announce his presence, but remained faithful the right words would come from his heart.

She sensed him before he said a word. She stopped playing and turned towards Jake as she laid the flute down on the bench beside her.

Her simple beauty awed him.

"Hello," she said with an innocent smile.

"Hi."

"My name's Lottie," she said, pointedly. "Do you play the flute?"

Jake walked in the cabin and towards her, struggling to contain his emotions. "No. No, I don't play anything, really. A little piano. I'm a whiz on the kazoo, though," he weakly joked.

Lottie's free and open laughter broke Jake. He dropped into a wooden chair near the bench, put his head in his hands, and began to sob.

Lottie rose from the bench and approached Jake slowly. "Why are you crying?" she asked.

Jake could not look at her, let alone respond. He had no words.

Lottie put a hand on his shoulder. "It's all right. It's all right, Daddy, I forgive you."

Jake sniffed, raised his head, and stared at her brown, big, loving eyes. He realized she knew the truth. His tears stopped.

She knew everything.

And she just forgave him.

"It's all right. Uncle Albert's been taking care of me until you returned." She put her arms around Jake and hugged him tightly. "I love you, Daddy!"

Jake's laughter echoed joy, sadness, understanding, and a spirit freed as he rocked Lottie, enveloped by the warmth generated by the fireplace and the love of two souls.

Thirty-Two
Truth

Albert's Dock
Morning

The sun rose over the lake, a new beginning in a place of new beginnings.

"That's what it's been about this whole time, the guilt," Jake said, looking at the reflection of the morning light dancing on the nearly still water.

"Aye, an' forgiveness."

"I couldn't change anything, anything," he said as he threw up his arms. "Each time, every time I tried, in the end it was the same result. I knew I couldn't change what was going to happen, that I couldn't control events, even with past knowledge," Jake continued as they walked on to the dock.

"Ye changed one thin', Jake."

Jake stopped and stared at Albert. "What?"

"Courtney. Ye stopped her from havin' th' abortion."

Jake rolled his head a bit to the right and shrugged his shoulders slightly. "Yeah, I guess so. But somebody else probably convinced her anyway not to go through with it the first time."

Albert did not respond as they continued to the dock.

"And you've been, uh, you, you're, well somehow you're a part of all this," Jake said, breaking the awkward silence. "Are you . . ."

"I'm a player, that's all, Jake," Albert interrupted as he sat on the dock and opened the tackle box. "I'm just here t' help. Yer guilt is yer own, and ye've helped yerself with the other situations, but really this is the one that's truly tied yer soul."

"The guilt. Yeah, I had never felt so much guilt as I did after the abortion," Jake said as he cast his line from the end of the old wooden dock jutting out over the lake.

"Aye. I told ye I'd take care o' her until ye were ready."

Jake remembered, again, when he met Albert the first time at Spanky's. "You've done a fine job. She's incredible on that flute," he said as he gazed towards the shore where Lottie was playing. "Did you teach her?"

"Me? No!" Albert said with a hearty laugh. "Ah haven't got a musical bone in muh body, Jake! No, it was entirely her idea," Albert replied as he lit his pipe. "She knew that ye loved the sound of the flute and wanted to learn it for yer arrival.

Jake turned from staring at the fishing line and studied Albert's face. It was strong yet kind, weathered yet fresh, innocent yet knowing. "So, she knew I'd be coming?"

Albert nodded. "We both knew."

Two geese flew overhead, their dark features contrasted against the bright blue sky. Jake surveyed the surroundings, awed by the beauty of the colors of the changing leaves, the luscious green pines, and the white snow-capped mountains in the distance.

"Albert, I have to know. Did I make a difference in Courtney's life? Did someone else convince her not to abort?"

Albert stayed silent as he adjusted his lure.

"Did I make a difference in her life? Did I save a life?" Jake asked again with more intensity.

Albert let out a slow sigh. "Yes, Jake. But ah think yer missin' the point."

"So she didn't have the abortion after all. Why was I able to change that, and nothing else?" Jake continued on his own train of thought.

Albert gazed at the lake, the mist still rising off its surface, energized by the early morning sun. "When ye make a case for someon' else, ye make it for yerself."

Jake joined Albert in contemplating the vastness of the body of water reflecting the known while concealing truths below. "I had to make that decision, before I could meet Lottie."

Albert gave a sideways smile. "Aye, Jake, now ye are beginning to see the whole picture."

"God, I miss her, Albert. It's strange, I mean I never knew her, but somehow that's how I thought, well how I knew she'd be."

"Aye, she's a princess."

Jake turned to Albert with an inquisitive expression on his face. "Why didn't you simply tell me? Why all of this, this, well, I don't even know what 'this' is."

Albert sighed. "I tried, Jake. I told ye when we first met not t' do it, remember."

Jake hung his head down. "Spanky's."

"Aye. I told ye that if ye didn't want yer child I'd take care of her."

"But it wasn't that I didn't 'want' her," Jake protested. "I did, so much! We were young, we were scared. I do want to love her and take care of her."

Jake stared at his reflection in the water. "I made a mistake. A big mistake."

"I know. But ye've been remorseful for it, even sought forgiveness."

Jake shook his head. "Forgiveness for that is too much to ask."

"No Jake. Believe me, I know about guilt, the exact guilt yer feelin'. But mistakes are made. That's just how things are. It's the lessons ye learn from them that are important. God doesn't expect perfection, but he expects respect. Asking for forgiveness is th' respect I'm meaning. His grace is the most endless, perfect gift, but we have t' accept it."

He shifted his stance as he cast a line. "Besides, Lottie is fine, she's growing up still. That hasn't changed, as ye've seen."

Jake was visibly upset as he turned to Albert. "How is that possible? I took away her life!" he said in anguish.

"Ye asked for forgiveness Jake, and since ye were sincere ye were forgiven," Albert reiterated.

"Funny, Albert, but I don't feel that way," Jake replied in sarcastic desperation.

"Jake, that's because ye haven't learned the most important lesson. Ye haven't forgiven yerself.

Ye have for everythin' else, but not this. Ye haven't been able to go on at all, and never will, until ye do."

Jake's line seemed to twinge as if a fish took the bait, but the movement stopped. "I guess I don't understand why I was granted this second chance."

Albert reeled in his ineffective lure. "Jake, ye keep thinkin' and talkin' of a 'second chance' that ye had." He cast the line out into the lake again. "God doesn't give second chances, that's limiting Him to just two. The chances he offers are as infinite as His grace. Ye always have a chance t' forgive, even yerself, but ye can't truly forgive others, or expect t' be forgiven, if ye can't forgive yerself."

Jake declined to continue to fish or respond to Albert as he sat down, feet dangling from the dock over the water. He studied himself, in silence, possibly deeper than he ever had in his existence.

*　　　*　　　*

"Albert, the pie was fabulous," Jake said as he laid his napkin on the kitchen table. Lottie nodded enthusiastically in agreement.

"Thank you," Albert said as he rose. "Lottie, don't forget yer chores. After ye are done, then ye can play for yer father."

Lottie began to gather the dirty dishes for cleaning as Jake walked outside, with Albert close behind him. "This is quite a beautiful place," Jake noted.

"Aye, that it is, mate," Albert said as he lit the tobacco in his pipe. "So how ye feelin'? About the whole thing, I mean?"

Jake sat down on a rocking chair on the cabin's porch. "Good, really good. Like I've finally found my place." He stretched his hands over his head. "What you said about forgiving myself this morning, I really thought about. When Lottie and I were walking this afternoon and she was talking about the different animals and trees, I came to the realization that I had forgiven myself. I don't know when exactly, or how, but I felt it when talking with her."

"That's good. Ye found yer place, then"

"Yes. It's here, I'm home."

Jake accepted he was dead, and this was heaven. He did not understand how he got here or why, nor did he care. "It's here" he said again.

"I dunna think so, laddie."

Albert's response surprised Jake. "Huh? I don't understand. Isn't what this is all about? Aren't I here to take care of Lottie?" Jake asked.

Albert shook his head slowly. "Not entirely, Jake."

Jake stood up and put his hands on his hips. "Wait a minute. You take me all the way here, show me this, show me that my daughter, who was never born on, well, wherever, that she forgives me and still loves me? And now I have to leave her?" Jake threw up his arms. "I can't abandon her again, Albert."

"Jake, ye don't have to. But this is not just about ye. Think about it. There is someone else whose soul is in just as much torment as yers is over this."

"Someone else?"

"Aye, Jake. You know what I mean. This is not just about ye," he said, again.

Jake understood all too well. "Nina."

"Aye, Nina. She's hurtin' as much as ye about this."

Jake threw up his arms in exasperation. "Well, that's great, Albert, but Nina and I aren't exactly on speaking terms, at least not in, well, I really don't know what is real anymore. I had the most marvelous dream, or experience, or whatever, where I met her again in school and all was all right, but the last I talked to her, I mean, in reality, well, we didn't talk to each other, we yelled at each other."

Jake turned his head away from Albert and concentrated his gaze out the window and on the boat dock. "Look, dreams are nice, but like I said Nina and I are not on speaking terms. In fact, we're not on any terms. She ran away, found her own life."

"She ran away, did she?" Albert said as he leaned forward. "Tell me, Jake, how much did ye push her away?"

Jake whirled around to face Albert. "Push?" he defensively asked.

"Push. Ye pushed her away."

"No, no I didn't," he protested.

"Yes ye did. Ye pushed her away, because ye were scared, upset, and couldn't get rid of th' guilt."

"No!"

"Ye blamed her, Jake," Albert insisted. "It wasn't right, ye shouldered her with all the blame."

"No, that's not how it was . . ."

"Ye can try t' run an' hide it from me, Jake," Albert interrupted. "Or from anyone else for that matter, but ye can't hide it from yerself. Ye said ye forgiven yerself, but how could ye if ye haven't come t' terms with th' truth of what happened?" Having made his case, Albert rose and walked towards the door, paused, and turned back to Jake.

"Whatever happens, Jake, remember, forgiveness leads t' unnerstandin', and inner peace, for everyone," he said before continuing back into the log cabin, leaving Jake alone on the porch as the last of the twilight faded.

Jake Stockman had been alone many times in his existence before, but had never faced loneliness this deep, this cold, and this true as he did the moment Albert shut the heavy wooden door.

Thirty-Three
Devotion

Buffalo, New York
Friday, May 29, 1992

Nina Thater Stockman stared with longing sadness at Jake Stockman lying unconscious on the hospital bed, a routine repeated countless times over the past few weeks. She remembered him as full of life, now reduced to merely a physical shell. How out of place, she considered, his body devoid of his energetic soul.

Jake lived, but only in the physical sense, and only because machines dictated such. The sterile hospital room contained no reflections of Jake's true nature and spirit. "How unfair, how undignified to have to lay there with all of those tubes and wires sticking out of you," she thought.

Today the doctors began the process of bringing Jake out of the coma induced after the accident in an attempt to stabilize him and minimize brain damage. His body had responded well to treatment and the swelling had eased, allowing an estimate upwards of an eighty percent chance of a complete recovery. Uncertainty persisted, though, of the existence or degree of permanent damage from the hit to the head by the vehicle in front of The Oasis. Machines spoke of normal brain functions, but only consciousness would reveal the truth.

But Jake was not awake, yet.

Julie Stockman returned to Jake's room with two coffees and handed one to Nina. "Any word?"

Nina shook her head as she took the cup. "Thanks, Mom. No, there's been no change the past thirty minutes. Every now and then a nurse comes to check but it's going to be awhile before we should expect any signs of him coming out of it."

Julie sat down next to Nina in a chair borrowed from the empty patient bay next door. "I know that things didn't go well between you two, but I want you to know how much I appreciate you staying with him these weeks. I'm glad you're here." She motioned towards Jake with her head. "And I am sure he is, too."

Nina weakly smiled. "I'm just glad he didn't take me off as an emergency contact."

"I know. I guess it wasn't the best time for me to take a month long pilgrimage to the Holy Land. When they said it was away from all communication so we could fully immerse ourselves in the experience, they meant it."

"You couldn't have known Jake was going to get hit by a truck, Mom."

They stared at Jake in silence, both aware of a certain level of awkwardness between them. Julie had returned to San Diego from a four-week church sponsored trip to Israel the day before. She had listened to only the first three desperate messages from Nina before calling for a cab back to the airport. Two connecting flights and over fourteen hours later she had arrived at the hospital.

They last saw each other a few years ago, before the breakup, at the party Nina gave to celebrate Jake's promotion to Materials Engineer. Julie did not learn of the troubles in their marriage until months after Jake had moved out of their home.

After a few minutes of unease, Julie broke the quietness. "We never got a chance to talk, Nina, and I'm sad about that. I wanted to call, but didn't want to seem like I was trying to interfere. I was very sorry that things didn't work out"

Nina sighed. "I know you were. And I wanted to call, too. Sometimes, though, it seemed we were going to get back together, so I'd wait for that time when we could tell you together." She hung her head down. "But obviously that never happened."

Julie put her hand on Nina's knee. "One thing I do know, though, was it wasn't for lack of love. That's why you're here. Maybe not what brought you here, initially, but what kept you here all those long nights."

Nina nodded her head in agreement.

"I know Jake can be stubborn and driven sometimes. But I also know that when he first met you, he knew you were the one for him. I remember how excited he was when he described you. I could hear it in his voice. He really loved you."

She paused.

"And I bet he still does."

*   *   *

Sleep would not come, perhaps because of the coffee, or the sounds of the medical equipment, or the growing anxiety over understanding that if Jake did not wake up and emerge from the coma soon, he quite probably never would.

Nina sat alone in the dark with her eyes closed. Julie had left for the hotel three hours earlier, succumbing to the exhaustion from the extensive traveling. In solitude with her thoughts and fears, Nina prayed.

During many nights such as this, sitting in dark silence with only the hum and beeping of the machinery as companions, she gradually rediscovered a part of herself she believed no longer existed. With all of their superficial arguments, volleys of mistrust bombs, and total blockage of meaningful communication, her prideful defenses had prevented such honest reflection before. Now, with Jake helpless, she lowered her own protections. She chose to embrace rather than ignore the opportunity to explore herself.

Her ability, and her choice, to forgive herself for the affair represented a major milestone of her recovery, one she once thought unachievable. The intense liberation from the self-loathing provided her with a measure of inner peace.

But forgiving herself had not come easily to Nina. She had convinced herself the marriage would fail at some point anyway. Still, she regretted providing the impulse that pushed the end to the forefront, although not without some benefit.

"Maybe the affair was my only way to find my peace," she had thought. "The only way."

Despite living together, they communicated little in the year before separating. The times she had tried to open up to him he either steered the conversation to the guilt they shared, inferring everything was her fault, or simply dismissed her, preferring to focus on his work and his career, chasing a ghost of fear of failure he had never let go of. His distance and lack of desire to talk had left her frustrated, rejected, and abandoned.

She had allowed those feelings to drive her deeper into depression. By participating in the church support group, though, she had found comfort and strength when she learned she possessed the power to choose how to respond to her emotions. She understood feelings themselves were neither good nor bad but rather a gift from God, with benefits and impairments. She finally stopped trying to control her feelings, and took ownership of how she reacted to them.

Yet before reaching out for positive assistance, she had let the depression rule her, seeking solace through instant gratification. She never planned to have an affair with Lucas Robinson after meeting him again, but the short-term comfort had virtually intoxicated her.

Even though learning of her indiscretion provided all Jake needed to blame all of their problems on her, she could not fault him for such. She had made the final mistake, albeit in a long line of mutual blunders, and she carried guilt for such ever since.

The freedom self-forgiveness brought allowed her to see what Jake had been hiding from her at times before, his self-blame for the breakup as well. Jake had realized while struggling to prove himself in his career he had withdrawn emotionally from Nina. He may not have tried to tell her, but she had not tried to listen, either. But she understood, now, through his actions and words, that he had carried a guilt burden as well.

They suffered the same, yet separate.

She sighed as she wondered who ultimately left first. "What does it matter, anymore," she said sadly to herself as she watched Jake's chest rise and fall from his steady breathing.

Both had tried to deal with the heavy burden of the abortion on their own instead of working through the pain together. Both ran away to their own castles and pulled up the drawbridges when they had needed each other the most.

Julie was right. Nina still loved Jake, she admitted to herself. She had denied her true feelings as her defense mechanism, her method to avoid pain. When he awoke, she would tell him the truth, with no expectations, she promised herself.

Questions and fears filled her head. No one could predict Jake's condition even if he regained consciousness. An eighty percent chance of a full recovery meant a twenty percent chance Jake might not be the same. The twenty percent loomed quite large in her mind.

Jake would not have been out with Tom had they not fought at her apartment, she bitterly acknowledged. They could have avoided the accident, if they had been civil to each other. "He always goes running for the beer, the escape," she thought. "Could haves, should haves, what price do you, do we pay for our stupidity?"

In their moment, her at his side, she recalled what Jake once said about their marital problems and hurt. He postulated they experienced purgatory on Earth for their one shared mortal sin. She had discounted such as a ridiculous notion at the time. Yet the silence of the nights next to an unresponsive Jake over the past few weeks led Nina to reflect more often on the possibility.

"Maybe he was right."

Thirty-Four
Return

The Lake
Sunrise

Jake awoke early in the morning, well before Lottie and Albert, and walked down to the dock, bathed in the purple and orange glow of pre-dawn twilight. The sun, minutes away from rising above the horizon over the northeast corner of the lake, provided more than the needed illumination to navigate the path. Though Jake figured he could determine the approximate latitude of this location using a compass and some keen observations, he did not care.

This place was not about logic.

If what surrounded him was real and he was in fact dead, all of the physical appearances and attributes, including location, were irrelevant. The coordinates of the cabin did not matter.

The dreams had provided a glimpse of his final resting place. Having arrived, he did not need a map to navigate heaven.

He also now understood his purpose, and his destiny.

He stripped all his clothes off and stood naked on the dock, not the least bit ashamed or self-conscious. The wetness called out to him, and he dove in, his body disrupting the early morning calmness of the lake, sending concentric ripples emanating from the point of immersion.

As he swam, he noticed the shimmering sharp points of reflected light on the water brought on by the sun now peeking out over the lake, and they mirrored reflections within. He retained all memories, including those of "The Transferal." The entire experience had been akin to watching a movie, showing him his serious mistakes and the influence those errors in judgment had on his future decisions, actions, and directions. He relived the missteps that had led to his greatest guilt, despite all of his attempts to navigate around them.

In high school, he decided between a life of mediocrity and not living to potential or striving for something greater. He did not remember exactly when or how he began to pull himself out of the descending spiral the first time, but he now understood why. He had built his life on a somewhat narcissistic foundation constructed of expectations of entitlement, and yet never had achieved fulfillment, preferring to accept what society handed him.

Only when he had recognized and accepted the need to work to earn what he desired from life had the spiral reversed. Jake had become a man bent on creating his own opportunities, fuel for success as he embarked on his studies at the University of Buffalo, both times.

He had never seen the drive towards self-improvement as a curse as well, however, until "The Transferal." His passion to excel in his career had not been devoid of the narcissistic foundation, rather represented another shade of selfishness. Only through reliving the past did he gain insight into the effect his focus on his own desires had on those around him. The revelation stung, as worthwhile lessons generally do.

He remembered the intense attraction and soothing comfortableness in the early days with Nina, the second time still fresh in his mind from "The Transferal." Love had bloomed, and he accepted himself inside as a person. Accomplishments in his career or social status no longer mattered, as she loved him as is. He never really saw her through his need to control his destiny, sprouted from seeds of insecurities, before.

Jake realized his self-centeredness and need to go it alone had prevented him from moving past the abortion, his second mistake, the most egregious of all of his missteps. Only when he opened up and asked God to forgive him did he find a hint of freedom. But the chains were completely removed when Lottie spontaneously forgave him as well.

The abortion had provided the first convenient excuse to vent all of his frustrations, all of his guilt on Nina, instead of "manning up" and asking forgiveness for his own actions. While he never blamed Nina outright for the decision, he had inferred such, too many times. "Classic avoidance of responsibility," he thought as he turned to swim back to the shore. He grieved his past, hurt by the stark insight that he had placed much unearned and undeserved culpability on Nina.

Given the chance, again, he would confess his error to Nina. She deserved better than how he had left the situation.

Jake recalled the day he found out about the affair as he stopped swimming near the dock. He laid back to float on the water and to reflect further in his humanity. Hurt and anger had blinded him then. How he dealt with those feelings and the ensuing breakup marked his third major mistake.

His internal struggles had often manifested themselves externally, and she had continued to be a convenient outlet for his need to vent his disappointments about himself. He used to count the Gulf War in the list of outside influences responsible for the end of their marriage, but realized such as yet another excuse, another internal example of running from pain. His failure to deal with his own issues had blocked his deep, strong love and devotion for Nina.

"Albert was right. I did push her away," he thought. "I should have just forgiven her, and asked her to forgive me. I thought I didn't, couldn't trust her. But it was myself I could not trust, or forgive."

"The Transferal" had brought him back to high school, he now understood, because his teenage years were when the effects of his first major mistake took root. Reliving past decisions led to a greater understanding of why he chose the paths he did and, more importantly, their consequences.

He had to relive those mistakes, to see what his choices had cost his soul. He had to relive those mistakes, to learn how to ask for forgiveness. He had to relive those mistakes, so he could forgive himself. He could never learn from any of his mistakes if the outcomes were different.

He understood why he could not change anything about his life in "The Transferal."

He gazed with little impulse towards the shore, not more than ten feet away. In this water, he found his home. Not geographic, not chronological, but rather the comfort of purpose within his heart, filled with peace and contentment.

In this water, he baptized himself with the wholeness of truth and love.

He was home. Finally, home. Still, he did not feel complete. Something was still missing. And he knew exactly what that something was.

Jake swam the last few feet to the dock with vigor, hopped out of the water, and toweled down. He grabbed his underwear, jeans, and tee shirt, and dressed after the early morning swim. Fully clothed, hair still wet, he returned to the porch of the cabin as Albert walked outside.

"Ye up early, Jake. Went fur a swim, did ye?"

"Yes. Wanted to try the waters before I left."

"Then ye made up yer mind?"

Jake nodded as he sat in a chair on the deck. "Lottie's in good hands here, and I know I'll see her again. I have to go back to Nina. And I know why."

Albert smiled. "Ye've come a long way, Jake. We'll be wait'n fur ye."

"Will I see you again? I mean, back, back there?"

Albert shook his head. "I dunna think so, lad. My job there is done. Besides, th' young lass will be quite a load to handle as she grows up."

"I'm sure you can do it."

I helped ye, didn't I?" Albert winked.

Jake smiled. "Yeah, you always have, Albert. You always have."

Lottie, still dressed in her pink ruffled nightgown, emerged from the cabin's front door and stopped next to Albert. "Are you leaving, Daddy?"

Jake rose out of the wooden chair and bent down in front of Lottie. "Yes, honey. I'll be back here soon, but right now I've got to go back. To Mommy."

Lottie flashed a wide grin. "I love Mommy!"

Jake returned the smile. "I do, too. And I'll tell her you said so."

He hugged Lottie with all the love and passion a father has for his child. But as he released her, a sharp pain emanated from his chest, and he bowed over, emitting a muffled groan.

"Ye alright, laddie?" Albert asked, his face contouring to reflect his concern. Lottie put a hand on Jake's shoulder.

The discomfort passed, and Jake stood up erect. "Yeah, I think so," he said, rubbing near his sternum where the sting seemed to come from. "Not sure what that was all about."

Lottie returned inside and began to play her flute. As the melody wove itself through the air, Albert withdrew his pocket watch and checked the time. "Ye had better hurry, Jake. Ye dunna have much time. Th' bus leaves soon."

Jake nodded. "I know." He felt another twinge in his chest, but not nearly as strong as the first. He extended his hand to Albert. "Thank you, for everything. Here, and there." He glanced over his right shoulder.

The mentor accepted Jake's hand offered in friendship, and they hugged. "Thank ye, lad," Albert said as he turned and began to walk away. Just before entering the cabin, he stopped and looked back at Jake.

"And Jake . . ."

"Yes?"

"In forgiveness there is peace. Ye found yer peace, dunna lose it. Now ye have t' help her find hers."

"I will," Jake replied with sincerity and conviction.

He jumped off the porch, ran down the dirt path, and diverted to the right. He retraced the route he had taken through the woods when he had arrived at the lake.

As he navigated the brush, thicker this time, sharp pain again rocked his body, originating from everywhere and nowhere at the same time. He stopped and fell to the ground. He began to sweat profusely as the sky rapidly darkened.

Fear overtook him. He turned to look ahead and could make out only two faint yellow lights like cat eyes in the darkness that seemed to be closing in on him.

"No. I will not give in again."

He stood up and redoubled his efforts to reach the light, fighting the scorching invisible swords cutting through his chest. He progressed forward, stopping in pain several times, yet managed to continue his quest towards the twin lights, until a shock so massive paralyzed him in his tracks. He fell without control face first to the ground.

*   *   *

Medical personnel rushed past Nina within seconds of the alarm sounding. A nurse hustled her out of the room.

She heard them trying to resuscitate him.

She heard their frantic efforts, repeating the same commands.

"Clear!"

Thump.

Jake was dying.

*   *   *

Jake, lying against the moist earth, caught his breath and found sensation and movement had returned to his legs. The shocks of pain had stopped, and while strong, dull aches remained, he managed to find the strength to stand.

A certain purpose again enveloped his person. He had to reach the bus. He continued the struggle to get to the twin lights at the edge of the woods, now not more than twenty feet away, before it was too late. He nearly collapsed again as he emerged from the trees, but kept his balance, determined.

The brightness from the bus's headlights bathed him in a spiritual glow. The engine revved, and the door began to close.

"Wait!" he shouted as he lumbered towards the bus.

The driver reversed the door and smiled as Jake climbed on to the bus. "For a moment there I didn't think you'd make it."

"Neither did I," Jake meekly replied through heavy breaths as he dropped into the seat behind the driver, beads of sweat rolling off his forehead. He inhaled deeply several times as the bus began to pull away. All pain had left him.

Jake Stockman was exhausted, more than he had ever been in his life. He closed his eyes and, in his fatigue, he welcomed this darkness, knowing it would lead him back to the light.

*   *   *

"For a moment there I didn't think he was going to make it," Dr. Herbert Weinstein said to Nina.

She dried her eyes with the tissue clenched in her hand. "Then he's going to be ok?" she asked, voice unsteady and unsure.

"I think so. The cardiac moment was likely a side effect of the induced coma. It's rare, but does happen. Once we were able to get his heart started again, he stabilized quickly."

Nina nodded, not understanding but accepting the apparent miracle. "Can I see him?"

"Not yet. But in a little bit," Dr. Weinstein replied.

"Thank you, doctor, for everything." Nina squeezed the doctor's hand, and he smiled as he rose from the bench to leave.

Nina looked up from the pew at the altar in the hospital chapel and stared at the cross. "Thank you Lord, thank you for not taking Jake yet," she prayed aloud, her hands still trembling.

*   *   *

The feeling of dry cottonmouth was the first sense he consciously experienced. The sound of regular beeping was the second.

Jake slowly opened his eyes. Two round, blurry, dim lights shined in front of him. He struggled to focus on the twin illuminations, and they became clear. He recognized two monitor screens, and realized one as the source of the beeping. The noise emanated in unison to the peaks of the solid blue line travelling across the screen.

He understood. He was in a hospital room.

His eyes travelled away from the hypnotic display and focused on a chair to his left, occupied by a sleeping woman.

A beautiful woman.

He knew her.

He loved her.

Jake Stockman moved the target of his eyes from her face down her shoulder and her arm to her hand holding his.

He remembered how to move his fingers.

He gently squeezed her hand, and Nina Thater Stockman woke up.

PART VII
Second Chance

Thirty-Five
Forgive

Buffalo, New York
Thursday, June 4, 1992

The prospect of leaving his room to enjoy lunch thrilled Jake. Although prepared in the same manner as meals served in rooms, something about dining outside on the veranda beside the hospital cafeteria made the food much more appealing. The temperatures in the mid-seventies and just a few puffy cumulous clouds in the sky blown in from Lake Erie on a gentle southwest breeze made for a fabulous scene. He took in a deep breath, enjoying the sweet smelling Buffalo summer air for the first time since the accident in May.

His gait unsteady, he managed to carry his tray from the cash register to the table despite Nina's offer to help. He appreciated her willingness to assist, but he wanted to handle his food himself. After a month of having no control over events happening to him, he needed to gain dominion over his destiny again.

He needed to be in control.

He retained all memories, and those experiences had culminated in joy upon seeing Nina at his side when he had emerged from the coma. The fact she had stayed by his bedside most of the time since the accident bolstered his happiness.

Yet a chasm still existed between them, bred from humanity and pride. Feelings of initial closeness waned somewhat in the days following, and he did not understand why, but the all too familiar coolness had returned.

He fought to navigate a fork filled with spaghetti to his mouth. The doctor had warned him relearning and mastering certain motor skills would take time. He dismissed the lengthy recovery prognosis, however.

"Do you want some help? Nina asked, again, seeing Jake struggle.

"I got it," Jake replied in frustration as spaghetti landed against his lip.

Silence descended on the pair. An intangible clumping of thoughts and words and feelings and mistakes and regrets wove a tapestry blocking rays of meaningful communication. He could not talk to her about the weather, let alone "The Transferal."

Once, only hours after regaining consciousness and high on pain medications, he started to relate to her his experience while in the coma. A minute into the conversation, however, the hospital fire alarm had sounded, mandating patient evacuation.

In his medicated state, he had imagined Lucas standing in the hallway while the orderly wheeled his bed back to his room in ICU. The thought of seeing Lucas, coupled with the memory of Nina's previous encounter with Lucas at JCPenney from "The Transferal," had overshadowed his desire to talk further. He closed up upon himself.

Sometimes a fool does not know just when to let go.

He lowered his head and mindlessly twirled his fork in the spaghetti. They had spoken less than a dozen words to each other since leaving his hospital room.

With a loud sigh, Nina pushed her tray away from her body, her meal half eaten. She rose and left the table without speaking a word. Jake lazily watched her traverse a silent path back through the cafeteria. He wondered if she realized, or cared, how much her chosen silence hurt him.

*   *   *

Nina refused to sit across from Jake anymore in awful silence. She did not want him to see her tears. The sanctuary the women's bathroom promised seemed too far away after rising from the table, but she reached seclusion before relinquishing control and letting her emotions flow. She sat inside a stall, the thin metal walls providing enough privacy for a good cry.

"Nothing has changed. Why does he always do this?" she asked no one in particular in the deserted restroom. "Doesn't he realize what he's doing? He doesn't have to go it alone. He's closed himself off from me again."

She had spent too much time wishing for people in her life to change, to stop hurting her. "That isn't love," she thought with resentment. She had worked too hard to regain her self-respect.

She blew her nose, emerged from the stall, and walked to the vanity. She studied herself in the mirror, and wiped the remnants of mascara from her face, diluted from the tears. A sense of hopelessness enveloped her as she began to apply fresh makeup. "Why bother? He doesn't need anyone else."

"He doesn't care."

*   *   *

He turned his attention away from her as she returned to the table. She gave no indication of her thoughts or feelings. She sat down as she had left, quiet and calm, with no eye contact.

Albert had insisted Jake needed to return to ease Nina's pain, but did not tell him how to do so. "Albert, real or imaginary, was wrong," he thought. "I can't ease her pain if she shuts down communication again."

"Please, God, show me what I am supposed to do."

Nina put one last bite of spaghetti in her mouth and stood up before swallowing. She looped the strap of her purse over her shoulder.

"I'm going to head out. I have to stop by the library this afternoon to do some research for my paper," she said tartly.

He nodded, resigned to the chasm. "I understand," he said softly, not knowing what else to say, but desperately wishing he did.

"Is there anything you need from me?" she asked out of politeness only, well aware of his likely answer.

"No, I'll be fine," he replied.

She did not respond.

He stared at her eyes, cold, devoid of emotion with the exception of sadness.

Revelations often occur in an instant, a moment not to be wasted.

He dropped his pride in an instant. "This isn't about me. This never was about me. And yet I made it all about me. I thought I had to do it all. I had to control everything, when in reality I am still just a powerless man . . ."

This could be their moment.

She started to walk away. He decided not to let her leave, not this way.

He needed her.

He called out to her.

"Nina!"

She stopped and turned to face Jake, her expression frozen and drained. "Yes?"

He walked slowly to her, stopping at arm's length.

Words of honesty came to him, and fear left. "Thank you for today. And for yesterday. And for staying all those days I was out."

She turned slightly more towards him.

"I know I've been distant, and I'm sorry, he continued. "I'm not dealing with this very well. But I am looking forward to seeing you tomorrow. Will you be here?"

His words surprised her, and her lips formed a slight smile. "Do you really want me to come by?"

"Yes. Yes. I need you. I need your help," he said with truthful sincerity, as he surrendered all remnants of control.

She faced Jake head on. "It'll be later in the afternoon, but I'll be here. Is that ok?"

Jake smiled and extended his left hand to hers. She reached out and touched his fingers.

"Of course. You can bring your books and work on your paper here too if you'd like. And if I can help, I'd like to."

Her smile grew larger, as the coldness thawed. "Kinda like those times at the library, eh?"

He recalled when they used to meet at the University at Buffalo's undergraduate library to study or just hang out. He grinned. "Yeah."

*　　　*　　　*

Nina desired a nice, long warm bath with a glass of wine to unwind her tense soul. "Maybe some soft music, and candlelight, and definitely bubbles," she thought. She perceived a melting of the emotional ice between her and Jake, and she wanted the warm feeling to continue. Her body called out for comfort and her spirit for protection and peace.

With classical music playing in the background, she eased out of her robe and entered the tub. She gently sat down in the water, and her body savored the warmth. She took a sip of wine, sat back, and closed her eyes, immersed in relaxation.

After several soothing minutes, she opened her eyes. Her gaze landed on the scar on her right inner thigh, the result of a cigarette burn when she was four years old, punishment for letting the dog outside against her father's wishes. The skin had healed well and the blemish was hardly noticeable to her anymore. She never let go of the emotional scars, however.

Perhaps the bath, or the wine, or the desire to end a long battle comforted her, as safety and contentment enveloped her as she rose from the water. She dried herself carefully with the plush cotton towel, and then draped her white terrycloth robe over her body.

Her time had come.

With meaning and naked honesty, she said the words aloud.

"Daddy, I forgive you."

A simple expression unlocked her chains and released her from her lifelong prison. Effects from the warm water or wine did not match the contentment she now experienced.

She removed the robe and slipped into a pair of silk pajamas, a gift from Jake years ago on their first anniversary. As she eased herself under the covers of her bed and stretched out on the mattress, she reveled in her peace.

She knew the direction she must take. Pride held no place in her journey.

She drifted to sleep, lazily aware of a flute rendition of "Amazing Grace playing on the stereo.

*　　*　　*

Out of the corner of his eye, he saw the words.

The floor nurse did not wake Jake up for breakfast, letting him sleep later, as the previous shift staff had reported he had spent much of the night out of bed pacing the halls. He had tried in vain to figure out how to help Nina find her peace while he struggled to find his own.

He recognized the coldness between them thawed somewhat the day before, brought on at least partially when he relinquished his need to control. Yet the serenity Jake craved still eluded him. Submission to fate did not fill the void, nor did obsessing about the missing elements until past three in the morning.

There were new words, in his handwriting, on the pad on the nightstand.

He raised himself in the bed. The nurses had left the blinds closed to keep out the mid-morning sun in deference to the sleeping Jake. He turned on the overhead light as brought the notepad from the table into his field of vision.

He blinked his eyes as he stared at the paper, and recalled the dream of the lake from a few hours prior, his first since emerging from the coma. The sentence, so beautiful in simplicity and so clear in meaning, spanning the entire page, provided the answer he sought.

"In forgiveness there is peace."

"Always listen to your dreams, as they are the mirror to your soul and always speak the truth," he thought.

This was his moment.

He understood.

He had laid a large burden of underserved guilt on Nina for everything wrong between them. He had promised himself he would ask Nina for forgiveness if given the chance, yet he had not followed through.

Now everything was different.

The kiss at JCPenney did not matter anymore.

The affair did not matter anymore.

Lucas did not matter anymore.

Only she mattered.

Thirty-Six
Peace

Buffalo, New York
Friday, June 5, 1992

Nina surprised Jake with a bouquet of flowers when she stopped by the hospital to visit in the evening. Jake laughed, as he had ordered a dozen roses sent to her apartment not long before.

"Jake, I just wanted to say I'm sorry for being distant. I want to give you some space, and I know this has been hard on you. But I've thought a lot since your accident. I know there've been rough times, but I don't want to feel like we're on opposite sides of the world."

Jake thought of the notepad by his bed. "Nina, there's nothing to be sorry about. I know I spoke some pretty bad words in the heat of battle that I didn't mean." He hung his head. "I'm sorry for that."

"We've both kinda used each other as a target to vent our frustrations and guilt, and we've been caught up in that cycle for a long time," Nina responded. "But I think that forgiving others, while it can be difficult, is much better than holding grudges."

She paused before taking a deep breath and continuing. "I forgave my father last night."

"In forgiveness there is peace," Jake thought, sensing a door opening. He leaned forward. "That must have been difficult," he said.

"It was, and yet it wasn't. I was taking a long bath, and it was very peaceful. And it just sort of hit me that I've been harboring such anger all these years and that it was eating me up. Once I said 'I forgive you Daddy,' I felt so much lighter, really like a burden was lifted from me."

Jake winced inside, recalling Lottie saying the exact words to him. He rocked back in the hospital chair. "I've been thinking about forgiveness a lot recently, I have to admit. And I want you to know that I agree with something you said before, that we've been using each other as targets for venting our pain from guilt."

He paused before continuing. "Nina, I'm so sorry for doing that – laying all of that shit at your feet."

Nina sighed as she looked out the window. "Do you remember the conversation we had when I found out I was pregnant?"

Jake nodded his head. Remembering always hurt. "Yes."

"I sometimes think that so much of the 'badness' between us started at that moment. Like we both felt guilty but blamed the other for our own feelings of guilt. That's when we started taking it out on each other."

He looked down. "We took it out on each other partially because we never forgave ourselves."

Nina thought in reflective silence for a moment. "And each other. I think you're right."

"True, complete peace can only come when we forgive ourselves," Jake responded. "We can completely, truly forgive others, but if we haven't taken that step to forgive inside, we can never be at peace. I've learned that recently, and it is hard sometimes."

"Yes, very hard," Nina agreed. "And I do forgive you, Jake, and I think inside I did a long time ago. But I often think about what could have been, if we hadn't made that awful mistake. That guilt sometimes feels so strong that I can never see myself getting through it to forgive myself." A single tear formed in her right eye, and dripped down her cheek.

"I can't get through that. I've tried, but I can't."

The door completely opened.

"This is the time," he thought.

"Have faith."

Albert said he must ease Nina's pain. His suffering eased when he experienced the lake, the cabin, Albert, and Lottie. The words he wrote on the pad last night did not come from a dream. Albert spoke loud and clear, again.

"The Transferal" was never just about him.

Jake stood up, confident and sure, and motioned for Nina's hand. "Nina, let's take a walk. I'd like to tell you a story . . ."

*   *   *

After he finished recounting the tale, moments passed in silence between the two, but not an awkward stillness as in times past. Jake waited for the response he expected, an agreement with Dr. Weinstein's assertion the source of his experience the result of the drug-induced coma.

He did not anticipate the words she spoke.

Nina let out a long breath. "I was never going to tell you this, but it took a lot of trust from you in me to tell your story. So, you deserve to hear this. Remember I told you back then that it was too early to determine the sex of the fetus from the ultrasound?"

"Yes."

"That wasn't true. At least the doctor was pretty sure he could ascertain the sex, even though I was only at eight weeks."

She stared into his eyes. "It was a girl."

She took his hand. "I didn't want you to know because you had always raved about wanting a little girl. If you didn't know, I thought maybe you'd not hurt as much."

Jake nodded, in both shock and understanding. He put his head in his hands and ran his fingers through his hair as he lifted his head back up.

"That was her. That was Lottie."

"But how could it be, Jake? How could that be? How is that even possible?" she asked.

He leaned back against the bench, took a deep breath of the cool summer night air. "I don't know. But I'm pretty sure I had met the old man before. When you told me you were pregnant, and we started to talk about an abortion, remember I left in a rush? I was trying to gather myself, to figure things out."

"I ended up at Spanky's. I think I had a pretty despondent look on my face, and I chugged the first beer pretty fast. I sort of felt people were watching me." He shuffled his feet, remembering how he had told the same story to Courtney before, in "The Transferal."

"This old guy was there, never seen him before. He came over and sat next to me. He had this Scottish accent, and he asked me if everything was ok. I told him about us thinking about aborting and he tried to convince me not to choose that. He kept saying that we should bring the child to term, that it would be wonderful and everything would be all right, and that it was a gift from God."

Jake looked up at the blue sky. "He said that if we didn't want to take care of our child, he would."

He paused. "It was the same guy from the lake, Nina. The same guy who was taking care of Lottie."

An uncomfortable silence followed as Nina absorbed Jake's words. She wanted to believe, but her studies had taught her a medicated mind could produce powerful illusions.

Nina sat still, transfixed on two children playing catch about fifty feet away in one of the fields in the park next to the hospital. "Jake, is it possible that while you were in the coma you played back memories of meeting this person at the bar and imagined the rest?" she asked. "You had always wanted a daughter. Maybe this was your way of working through things, through the guilt, in your mind?"

Jake did not answer the question. "There is one other part of the story I didn't tell you yet. I wanted to stay at the lake with Lottie - I told you that part. But the old man said that I couldn't. I could not stay because I had to come back here, to you. I had to help to ease your pain. Albert said I had to come back to ease your pain."

Nina stared at Jake. "Albert? The old man's name was Albert?"

Jake nodded. "Not sure when he told me that, now that I think about it."

She focused on her black purse, and carefully opened a zippered pocket on its side. She reached in and withdrew a well-worn folded sheet of paper. Her hands trembling, she unfolded a handwritten letter, with a small newspaper clipping inside. She passed both to Jake in silence.

Jake read the note to himself.

Dear Nina,

It took much courage to come speak to me about your predicament. God forgives those who are truly repentant, and your honesty and the conviction you showed when we talked yesterday about your issue tells me that He forgives you. We are all blessed, and cursed, with the gift of free will, and sometimes we all fail, but it is though His grace and love and forgiveness that we are

Jake then studied the newspaper clipping, an obituary for a Father Albert Whelan of St. Ann's Catholic Church. The priest had died of a massive, sudden stroke, one week after the abortion.

*   *   *

Jake steadied the wheelchair with his hands when the elevator jerked downward. The chair moved, and Nina lent a hand for stability. Even though capable to maneuver under his own two legs, Jake ceded to the hospital policy of transporting all discharged patients in a wheelchair to the front door.

He did not need to be in control.

Nina had parked her car in the loop outside of the exit doors. Once beside Nina's car, Jake rose, accepting Nina's arm for comfort, if not balance, though he needed assistance with the latter. He had spent over a month in the hospital, the first few weeks in ICU in the induced coma, and a full recovery may take several months.

Glad to resume his life, his current physical difficulties mattered little to him. "Probably haven't fixed the damned roller specs yet," Jake mused as thoughts of returning to work on "17 Roll" entered his mind. He shook them off.

"I have higher priorities," he smiled to himself as he watched Nina climb into the driver's seat.

Both stood at the starting line of a new beginning, at peace, with each other and themselves. She had offered to help with Jake's rehabilitation as much as he needed, and he opened up to all assistance she would give. They may still make mistakes, but both accepted with thanks the gifts they had received.

Jake believed in the realty of "The Transferal" and the love waiting for them in a cabin by a cool, blue lake. He did not need a map to determine the location of their ultimate destination. Their home existed in his, no, in their hearts.

"In forgiveness there is peace," Albert had told him. As Nina brought her car to a stop in front of Jake's house, he concluded he truly was one with those words. Harmony came when they absolved each other, and themselves. God gave the gift of forgiveness of all sins a long time ago, but they only recently accepted it.

He steadied himself as he started to exit the car, and remembered he did not need to struggle alone. Warm comfort from understanding the need to face life's challenges with help from others had replaced self-centered pride. Nina smiled as Jake put his arm around her shoulder for support.

He grinned as they approached the front door of the house. He was home. Not just physically, but also spiritually home.

Thirty-Seven
Future

Buffalo, New York
Friday, July 3, 1992

First came friendship, then love, then a big mistake and much fighting. Separation and the void followed, where self-indulgences and posturing clouded sharing and compassion.

Then the accident occurred, the "The Transferal" happened, and forgiveness emerged.

Those events existed in the past. This evening Jake and Nina concentrated on the future, one they again agreed to share together. Tonight they planned to celebrate their engagement, and Jake thought of no more appropriate a place to take her to make their recommitment official than The Oasis. The lessons of "The Transferal" began, and ended, there.

Tom had secured a table, as usual, but also by design, enlisted by Jake to perform the same favor as years ago. After he ordered the third round of drinks, Tom covertly slipped the item into Jake's palm, relieved of his safekeeping duty.

Jake got down on one knee in front of Nina, not a surprise, but rather a confirmation of their decision made the previous night. He took Nina's left hand, and slid the engagement ring on her finger. "Nina, I love you. Will you marry me, again?"

"Yes!" she exclaimed as she stared at the familiar gold and diamond band, and her smile grew even wider.

"You kept it! I thought you had sold it!"

Jake grinned as the server delivered the beers to the table. "Somehow, I just never got around to it after you gave it back to me."

"Let us toast to the soon to be newlyweds, again!" Tom triumphantly exclaimed as he raised his glass. A cheer filled the bar.

As he drank, Jake relished in the perfectness of his world. He had found his peace in the forgiveness Albert had spoken of, and helped Nina find hers as well. He discovered a love with Nina deeper than anything they shared in the past. And despite his logical, engineering mind protesting otherwise, he accepted on faith the existence of a very real place where Lottie thrived, and where they would meet again, someday.

With reestablished priorities, no longer did he put his career at Buffalo Steel ahead of his love for Nina and for God. Earlier in the evening Jake had received a call from Chuck informing him of a problem with one of the furnaces, necessitating Jake's return to ensure the repairs met specifications. He immediately refused. In his past life, Jake would have returned to work, but not now.

This night was their moment.

"Besides, it's time to let one of the new kids get their feet wet," he thought.

Jake set down his beer after the toast, recognizing his medication's diuretic effects. He rose slowly from his chair, still weak from the accident, and paused on the ascent. Nina noticed his hesitation and lightly touched his right forearm.

"Do you need a hand?"

Jake steadied himself. They both understood his recovery was progressing slower than Dr. Weinstein's expectations. He smiled at her to ease her concern. "It's alright. I'll be ok."

"I love you, Jake. I am so looking forward to our life together, again!" Nina said as Jake stood fully erect.

He saw hope, love, and his future in Nina's eyes. He leaned down to kiss her. "Me too, and I love you too!"

Jake turned and walked towards the restrooms located at the back of The Oasis beyond the bar. He paused as he passed the pool table on his left, and overheard two college age males agreeing the winner would buy the next pitcher of beer. Jake shook his head and smiled to himself.

"No more alcohol related bets for me, ever," he thought as he resumed his trek to the restroom.

*   *   *

A one-page montage of rather clean adult jokes and riddles hung above the urinals, and Jake chuckled at the memories the poster provoked as he stepped up and unzipped his fly. He and Tom would quote from the collection, replaced monthly, during their college years when they had frequented The Oasis almost daily. Jake memorized a couple of the jokes to repeat to Tom and continue the tradition as he peed.

He slowly washed his hands at the sink. While shaking off the excess water over the basin he checked himself in the mirror. He studied his eyes. They showed much experience, betrayed much pain, and yet shone with much hope, he thought. Physical, emotional, and spiritual recovery resided in those eyes.

He again turned his focus to the future, his destiny, and his peace.

As he dried his fingers, a sharp shriek of panic pierced the air. He whirled at the sound, the moist paper towel falling to the concrete floor.

The shout from a man echoed throughout the bar and permeated the restroom walls. "Don't move!"

Jake's adrenaline surged at the crack of a gun firing a single shot, followed by more screams of terror.

Fright further heightened his awareness as he slowly moved towards the men's room door separating him from the situation unfolding. He opened the door a crack and peered out.

Nina and Tom sat motionless at the table where he had been a few moments before. A man, his back to Jake and dressed in a standard military issue olive green field jacket stood over them, a semi-automatic pistol prominently displayed in his gloved right hand raised above his head. The man did not try to hide the gun, rather he flaunted the weapon, as some token of superiority.

The man laughed as he threatened Nina. Jake recognized the voice.

"This can't be happening!"

Thirty-Eight
End

Buffalo, New York
Friday, July 3, 1992

Lucas Robinson roughly jerked Nina up out of the chair, held her close against his body with one arm, and pointed the gun at Tom. "Don't move, hero. Just tell me where he is."

"Lucas, stop!" Nina pleaded. Jake saw the distress in her eyes from across the room as he continued to peer out though the slightly open bathroom door.

"Damn it, Nina, if I can't have you no one can!" Lucas pulled her violently as he turned to face the bar. He fired another shot, shattering a liquor bottle two feet above the bartender's head.

"Touch that damn phone and you're dead!"

Lucas placed the gun barrel under Nina's chin. "Where is he, sweetheart?" he asked again, this time with a sadistic smoothness.

Lucas licked his lips and looked around with a wild, primitive grin. All eyes in The Oasis focused on him. He relished being back in total control, unlike the night weeks ago. That plan had been almost foolproof, and yet he had lost his discipline and screwed up executing it. He was glad his father did not know about his failure.

He had spent a long time scheming how to remove Jake from what belonged to him. By following Jake, he had figured out when Jake would be the most vulnerable, in front of The Oasis on a Friday night. All Lucas had to do was bide his time and wait.

That night Lucas had floored the accelerator as Jake and Tom had stumbled out of the bar and into the street. Yet, in his excitement, he had given the engine too much gas. The resulting fishtail provided a split second of warning for Tom to push Jake out of the path of a direct, lethal strike. Instead the collision, Tom in the chest and Jake on the head, was forceful enough to maim but not kill.

At least neither of them had identified his truck. He had injured both enough to guarantee so, he realized with some measure of satisfaction.

But he had still lost his discipline, and his control, and his destiny, that night.

Lucas Robinson was sure this time he was on the right track and had a second chance to get what rightfully belonged to him, but he had to work a bit harder to complete the job. He savored his immediate success as he surveyed all of the frightened eyes on him. "Good. They all know I'm 'The Man.'"

Now he had to complete the job. His father had always instructed him to finish strong.

"You're the reason why this had to happen," he shouted at Tom from across the room as he leveled the gun at Tom's chest. "Now you're gonna pay for that." Tom had only a moment to utter an incoherent sound before Lucas fired the weapon. Tom fell forward in the chair, his forehead breaking his glass.

Lucas thought about what his next move should be. His second attempt to kill Jake had also been ineffective, due to poor planning again. He had tried but failed to get close enough to Jake after pulling the fire alarm handle at the hospital a couple of weeks earlier.

Success would only come this time if he kept strong and focused.

"In discipline, there is control, and when in control, you own your destiny," he thought

He centered his attention back to the situation at hand.

There was no easy way, and this was no easy time. He hated to threaten Nina, but he had to complete his job. He must win. "She'd want me still if she didn't feel sorry for that ass," he convinced himself again as he straightened his field jacket.

"Where is he? Where *is* he?" Lucas shouted frantically at Nina, sweat beading on his face. He pointed at the two partially filled glasses and the broken one on the table, a chunk of the latter embedded in the unconscious Tom's forehead. "I know he is here! There are three glasses!"

His eyes darted back and forth in a wild frenzy as he processed the visual scan, pausing twice in the general direction of the restrooms where Jake hid.

*   *   *

Jake watched Tom's blood mix with the ale on the table, frozen by horror and circumstance. He had no idea what to do. He released the pressure holding open the bathroom door and searched around for an escape route. He surmised the small window above the urinals would not accommodate his size. He needed to find another way out to get help, as going back into the bar was blatant suicide.

He looked around again, panic-forced adrenaline pumping through his body. His gaze returned to the window, then the door, then back to the window. Jake feared Lucas would soon migrate to the back of the establishment and figure out he was in the restroom.

"Not much time. There must be a way."

The partially boarded up hole contained inlaid security glass and a rusty inoperative exhaust fan on the left side. Over a dozen screws secured the plywood, and the vent would not budge when Jake pulled on the front grill.

He switched his focus to the pockmarked tiles a couple of feet above him. "If there's enough room between the false and real ceilings maybe I can escape that way," he thought. His arms shook as he climbed on top of a commode and pushed aside one of the tiles.

*   *   *

Lucas glared towards the back area of The Oasis as he roughly grabbed Nina again, his patience exhausted. He forced the gun against her right temple and dragged her with him towards the restrooms.

"Lucas, you don't have to do this!" Nina said as Tom rose from the chair and staggered from the table, out of Lucas' sight.

"Oh, but I do, I do, Nina! Don't you see how much I love you? I'm doing this for you! All of the fucking shit he put you through, you told me that, remember? I'm saving you from him!"

*   *   *

Jake's head cried out in pain and he almost lost his balance, but he managed to brace himself against one of the stall's walls for support. Three feet separated the false and true ceilings.

Jake hoped the top of the stone and mortar foundation, a ledge a foot wide, would provide suitable footing. Gripping a beam above, he hoisted himself up through the hole, ignoring the agony in his head. He swung his butt onto the outcropping in one motion.

He leaned forward and carefully replaced the pockmarked tile back in its original configuration. Light from the florescent fixtures throughout the restrooms and kitchen leaked through vent holes and cracks, providing an even faint blue white glow in the space.

The bathroom door slammed open.

"I know you're in here, ass wipe!"

Lucas swore as he kicked each of the stall doors open, revealing nothing. Jake crouched motionless above, in dread.

Lucas cursed again as he rushed out of the restroom. Jake discerned sounds of a struggle and a faint, muffled cry from Nina moving away from the bathrooms and towards the small kitchen.

The dim space between the false and real ceilings was the loneliest of spots.

Lucas pushed open the door to the unoccupied kitchenette. Manic infuriation oozed from his voice. "Jake, I know you're here somewhere! I'm gonna kill you!" he yelled.

Jake realized Lucas would likely take his frustration out on Nina very soon. He had to do something, now. He changed his strategy from escape to encounter, and slowly crawled along the top of the foundation towards Lucas below.

Nina screamed again. The sound of metal against bone followed, and then heartbreaking silence. Jake crouched on the ledge.

Through a hole from a missing tile corner, he saw Nina on the ground. She struggled for balance, supporting herself with her left hand, the ring still prominently displayed on her finger.

"I know he's here. You can't be with him!"

"No, Lucas, listen," she said as she fought to raise herself. "Lucas, Lucas why are you doing this? Lucas, listen to me, I still care for you!"

"Bull fucking shit! Bull fucking shit!" Lucas shouted with increasing fury. "I know you're here with that bastard! He fucking wrecked everything, man, he fucking wrecked everything!"

"No, No, listen to me! Listen to me, Lucas, it wasn't working, it just wasn't working at all. Will you just listen to me!" Nina pleaded.

"No, you listen to me," Lucas calmly said as he looked directly at Nina. "I love you, Nina. I love you very much. But I swear to God, if I can't have you . . ." Lucas noticed the engagement ring, ripped it off her finger, and flung it across the room behind him. "But if I can't have you . . . I want you, I need you, I don't know what else to do." He started to raise his right hand holding the gun.

Jake stayed silent. Nina needed him now more than ever. A sense of clear purpose again enveloped him. Before, he had left her. This time, he would not.

"Faith," he thought.

"Lucas," Nina pleaded from nearly beneath Jake's feet.

"Shut up!" He whacked her roughly across the face with the butt of the gun's grip.

"No, this won't work," Jake concluded, with a sense of calmness. He reversed direction and crawled the few feet back to where he had raised himself up. He removed the ceiling tile in the bathroom, and dropped down on to the toilet.

Jake Stockman walked out into the bar, silent, and turned towards the kitchen, oblivious to the incredulous stares of the patrons and the bartender on the phone.

"Jake, don't," Tom struggled to say from lying atop the blood stained pool table.

Jake continued peacefully, not out of courage, but love. He did not hesitate as he as he opened the door, and he spoke no words as he faced Lucas.

"There you are, you weak son of a bitch!" Lucas said with a wicked grin as he held Nina with one hand and the gun in the other. "So, who's 'The Man' now, college boy? Who's 'The Man?'"

Nina stated wide eyed at Jake, blood dripping from her hair.

"Lucas," Jake started.

Lucas leveled the gun at Jake. "Don't move. I wanna kill you just where you are," he proclaimed as he laughed. "Hell, it's even an easy clean up, all they have to do is wash your blood off the floor with a hose!" he cackled as he pointed to the drain with the gun.

Jake leveled his hands, palms open, all of his discomfort and fear gone, replaced by calmness and serenity. "Lucas, you don't have to do this."

"Oh, but I do. I do! Someone as weak and pitiful as you couldn't understand. No, you're gonna die, and I'm going to enjoy doing it. Nina, say goodbye to this ass."

As Lucas began to point the gun at Jake, Nina bit Lucas' empty hand.

Lucas screamed in pain and whirled around, releasing his grip on Nina in the process.

Nina grabbed an iron frying pan and hit Lucas on the back.

Lucas fell.

Jake jumped towards Lucas.

Lucas squeezed the trigger as Jake landed on Lucas's firing arm.

The sound of a single shot echoed through the kitchen.

Screams emanated from the bar, followed by an eerie silence.

Lucas lay motionless on the ceramic tile floor beneath Jake, unconscious. The firearm remained cradled in the palm, no longer gripped.

Sirens wailed in the distance.

Jake heard the muffled coughs, the moan, and the stifled cry.

He rose and turned to Nina, slumped in front of a wooden cabinet. Blood dripped from her mouth. She struggled to move.

He moved to her.

He sat beside her and cradled her head in his arm, her back resting on his knee.

He noticed the growing red stain on her flowered dress coming from the bullet wound to her chest.

"Oh, my God, no. *No!*" He looked up, then back down at Nina, then up again. "Please, let this still be a dream!" he shouted.

He turned to her at his side. She stared at him with those beautiful eyes he had fallen in love with so many years ago. A tear formed at the corner of one, then the other.

She tried to speak, but coughed.

"Don't worry. Don't worry, you are gonna be all right . . ."

The sirens grew louder.

The kitchen door opened. A man and a woman started to enter, then stopped. One began to cry.

Nina swallowed, her face betraying the great effort to speak. "Jake . . ."

"Shh," he whispered as he gently rocked Nina, vaguely aware of the crowd that had migrated from the bar. One picked up the gun and pointed it at the still unconscious body of Lucas Robinson.

"Will somebody call for a fucking ambulance? We need an ambulance!" Jake shouted hysterically.

Nina closed her eyes, opened them again, and stared straight into Jake's. A whisper emanated from her lips.

"Jake . . ."

Jake leaned over Nina, consumed with hopelessness. His eyes focused squarely on hers.

"Nina, sweetheart, it'll be fine, it's gonna be ok, I love you . . ."

"Jake," she weakly whispered again as she motioned Jake closer.

He leaned in.

"I hear - I hear a flute playing . . ."

Jake Stockman let out a loud, soulful wail of grief as he felt the life leave Nina Thater Stockman in that last breath.

Thirty-Nine
Home

Myrtle Beach, South Carolina
Wednesday, June 7, 2017

Jake laid the notepad down on the desk, wiped a tear from his right cheek, and stroked his beard thoughtfully. The agony of reliving Nina's death struck at his core, as poignant as the day she left in his arms.

"That bastard," Jake thought as rose to grab a Sam Adams from the fridge, shaking his head. He picked up one of the many readily available openers and popped the top of the beer bottle with much more force than necessary.

"He got what he deserved."

He had no more words to write. Continuing with the trial or his subsequent spiral into the alcoholic abyss that cost him his engineering career and almost his life added nothing, he thought. Lucas had never displayed any remorse or emotion during the proceedings, except for the evil smile directed at Jake at the conclusion of the sentencing.

The story always ended the same, and yet never ended for Jake. For twenty-five years, the pain had eaten at him from deep within.

It had stifled his life. It had stolen his soul.

Every annual flight to Buffalo to visit Nina's grave on the anniversary of her murder constituted a renewal in pain and anger for him. From the day they laid her to eternal rest in that spot, the aching from losing her had never eased. Loneliness, loathing, and depression had become his lifelong traveling companions.

He picked up the pad, scanned the contents of the last page, and slammed it down on the floor in disgust. No happy conclusion existed, no fulfilling end to the story. Writing about it did not produce the desired relief from years of suffering in his personal hell.

He wanted the liberation a miraculous pardon from his prison would bring, but no such freedom awaited him. The three weeks of revisiting the past provided a poignant lesson in reality.

"These are my last words, I won't write again," he vowed again to himself.

He walked through the open door of the bungalow, stretching his arms above his bare torso as he moved. The sea still roared, but with no inspiration, no encouragement, no understanding.

And no forgiveness.

He felt only pain as he sat in the beach chair. He pondered the true value of the hurt from reliving the past in such detail.

*   *   *

Thursday morning brought another jog through the sand, another egg breakfast, another coffee, and another hangover. And so began another unremarkable, lonely day in the ordinary life of a bitter man who had not fully learned a lesson delivered ages ago.

The mail came early, or Jake woke up late, or a combination of both. Jake did not keep meticulous track of the hours anymore. He had no reason to do so.

The mailbox held nothing outstanding, like every other mundane day. He lazily took inventory of its contents - the electric bill, a postcard from Steve from Washington D.C., and an ad enticing him to return as a DirectTV customer, even though he currently subscribed to the service.

He chuckled as he read the postcard. Steve completed his goal of attending a baseball game in every active Major League Baseball stadium with the Nationals at home against the Mets the week prior. "Good for him," Jake thought.

As he did with all of the other postcards from Steve he proceeded to file this one away in the old shoebox in his beat up wooden desk, the last remaining piece of furniture from his Buffalo days. He opened the middle drawer, and noticed a yellowed piece of paper wedged between its joints. Carefully, purposefully, he removed the scrap and read its contents.

"In forgiveness there is peace."

He dropped on to the couch, clutching the note he wrote ages ago in the hospital during his recovery.

With Nina's murder, all of his understanding of the reasons for "The Transferal" had left with her. "If it had been real, why had she died? I helped her find the path to peace. Then she was killed, all because of me," he thought for the countless time in the past twenty-five years.

There was no peace.

He stood up and returned to the desk. The lower drawer contained his small collection of photographs. He preferred hard copies to digital media for important images, to be able to hold a physical artifact of the most intimate and special memories. He thumbed through them until he found the object of his search.

He held the picture up at eye level, and studied the image of Courtney and Leslie from Leslie's fourteenth birthday party. He turned over the print and read the writing he knew by heart.

"Isn't she beautiful? Every day I thank God you talked me out of it!"

He helped her in "The Transferal," not before.

He looked at the note again, written all of those years ago in a hospital bed.

"In forgiveness there is peace."

He knew what he should do, what he had to do. He had always known.

But he could not bring himself to do so. "Not possible, not now, not yet."

He shook his head and sighed as he grabbed his flight bag. With his hangover gone, he had a lesson to teach.

*   *   *

"Good job."

"Thanks, Jake."

"Now, remember, if you leave here with one thing, remember this. A side slip and a forward slip are the same thing. It all depends on the extent of the cross controls. Full rudder will enable you a full slip attitude, and that's what?"

"A way to lose altitude fast," Paul Corrigan replied.

"Right. Again, good job. Next we'll start on our navigation, so start studying GPS procedures and the local VFR waypoints."

"Right."

"Your logbook is filled out. I'll see you Wednesday."

"OK, see you later, Jake."

Jake watched the teenaged student pilot leave the briefing room at the Myrtle Beach airport with slight amazement. He did not recall anyone so young learning the fundamentals of flying an airplane so fast. "Of course, the kid won't taxi with the yoke since he doesn't drive yet, but that's good. Eliminate bad habits before they start."

Jake had hoped to have enough time to complete Corrigan's training, but he could not push back his mandated physical exam any further. His piloting skills were still sharp, but the FAA did not care. Regulations would demand revocation of his license because of his condition once the FAA became aware of its acuteness.

*   *   *

A single light above the desk illuminated the otherwise dark room. The analog wall clock read twelve thirty-four AM. "Ticking off the time that we'll never share," he thought.

He stared at the open bottle of brandy on the shelf in front of him. He had not poured nor drank any alcohol this night.

"Every time, I escape to it. I always have."

He looked down at the manuscript again, and then at the note with those words.

Albert's words.

"In forgiveness there is peace."

"Albert told me not to lose that peace . . ."

Yet he had lost the peace, long ago. He always ran away, in some way. He wondered if he had the strength to follow through this time, and finally face the truth.

He rocked back and forth in the desk chair, clutching the manuscript tightly against his chest, the struggle within difficult to endure. He closed his eyes, arched his head up, and moaned aloud. "It's so hard, Albert."

Lucas Robinson had spent nearly twenty-five years in prison, and yet during those two and a half decades never showed any remorse or guilt. Jake had hoped for some sign of repentance as the key to his own peace.

It never happened.

The emptiness of the past twenty-five years ate at him as he fought the truth he never accepted. True forgiveness is not conditional. He would have found the solace he craved had he given up the requirement of atonement.

But his heart was hard.

The message had always been forgiveness brings peace, not requested forgiveness brings peace.

Jake had a good reason to despise Lucas, if such really existed. And he had, for years. He had disciplined himself to hold on to the hardness of his heart.

He had controlled his pain by stifling it.

"In discipline there is control, and when in control, you own your destiny."

"No . . ."

He realized, again, in the loneliness of the early morning hours, that he had control over absolutely nothing. The realization though that he had a choice how to deal with the eternal pain comforted Jake.

He thought of Nina, and her father.

He thought of Lottie, in the cabin.

He looked at the bottle.

He trembled.

Then, mentally and spiritually, he released his grip. He let go. Relinquishing control unlocked his heart for the first time in decades.

The warmth he experienced reassured him.

The hardness in his heart eased.

In the dimly lit beach home, early in the morning, he surrendered, and spoke the words loudly, with conviction.

"Lucas, I forgive you."

He keeled over and cried, not out of pain, but of newfound freedom, from a soul released after years shackled with self-imposed chains.

*   *   *

He pondered his physical changes as he stared at himself in a mirror early the next day. The beard was not him, and would have to go. He liked the slimmer image, but he accepted the cold fact his issue contributed more to his weight loss than any other factor. Even with returning to a full, varied, healthy diet, keeping pounds on became tougher day by day.

With no hesitation, he grabbed the full plastic garbage bag, walked out the front door, and lifted it up to the top of the canister at the curb. The glass of the bottles, most still unopened, clinked loudly as he dropped the trash into the bin.

The sun rose over the gently rolling waves of the Atlantic Ocean. Jake allowed himself many minutes to enjoy the simple beauty of the most natural indicator of the passing of time. He knew he was finally free. "They know it too," he thought, as the image of the cabin by the lake filled his head.

He sighed as he stared out across the ocean. His life journey not quite complete, but with the finish line drawing closer, he sat down in the beach chair with the manuscript one more time.

He believed in what had happened, and although it took him twenty-five years, he found peace because his experience showed him how to finally let go of his pain. But he could not prove to others the reality of "The Transferal," nor did he care. He wrote about it for himself, not for publication.

He long ago banished the logical thinking of the engineer's mind to try, in vain, to find clear-cut answers to everything. No matter how deep man delved into the question of the ultimate meaning of life, some things remained beyond human comprehension.

Some things just required faith.

Only after reliving the experience in its entirety, an exercise he had steadfastly avoided for twenty-five years, did he grasp the real meaning of the lesson. The "The Transferal" had happened, with God the true author of the story. He chuckled to himself as he pondered whether God would impose a copyright infringement suit on him for plagiarizing His work.

He reversed his earlier stance. A few final words to write remained after all. He clicked the pen, wrote the last lines of forgiveness, and closed the notepad.

It was done.

He felt an intimate closeness with God, and with them as well.

*   *   *

It had been too long.

Jake bent over, slowly, habitually ignoring the pain, his physical failings preventing a more rapid descent. He placed a single rose on the stone marker, as he had done for countless number of years on this day. He ran his hand along the characters carved in granite, forever recording her name and the dates of her birth and death. He winced as he remembered the latter.

He stared at the dash between "1967" and "1992." "She lived the dash, fully. I wish I had done the same."

He learned he had failed the medical exam ten days earlier, as expected. The FAA revoked his license to fly within a week, a rapid response for an agency mired in bureaucracy. This time, his final trip north, he instead drove from Myrtle Beach to Buffalo, a difficult endeavor for his weakened body. But he would never, ever miss their date.

They were together, two souls at peace, as was Jake's.

He knelt down, straightened his jacket, and stretched out on the ground next to the tombstone. Lying on his back, he smiled at the sight of the puffy clouds and the blue sky through the treetops, in tranquil unity with everything and more, equations, emotions, and faith, all intertwined.

He missed them with all he was, and all he could do was wait. He would be with them again, and he yearned for that time.

And as he closed his eyes, with the warmth of the afternoon sun surrounding and comforting him, he let himself slip into a restful sleep. Eventually, he opened his eyes, and turned his head. He recognized the hill, with the brilliant fall colors painted on the leaves, and the lake, only a few feet from him. His eyes drifted to a boat nearing the dock with three occupants - an older man, a young woman, and a beautiful lady.

He stood up and began walking towards them. As he made his way down the wooded path to the dock to greet the arriving boat, no aches remained, physical, mental, or spiritual.

All three saw him coming. They waived in eager anticipation, eyes shining.

He smiled, and the smile grew larger and larger. His walk became a jog, then a fast run, the fastest his legs had ever carried him. And as he approached them in a sprint, he knew.

He was home. Finally, simply, completely, he was home.

www.ingramcontent.com/pod-product-compliance
Lightning Source LLC
Chambersburg PA
CBHW020323140726

47905CB00012B/161